PER
Immigrant & Pioneer

by
E. Palmer Rockswold

published by

Adventure Publications

distributed by

Adventure Publications
P.O. Box 269
Cambridge, MN 55008

ISBN 0-934860-18-9-814

INTRODUCTION

Let me, with great pride, here introduce a remarkable man, *Per*. His story, told with honesty and sensitivity by E. Palmer Rockswold, says much about the values that built our nation. It is a quiet tale of courage and strength, a celebration of the people.

Though based upon the experience of one Norwegian immigrant during the late 19th Century, *Per* embraces many elements common to the pioneer heritage. The novel emphasizes optimism, hard work, dedication to a better life, and family values. The author has portrayed through Per's life the bedrock upon which our American commonwealth grew and prospered. In these turbulent and troubled times, it is well to remember the sources of our nation's greatness.

This novel also incorporates painstaking research. The details of pioneer life flow easily from the story, and the net result is a work of imagination that is also accurate history. E. Palmer Rockswold has integrated fact and fiction with care; his style emphasizes a stark reality that Per, if he lived, would think honest and true.

As I read this novel, I came to respect and honor *Per*. As you read Per's story, I hope that you, too, will celebrate the proud heritage of struggle that belongs to us all.

Larry Remele, Historian-Editor
State Historical Society of North Dakota

ACKNOWLEDGMENTS

Many people have contributed in some way toward the writing and publishing of "Per" (Immigrant and Dakota Pioneer). A special thank you to Alma, Lewis, Clara, Selmer, Aunt Alice, and Cousin Inga of Oslo, who all provided me with bits and pieces of information carefully stored in their memories. Also to Per, who was kind enough to drive us to "Elvestuen" in his automobile some years ago.

Thanks to my sons, Gaylan, Gordon, Grant, and Gary, who initially supported me in this crazy venture. Also to Mary, Sue, Joyce, Sarah, Alf, and the many others who encouraged me along the way. My sincere appreciation to the "readers," Susan Briney, Trish Haugo, and Shirley Lewis for their input. Carol Bly, Laurel Reuter, and publisher David Nordell are professionals who have given of their time. Please accept my gratitude.

Very important also was the super reaction and help of Robert L. Carlson, Ann Rathke, Larry Remele, and others of the North Dakota State Historical Society. A special thanks to Larry for writing the introduction.

Last of all, may I express my admiration and gratitude to Per and Serianna and to all the other immigrants and pioneers about whom this historical novel is written. Their struggles for citizenship and a better life in America paved the way for those of us who are their descendents. Per and Serianna were steadfast believers in and staunch supporters of book learning. They would be amazed and most pleased at the level of education and the degree of productivity of their fifteen grandchildren.

E. Palmer Rockswold

CONTENTS

CHAPTER ONE

A Blacksmith's Apprentice   (1880)

"Clang! Clang! Clang! Clang!" pealed the steady bell-like tones of the great steel faced anvil, as Per pounded vigorously on the red hot iron with the blacksmith's hammer.

"Hit harder, Boy! Hit harder!" exhorted the older man, his piercing blue eyes gleaming.

"Zing!" Suddenly the seven pound hammer let loose from the shaft and flew through the air like a small cannon ball, barely missing his father, Erik's head. It crashed into the wall and fell to the floor with a thump. Per looked up in dismay, fully expecting a tongue lashing.

"Pick up your hammer, Boy," said Erik quite calmly, as he strode out of the shop and toward the house.

Per looked up to see the other apprentices standing stock-still as if transfixed. Evidently they had seen the near miss and heard the crash of the hammerhead.

"Good Lord! He could have been killed!" exclaimed Halvor, finally finding his voice.

Per found himself shaking, but the younger men recovered quickly.

"He could have been brained with the hammer," agreed Trond, with a look of pure delight, as he contemplated the idea.

Erik, Per's father, was a master blacksmith, and the boys were his apprentices. For the first year, the young men received board and room for their work, but no wages. Each of the next three years, they got the equivalent of a few dollars. Per, now in his fourth and last year, was paid what amounted to about five cents a day.

Per's father had the reputation of an exacting master. Apprentices found that they couldn't work hard enough or diligently enough to completely please him. Yet opportunities in Norway for young men were limited in 1880, and usually more boys applied than were needed. As a result, Erik was able to be selective on the basis of muscle and brawn even if not of wit and brain. He had little sympathy for weaklings or shirkers, and no such apprentices lasted long under his supervision.

Per's father was a large and powerfully built man in his early fifties, still in excellent physical condition. He was a driver and a pusher, who considered tender emotions a luxury if not a weakness. In spite of the dark circles about his eyes and the square set of his jaw, there was a certain attractiveness in his features.

The blacksmith shop in which Per worked was not only a repair shop, but also an ingenious and primitive manufacturing plant as well. Household utensils, hand tools, and simple farm machinery were fashioned of metal and wood. As the volume of business was good, the shop required six men. The same six also worked the small farm.

The old blacksmith shop had stood in the same spot ever since Per could remember. One of his earliest memories was the rhythmical ringing of the anvils in the shop. As an apprentice, he had learned something of the sweat and toil necessary for the trade. Some months earlier, his brother, Amund had worked in the shop. He had received no favors because he was the master's son. The same could be said of Per.

Suddenly Erik's imposing frame reappeared in the front opening of the shop, as he strode back into the building.

"What's the matter here?" he demanded gruffly. "Why are you all loafing?"

His voice seemed to lack some of its usual conviction, but the boys guiltily scrambled back to their posts. Per resecured the hammerhead safely to the handle. Then he began to reheat the iron to a cherry red.

"I better get this iron shaped and tempered," Per mumbled to himself as he pumped the cowhide bellows, "or I might not be spared next time."

Little more than seventeen years earlier, he had been born here in the eastern region of Norway.. This was the province of Kristiania and the district of Hadeland. The land lay near the cool waters of the Randsfjord, an inland lake. Low mountains, rolling hills, and patches of pines were visible from his home. Per thought Hadeland a beautiful land, both during the warm summers and the mild dark winters.

Elvestuen was the name of the small farm or *gaard*, which lay nestled in a scenic part of Brandbu parish, roughly 60 miles north of Kristiania. The gaard was near an *elv* or small stream, crossed by an old wooden bridge. Erik's father, Amund Kjos Olsen Elvestuen had left the place to Erik in 1868. That year, the father and younger children set sail for America on the Manila. Now Erik could be classified as a *bonde* or small land owning freeman.

There were several buildings on the little farm. Erik and his wife, Petronilla, lived in the square two story house with their children, Per, Anne, Engebret, and Kari. A stable for the animals stood some distance to the east. To the north and facing south was the large blacksmith shop. In it were sleeping quarters for the apprentices.

This was the place where the Elvestuens made their living. A few acres of rye and barley supplied the family with flour for *flatebröd*. The land supported four cows, and a half dozen sheep, several pigs, and one horse. Each fall they sold whatever small surplus there was at the marketplace. Erik's blacksmith shop, however, was the main source of income.

The Elvestuens were well off only by comparison to renters and cotters. Like most Norwegians of that time, they were quite class conscious, and keenly aware of differences between themselves and their neighbors.

Life in Hadeland had gone on thus for centuries; with an uncertain balance between the land and the people that it supplied. Since only a small portion of the land area in Norway was arable, Per was keenly aware of the growing strain that a doubling of population during the 19th century had placed on the scant supply of productive soil. Land ownership was therefore highly prized and eagerly sought. It carried status and respectablility that was difficult to match any other way.

Suddenly the boys heard the sound of a bell fom the house. "Supper! Supper!" yelled Helge. "I'm so hungry, I could eat a whale."

"Supper is ready," repeated another boy.

This was a favorite time of the day, and the boys hurried to wash up for the evening meal.

In a few minutes, the men were gathered around a large square table. Petronilla and Anne bustled about bringing in huge quantities of steaming potatoes, salted fish, carrots, flatebröd, and milk products from the kitchen. To the women, the hungry men seemed impossible to fill up with food.

Pertronilla was a traditional person for her times. She operated what amounted to a boardinghouse, with four apprentices besides her own family of six still at home. She was industrious and a good manager about the house. Beyond that she was quiet, kind and patient. Her habits were orderly. All those who knew her tended to feel kindly toward her. She felt intimidated by her husband, but living long before serious talk of rights for women, she said little of her feelings. Petronilla had long since learned to live with Erik's demands upon her. She dearly loved her homeland and could not bear the thought of leaving it. For this reason, she showed little interest when others talked of migrating to America.

If there was anything eccentric about Petronilla, it was that she was a bit fussy about keeping her house spotless. Since Erik was not in sympathy with this, she did her cleaning when she was quite sure he was not around. At one time, he had come upon her when she was down on her hands and knees, scrubbing the floor.

"What's the matter with you, woman?" he demanded. "This floor does not need scrubbing! Why can't you learn to do something more productive?"

For some moments the men ate in silence, except for the normal sounds of eating, passing food, and clinking of glasses and dishes. Erik was the first to break the stillness.

"The rye and barley will soon be ripe," he announced. "We

must be ready to harvest in a few days."

"I'll bring the scythes into the shop so we can sharpen them tomorrow," answered Per. "Only one needs fixing."

Cutting grain with a cradle and scythe was even harder work than that in the shop. Per could well remember how sore his muscles became on the first nights of harvest. After a few days the body toughened and grew accustomed to the grueling work.

His mind drifted off again. As soon as their own small harvest was finished, he would be working at the Kjos Estate, one of the remaining large farms in the area. Besides the Kjos renters, many harvesters would be needed to cut, bind, and shock the fields by hand. The year before, Per had received almost the equivalent of 20ᶜ per day. He knew these were very good wages.

Best of all he would be seeing Herre Kjos's daughter again. Per felt excitement just at the thought of her. He could clearly remember her as laughing and gay, blue-eyed, light-haired, and shapely. She was about his own age and quite willing to flirt with him. The year before, Per had been near losing his heart as well as his good sense, when his brother Amund had awakened him.

"You better not get any funny ideas!" he cautioned. "Just remember this, she is the daughter of a big land owner."

Per had been terribly hurt at the time, partly because he realized what Amund said was only too true. He could never hope to marry a girl like Sigrid.

At Christmas he had seen her again at a party in the big Kjos house. Per was included with the young folks who were invited. This time too he found his emotions difficult to keep in check. Sigrid had smiled at him in an inviting way, and he had responded by dancing often with her. He wanted to say something clever, but instead felt like a dolt in her company. Afterwards he was disappointed and angry with himself. All of this came back to him often and with a stab of embarassment.

As Per was leaving the house to do the evening chores, his mother motioned for him to come nearer.

"We have a letter from Amund," she confided; "he has much to tell."

"How is he? Is he all right?"

"Yes, he seems to be just fine."

"What is he doing? Where is he now?" Per was anxious to know.

"He has visited with grandfather and some uncles and aunts in Iowa. Now he has found a job with a Norwegian farmer near Decorah."

Per fairly flew out to do the chores. By working as fast as he could, it was only a short while before he was back in the house to read the letter.

Amund seemed enthusiastic about America, and he was pleased with the money he was earning. He told of driving four horses on the plow and harrow. This sounded fantastic to Per, thinking of their one horse at Elvestuen. Amund also spoke of a 240 acre farm. It sounded very large. Since Norwegians did not reckon land in terms of acres, Per did not get the full impact of size.

"Well, Amund is strong and ambitious too," Per said to his mother.

"If there's a way to get ahead, he will find it," she agreed.

About a week later, Per was slowly making his way along the edge of the Kjos field. His muscular arms worked in rhythm with the scythe, as he sliced his way through the tall, even grain. The yellow straw was laid in neat bundles for those who followed behind to bind and shock. The sun was high in the sky, and Per's face was sweaty from the heat and his labor. The smell of harvest was in the air, as he moved along in a row of six men cutting the ripe barley. The grain had to be dried and stacked. Rain might come.

On the first day at the Kjos Estate, Per had seen Sigrid. She had smiled and acted very friendly. That she liked him, was evident to Per. At first he did not get a chance to talk to her, but he hoped that might come later. The smiles she gave him were enough for now.

During the next several days, Per saw Sigrid often. He was pleased to believe she was deliberately crossing paths with him as often as possible. Much encouraged, he smiled and spoke to her whenever he could. Often when she brought water to the field, their eyes met and hands or arms touched.

Before long, Per began to look for a chance to be with Sigrid alone. With so many many workers around, this was no easy matter. He managed to say only a few words softly, meant for her ears alone.

"You are such a handsome girl, Sigrid," he said, blushing.

"Why thank you, Per," Sigrid dimpled with a pretty smile.

"And I like you so much that it hurts."

"Oh, Per, you are so nice and so good looking. I like you better than anyone else."

Per whistled to himself as he went back to his work. Surely Sigrid was the prettiest girl in all of Norway!

That same evening, as Per made ready to walk back to Elvestuen, he and Sigrid were drawn together like magnets. Per looked around and saw no one near. As they stood close to each other, Sigrid reached out to put her hand on Per's shoulder. In turn, he bent down to give her a kiss on the cheek. Instead she kissed him back with an invitation in her eyes. Forgetting everything else, Per gathered her tightly into his arms. As if in a dream, his lips met hers. This first kiss was soft, tender and loving; the second longer and more urgent, as she pressed against him.

"Sigrid, will you be my girl?" asked Per in a husky voice.

"Yes, Per, I would like that," she nodded in a direct answer.

Per's short but heady moment collapsed, as he looked up to see Herre Kjos standing at the corner of the house, in full view. He looked stern and displeased. More than likely he had been watching earlier.

On the following day, Sigrid looked troubled. She did not seek Per out or smile as they passed. He tried to speak to her and press her for an explanation. At first she did not want to answer his questions, then hesitatingly, she gave him the unwelcome facts.

"My father has forbidden me to see you," she said quietly, "and he has told me to stay away from you. I am truly sorry, Per."

Per was almost beside himself with anxiety. He knew only too well that her father had his reasons. The son of a blacksmith was certainly not a suitable man for Herre Kjos's daughter.

"Sigrid, I am going to America," he blurted out. "There I'll become a land owner, and then I'll send for you. Will you wait for me?"

For a minute, Sigrid looked up at him with a hopeful smile, then she lowered her eyes and walked away. She did not answer his question.

As Per went back to his work that afternoon, his emotions churned inside. By example he had learned that his people did not show their feelings. But on that afternoon, this was almost too much to bear. He was now glad that this was the last day of harvest at the Kjos farm. By nightfall they would be finished with the last field.

Over and over the same thought burned through his mind, "I must become a land owner. Then perhaps I can marry Sigrid. There is no other way."

Per was determined he would write to Amund the very next Sunday. As soon as he was 18 years of age, he would leave for America. There he would soon be a landowner, which would bring prestige and dignity. This should give him the right to marry even a *stor bonde's* daughter.

Back at Elvestuen, Per and Bjorn were set to stacking grain from the shocks. Per was careful to lay the butt ends out to the weather and the grain in the middle. He built the stack round with a domelike top. If the stacking were done right, the grain would remain perfectly dry. Since Erik was most particular about the stacks, it was a job to be taken seriously. To be sure, he would be out to inspect and criticize the work when it was finished. Per had come fairly close to pleasing his father the year before, and so he hoped that his stacking would pass inspection again.

When Sunday came, Per spent most of his time writing a letter to Amund. Writing was not difficult for Per, since he had spent a part of seven years in school and took to it naturally. It was the importance of the letter that took time. In order to get to America, Per would need a good deal of information about the long and complicated trip. Then too, he would need to borrow money from Amund or another relative in America since he did not have nearly enough money to buy the necessary tickets.

"Well, it's finally finished," he thought. "Amund will be surprised."

Per could not expect to get an answer for many weeks.

Towards evening of the same Sunday, Erik walked into the house looking very thoughtful. A frown creased his forehead, as he began to speak.

"I have just talked to Trygve," he announced, "and he told me that the government has sent his son, Erling, a notice of conscription."

It was evident by Erik's expression and demeanor that he did not approve. He was not one to believe everything government officials told people. In his opinion, most wars were begun by the aristocrats and the rich, but they were invariably fought and paid for by the common people. Most wars were unnecessary. Erik firmly believed that this was true of every country in Europe.

Military service was compulsory in Norway, as in every other nation in Europe. War was the usual method of settling differences between nations, and they always had old scores to be settled and new dissentions developing. Several young men from the Brandbu parish had migrated in time to avoid the draft, since consription tended to be quite unpopular.

"I feel sorry for Erling!" exclaimed Per. "He must be quite upset. I'm going to run over and talk to him."

As he walked along the path to his neighbor's home, Per reflected on the events of the day. Under the circumstances he thought perhaps it was just as well that he had already made plans to leave. He certainly didn't want to be drafted. Before Amund left for America, Per had learned that military draft was not used there except in the event of war.

"America certainly is far ahead of the Old Country in that respect," he declared out loud to himself.

Per was beginning to think more and more about the land across the sea. This was a country he had heard about since he was a small boy, and now before long it was to become his own land. He found this a very heady thought.

Up to this time Per's knowledge of America had been limited. He had read "Uncle Tom's Cabin," a best seller in Norway. Stories such as "The Sioux Uprising, "Custer's Last Stand" and others had found their way to European shores. Per also knew that Abraham Lincoln was a great American president, who had freed the negro slaves by proclamation. He had read some of the advertising of the steamship lines and railroad companies, which made great claims about the ease of obtaining land and wealth in the New World. Relatives living there had never fully verified these claims, but Per knew that some had come to own good sized tracts of land. The Elvestuen's received letters from Erik's relatives, who lived in Iowa. Neighbors had told of letters from their relatives in the United States. However, the information was sketchy and sometimes repeated rather than clarified the particulars of their situation.

From his father, Per had learned a certain restless discontent. As a freeholder, Erik and others like him had struggled against officialdom. The first small seeds of democracy had been planted in the Norwegian constitution of May 17, 1814. Erik and others also questioned the state church and clergy. They considered the state Lutheran ministers not too different from the Catholic priests of earlier times. Further, they believed that Hans Nielson Hauge, the lay preacher, was imprisoned, not because his teaching was false, but because he threatened the position of the ordained clergy of the state church. In Erik's mind, neither the state ministers or the government officials had very much compassion for the people of Norway.

The sound of the iron shod hoofs on the hard dirt road was monotonous, as the big horse plodded along. Per and his father sat up on the seat on the front of the wagon, which was loaded with sacks of grain. Following closely behind were Anne and Engebret herding the animals to be sold in town. The lambs and calves were smooth and sleek from the summer's ample grasses.

Per was looking forward to this trip to town, because he did not get there often. He had been to Roykenvik, which was much nearer Elvestuen; but that was only a post office and station, and not a town.

As was often the case, Erik was silent as they drove along. Feeling a need to talk with him, Per tried several times to start a conversation.

"I'm going to be 18, and of age in March," he volunteered.

"Yes, I suppose so," grunted Erik.

"I've been thinking a lot about going to America."

"Do you want to go?"

"Yes, I think I must go."

"Why do you say that?"

"Amund seems to like it fine there."

"All Amund cares about is making money."

"I want to become a land owner. Only in America can I have a chance to be one."

Since Erik had no reply for that, the conversation stopped.

Soon Per jumped off the wagon and waited for Engebret and Anne to catch up. He motioned to his brother to get on the wagon, and Engebret scrambled up on the back. He was looking forward to his turn to ride up front. Per walked along beside his sister, helping to keep the animals in a small cluster behind the wagon.

Although she was only 13, Per could see that Anne was mature for her age. Already she was a great help for her mother. Per was grateful for that. In one more year, she would be confirmed, and she would finish school at the same time. Then as was the custom, she would probably help at home until she was 18. After that she might get married or strike out on her own.

"Are you anxious to get to town?" asked Per.

"Yes, it's been a year since I was there last."

"Are your feet sore?"

"No, not yet, but they probably will be before we get to town."

The truth of the matter was that she was tired of walking, but she did not admit this to her brother. Soon it would be her turn to ride on the wagon. After that they would be in town. Driving animals was considered women's work, and Anne was glad Per was willing to take his turn.

By the time they reached town, it was late in the afternoon. After Erik had dickered intensely for a few minutes, he sold all the produce. They unhitched the horse from the wagon and fed and watered him. Then they made arrangements for the night's lodging. Only one room was rented for all of them, since they thought two rooms too expensive.

Together, the family made some purchases, which were necessary for the coming winter. Each one was then free to enjoy the sights and sounds of the town. Engebret and Anne each had a few carefully hoarded copper coins to spend. That the amount was small didn't seem to matter to them.

Suddenly Erik became very thirsty and headed for a *skjenk*. Accustomed as the children were to this, his drinking put a damper on their enjoyment. Often after indulging, their father became critical and quarrelsome. At home, it was usually the mother who took the brunt of his bad disposition that followed his intemperance. Per felt sorry for her, but he felt it was not his place to interfere in the matter.

Near midnight the younger Elvestuens went to bed, far beyond their usual bedtime. Erik had not yet come in for the night.

Perhaps an hour later, they were awakened by a loud banging at the door. They heard Erik stumble as if to fall and then curse loudly. Getting himself into bed seemed an insurmountable task. He swore and cursed again. A couple of times he began to sing loudly and out of tune. Finally, Per heard him lie still and begin to snore.

As late fall came to Hadeland, the sun gradually faded into the south and the nights grew longer. This was the time of the year the Elvestuens stored up food for the winter and the following year. When Per was not working in the blacksmith shop, he was helping fill the family larder. After the garden produce was safe in the cellar, he helped with the butchering. Petronilla needed beef and mutton for *rull*, a spiced meat roll, and dried beef. She also needed pork for salting and making into hams and bacon. Per and the other young folks stayed up very late several nights to catch trout for smoked, salted, and pickled fish.

Early winter was the time for the women to bake large quantities of *flatebröd*. Per's mother rolled out the dough like a large and very thin piecrust. She made the bread of rye and barley flour. Each piece measured about 20 inches in diameter. They baked the bread on top of the stove until it was crisp and dry. This way the flatebröd would keep indefinitely.

As the sun moved further south towards the horizon, winter came to Elvestuen. White snow covered the landscape. But even though the days were short and the nights long, the weather did not get quite so cold as one might expect for a country so far to the north.

During that winter, thoughts of Sigrid often filled Per's mind. He had heard she was away at school but was expected home for Christmas. As this was a time for sledding and skiing, the young folks often met on the hillsides. In hopes of seeing Sigrid again, Per went as often as he could.

On a Sunday afternoon, during the holidays, he saw her again on the ski slopes. It seemed as if everyone in the neighborhood was there, and he found speaking to her alone quite difficult. The two were soon very much aware of each other, and their glances met numerous times. Finally with some cooperation on her part, Per was able to address her in a low voice.

"Do you remember what I said when we last met?"

"Yes, I remember."

"I was serious about going to America. Will you wait for me?"

Just at that moment, several of her friends swept in on their skis, preventing Sigrid from giving an audible answer. Per was certain she had nodded her head. From that time on, he believed a promise or a bond existed between the two of them.

When Per's patience had been nearly exhausted, the letter from America came. Little Kari came running to tell him.

"Per! Per! Amund's letter has come!" she exclaimed, out of breath.

Happily Per caught her up and lifted her to his shoulder.

"I'll miss you, little sister," he said, holding her aloft.

"Hey, now I'm taller than you, Per. Please don't let me fall."

Per read and then reread the letter several times. Everything seemed to be there. The money he needed and the instructions seemed to be in order. In addition was a list of things he must not do. He was not to come alone, nor was he to carry much money. Above all, he was not to attempt to travel through the large cities by himself.

Immediately, Per began to make his plans for the trip. This was the major event in his life so far, and there were many necessary preparations.

Per's birthday was on the 8th day of March, and his departure was set for a few days following. Everything was ready. He had his home made iron bound chest packed with clothes and a few most prized possessions. His immigration permit had come.

On the last Sunday before Per left, several of his friends came for a farewell party. Petronilla fixed *Kjötboller*, since she knew this was one of his favorite meals. His mother knew how to spice the meatballs to make them taste just right.

As the time for his departure from Norway came closer, Per found he had mixed feelings about leaving. Up to this time, he had been too busy to think much about it. This was a serious step. Leaving the land of your ancestors and the home of your childhood, even for the best of reasons, was not a small decision. He often talked with Petronilla. His *Mor* was not happy about his leaving, and he found his feelings for her were deep indeed. She became symbolic to Per, during those last days, of all that was good in his homeland and all that he would leave behind, as he journeyed to the New Land.

CHAPTER TWO

Crossing the Atlantic

The salt tears blurred Per's vision, as he stood looking back at his native land disappearing in the distance. As the ship moved away from the dock at Kristiania, he had at once begun to feel homesick. The emotion swept over him like a wave. In the previous days, he had been impatient to get started, but now the impact of all he was leaving behind filled his mind.

His thoughts went back to his family as he had last seen them. He could see his sisters waving their handkerchiefs, and his brother waving his hand. His mother's eyes had looked so sad. She did not want him to go. Even his father had shown some feeling. Actually for a family who tried to hide strong emotions from each other, Per thought it had said quite an emotional "goodby".

Per's thoughts were heavy as he recalled his childhood. Now, standing on the deck of the ship, he was able to see a picture of the Elvestuen gaard just as it was when he played there as a child. He could see it all, the red tiled roofs, the upstairs windows on the house, the old gnarled boards of the stable, and the blacksmith shop opening to the south. Yes, and the dirt road leading to the old wooden bridge crossing the *elv* that gave the gaard its name. The Randsfjord, the mountains, the rolling pine covered hills, all of these were so vivid in his mind. Was he ever to see these cherished sights again?

"How beautiful it all was!" he excaimed softly, under his breath.

Most of all he would miss his family. How sweet little Kari had looked! What a sturdy lad Engebret had become, and how grownup Anne seemed for only thirteen. Then there was *Mor*. She had such kind and gentle ways. As always his feelings were mixed when he thought of his father, but now Per realized that he loved Erik too.

Inevitably his thoughts turned to Sigrid. Her merry eyes and flashing smile was as clear in his mind as when he had last seen her. But now, thinking about her was different than ever before. She had been his primary motivation for leaving Norway. For the first time, Per seriously wondered if he would ever see Sigrid again. That was a sobering thought.

Suddenly the chill spring wind from the sea brought him back to reality. Although warmly dressed, he shivered.

"Now its time to turn around and face towards America," he mumbled to himself under his breath. With that he stooped to pick up his iron bound chest and made his way below the deck.

A little later in the day, Per met another young man who seemed not much older than himself. Feeling lonesome, he wanted to make a friend.

"My name is Per Elvestuen," he said politely. "What is yours?"

Soren Björklund," the other answered quickly. "I'm on a business trip for my father. He lives in Kristiania. Where are you headed, Per?"

"I am on my way to America," answered Per simply.

Soren seemed impressed. Going to another continent was quite an adventure for anyone.

"What part of Norway do you come from?" he asked.

"From Hadeland, Kristiania Province."

"Oh is that so? Well, my father was born in Hadeland too."

"My family lives in the parish of Brandbu near Röykenvik."

"I've been to visit my grandparents in the parish of Lunner, near Roa many times!" exclaimed Soren.

Both of the boys were delighted to discover their common roots. From that time on, a kinship grew between them. Although one was from the city and the other from the country, the two boys hit it off very well. Per was so happy to have a traveling companion that he didn't mind that Soren was better dressed and more sophisticated. During the next hour, Per found that Soren could speak some English; also that he had been to the city of Newcastle on a previous trip.

On the second day at sea, Per watched again from the deck. The sky was clear, and he could see part of the coastline in the distance.

"We are looking at the last part of Norway we will see," said a man standing next to him. "One day I hope to see it again."

As Per thought about that, he had a second feeling of melancholy. If he could roll back the time and decide again, would he be able to make up his mind so easily? Eventually, he was able to console himself with the idea that some day he would be rich enough to return to his homeland.

After a while, he was able to turn his thoughts to more pleasant memories, including his last Christmas at home. How his family and their neighbors loved to celebrate Christmas! Per didn't really believe in the little *nisser* or any of the other trolls or goblins, but as a boy the stories had been pretty convincing to him. By reading, he had learned that Christmas was first set up late in December to replace the old pagan rituals and festivities the Norwegians had enjoyed centuries earlier. These celebrations had taken place just after the Vikings were certain that the sun had begun its long journey back to the north from the winter solstice.

Suddenly Per chuckled. *Yulebukking* may have gone back to heathen practice, but it was fun to dress up and go out in crazy costumes at night."

On Christmas eve, he went to church with his family. The Elvestuens (like most Norwegians) thought that the holiest night of the year.

Per's last weeks at home had been busy. During the short winter days, he had helped his family cut and haul wood to stack and cure for the following year. He had also prepared for the trip to America. First he worked diligently during his spare time to build a chest in the shop. This he made carefully of wood, bound with metal straps and corners. To the lid, he added metal hinges, and a hasp secured by a padlock. Into this trunk, he carefully packed the most necessary items for his journey. Luckily his emigration papers came in good time, as he could not have left without them.

Before his departure from Kristiania, Per had carefully followed Amund's instructions. For about $53 he purchased a contract and tickets that were to take him all the way to Decorah, Iowa. His baggage was carefully marked. Last of all, he exchanged the remainder of his money for American dollars.

On the ship that evening, the North Sea became turbulent, as the water rose and fell in rolls and swells. Per became so nauseated that he was unable to eat. To lie down increased his distress, so sleep was near impossible.

Stories had come back to them in Norway. Stories of dreadful experiences of immigrants making the crossing. In the past Per had wondered if these tales were actually true, but now, wide awake on the rough seas, he decided indeed they were true.

Per realized that with immigrants packed into the steerage beyond capacity, the adventure of a voyage to the New World must have turned into a nightmare for many. Some had told of seasickness in crowded quarters filled with filth and stench. Others complained of wormy food, spoiled meat, and water vinegared to cover the odor. He had heard that unless steerage passengers banded together to protect them, immigrant women were often raped by the ship's crew. Worst of all were the stories of dreadfull diseases that broke out in the underdecks of the old sailing vessels. Typhoid or cholera often raged out of control among the poor immigrants in the steerage. Victims of "ship fever" were buried simply, with a cold splash into the murky waters of the North Atlantic. Those who survived to send letters home were the lucky ones.

"I'm surely glad I have passage on a steam ship and not a sailing vessel," Per told Soren in the morning.

"That's right," agreed his friend. "Steam is safer and much quicker."

"I've heard the older sailing ships take six weeks or more."

"In the month saved, you can more than earn the difference in price."

Government subsidies paid to British, German and other merchant ship owners reduced the price of steerage passage. The object of these subsidies was to insure large shipping fleets in case of war; however, another result was that by the 1880's most immigrants were carried by steam ships rather than by sailing vessels.

Per was learning to appreciate his brother's advice. In one respect he had failed to follow instructions: he had come alone and not in the company of friends. At the time, Per felt he could not wait until others were ready to leave. Now he resolved to find traveling companions as soon as possible.

Early on the third day, the passengers sighted the coast of England. Some time later, the ship entered the mouth of the Tyne and proceeded up the river to the port of Newcastle. After docking, the two boys left the ship and agreed to meet again early in the evening.

Since Per's train was not to leave for Liverpool until morning, he set out for the boarding house provided by the steamship lines. He was not impressed, but the facilites were "for no extra cost".

Later, when he and Soren met again, they decided to see some of the city. Per had never been out of Norway nor seen a city except Kristiania. It was exciting to be with a person so knowledgeable. As the two walked along the street, they came to a pub from which came sounds of music, loud talking and laughing, and the clinking of glasses.

"Sounds like a good time in there," commented Per.

"It's a good idea not to go into places like that, especially if you are alone," advised Soren, confidentially.

"What do you mean?" queried Per.

"They are rough places here along the docks, and you could easily be beaten and robbed."

Several times Per noticed young women smiling at them or beckoning for them to approach. The women sometimes called out to them, but Per was not able to understand.

"What's the matter with those girls? Why are they acting so funny?"

"Oh, they are prostitutes. For a couple shillings you can go to bed with one," laughed Soren. "But I would be careful. You might get a sickness or you could be robbed of your money."

"I've heard men talk of women like that," admitted Per, "but this is the first time I've seen them."

"In cities like this there are people who will try to trick or cheat anyone who isn't able to protect themselves," Soren went on. "This is especially true around the docks."

After several hours of sight seeing in Newcastle, the two boys said goodbye to each other. They did so with regret, since neither ever expected to see the other again. In the morning Soren would take the ship back to Norway, and Per would be on the train to Liverpool.

Back at the boardinghouse, Per found that many men would sleep in the same room. Furthermore, every man was expected to share one of the double beds with another. Most of the men were already in bed or asleep for the night. Per removed only his outer clothing, then quietly slipped into bed with a sleeping stranger. For a long time he lay awake, thinking. He was glad that his money and papers were still safe in the soft sheepskin belt next to his skin. Some of the men snored loudly. . . Finally Per slept.

In the morning he awakened early. Soon he was relieved to find some of the men speaking Norwegian. At breakfast he looked the men over carefully and saw one dressed much like himself. After approaching him guardedly, Per was happy to find him a fellow countryman from Skien named Gustav Stensrud. He was on his way to Chicago. As Gustav too was alone, they soon agreed to travel together.

At the train station, the two boys met two other Norwegian immigrants. Both were from Stavanger and headed for New York.

"I've been warned that many are around who would fleece us if they could," explained Per. "Don't you think we would be smart to travel together through Liverpool and New York?"

"Andreas and I heard something about that too," agreed Torjus.

"Four of us together will be better protected," nodded Andreas.

Per found Liverpool a great city of smokestacks, factories, and slums. Being the city was one of the main European points of embarkment for America, the boys found the docks abounding with immigrants, sailors, commerce, and great ships.

As the many passengers streamed into the big ocean liner, Per and his new companions made their way with the rest. The hustle and bustle of immigrants and workmen was new and strange to them, and different from any experience they had known. The young men all agreed that their boat, the "Angelo", was a mighty fine steamship.

A little later as they found their way down into the steerage, it did not seem nearly so fine or so grand. They agreed that the steamship lines were not overly concerned about the comfort of immigrants. However, the price was low, and they realized that they were packed in to show a profit.

"There's an awful smell in here!" sniffed Gustav.

"What in the world is it anyway?" questioned Torjus.

"They say immigrants smell of ship after crossing the ocean in a steerage. This must be what they mean," explained Per.

"Oh, well," reflected Andreas, we'll soon be in America."

When the weather was favorable, the young men spent much of their time up on the part of the deck set aside for steerage passengers. His new friends made great sport in making overtures to the immigrant girls, who were also up on the deck. Sometimes Per joined in their fun, but more often he daydreamed about Sigrid. These dreams often included great holdings of land in America. In them he was *stor bonde* and Sigrid was his gracious wife.

Per did not suffer the hardships and indignities of those who sailed much earlier. Still, in 1881, it was not an easy voyage. The bunks were set close together in tiers and each just 24 inches wide. The steerage lacked any form of privacy. Overcrowding of human bodies resulted in strong and offensive odors like those that come from too many chickens in a crate.

The steerage steward soon earned the reputation of the most unpopular man on the ship. His "imperial majesty" looked down his long nose at the steerage immigrants as if they were less than human. At best they were only to be tolerated, at worst they were stupid, smelly foreigners.

From the beginning there was disatisfaction with the food. Steerage folks were used to simple fare, but what the steward dished out was unpalatable. At breakfast some found bugs in their oatmeal; at noon the meat was tainted; and in the evening, the fat pork was inedible. The meals continued with stale bread, oversalted fish, half boiled beans, and much more of the fat pork.

The steerage passengers tried to complain, but to no avail. The steward was unyielding. They found the ship's officers held complete power over the captive immigrants. On the high seas the steward's word was law.

One day during the noon meal, Per was to emerge as their hero and champion. The disliked officer again served the fatty pork. The resentment among the immigrants was unanimous. In a fit of youthful rebellion, Per suddenly picked up a big piece of the detested goo and threw it at the steward. As luck would have it, the greasy gob struck him full in the ear!

The haughty man whirled around, his face red with anger. "How dare you do that to me!" he yelled. "Who is responsible?"

Not a sound came from the group, as each one looked down at his plate.

"I say, who did it?" he demanded again in a loud voice. "You had better tell me or it will go hard with all of you."

Getting nothing in return except absolute silence, he glared angrily at them and stamped out of the room.

Per felt greatly relieved when everyone began to titter. For days afterwards, there was much quiet chuckling by the immigrants, who were in full sympathy with the act. If the steward made further attempts to discover the culprit, he apparently was unsuccessful. As Per came to understand the complete authority of the officers over the steerage cargo, he realized he might have spent the rest of the voyage in chains, had he been discovered.

His three companions had great fun over this event. They looked at Per with amusement, but also with a new respect. His position as leader of the four grew stronger because of the incident.

The following day, a spring storm came out of the northwest with tremendous force and fury. Both Per and Gustav grew seasick. Many of the young men were vomiting, and the resulting stench and filth added to everyone's misery. Per was fearful he would never feel normal again.

The main storm subsided, but Per and Gustav did not fully

recover until the ocean was quite calm again. Both of them tried to be cheerful in sickness, but the experience took most of the enjoyment from the voyage.

"I see you both quit feeding the fish," joked Andreas.

"It didn't look much like fun," added Torjus, sympathetically.

During the morning of the 12th day at sea, the passengers on the "Angelo" spotted the coast of North America. This news spread rapidly down into the steerage, and with much excitement the immigrants prepared to land. The four friends soon had their baggage packed and carried up on the deck. On the western horizon, they could now clearly see the land. Per shared the excitement with the others. He recognized the name "America" being said in many different tongues and dialects, as the people crowded to get a better look at the fast approaching land.

As the immigrants craned their necks, Per found his six-foot height an advantage. By standing on tiptoe, he could see over the heads of others. His mind was filled with strange and exciting wonder when he looked at the shore beyond the stretch of water. Here, finally was America! Here was the "Land of Canaan", his new home! Briefly he speculated as to whether they might see an Indian or negro, perhaps even a cowboy as they landed in New York City.

The excitement on board grew as land came closer. The immigrants watched as the great ship prepared to enter the bay. A pilot came on board to guide the ship through the channel and into port. Now they could easily see the shore on both sides. Numerous boats and ships, as well as islands seemed to fill the water. As the bay began to narrow again, the ship came to another halt. The people grew quiet wondering what was going to happen.

"The health inspectors are coming aboard," someone explained in Norwegian. "We are under temporary quarantine."

The ship's officers waved and shouted to make way for the health officials. Word was passed that if there was no sign of contagion, the ship would be allowed to dock. Then the cabin passengers would go ashore. The immigrants were to be processed. No cabin passenger was considered an immigrant.

"I wonder where we will get off," pondered Gustav.

For the fiftieth time, Per dug into his pocket to pull out his tattered letter and read a part of it.

"It says here that we'll be taken to a place called 'Castle Gardens'," he explained. "It's a big round building that can hold thousands of people."

The four boys gazed silently at the buildings of Manhattan Island. Per could plainly see this was a city far greater than either Kristiania or Liverpool. Now almost directly in front of them, they saw a large domed building with a big red, white, and blue flag on the top. Shortly the ship came to another stop. After some further delay, they saw smaller boats coming to unload the immigrants.

"Look, we are going to unload!" said Per. "Let's push ahead and see if we can be first."

Being more alert and agressive than most, Per and his friends soon found themselves on a boat approaching the large building flying the American flag. They realized this was Castle Gardens.

Inside the building, they found immigrants packed in by the thousands. People in front, people behind, people pushed together, until they seemed to fill up every space. Per saw awestruck children, women crying or praying, and men looking unsure. All were forming into lines and waiting in the midst of confusion. There were endless questions, inspections, and waiting. Some of the officials were helpful, but others plainly showed their contempt. Per reacted with anger when he saw older and less adaptable immigrants badly treated because they were confused by an interpreter who sometimes tried to trap them. He thought of his own parents.

"I've read that in America, all are supposed to be equal," he said, looking thoughtful.

"Not a poor steerage immigrant," retorted Gustav. "He gets a cold welcome, that's plain to see."

Although Per could see for himself people by the thousands, he was unable to grasp the immensity of the immigration movement. He saw only a few newcomers who came from the seaports of Europe to the shores of America, but could not comprehend the greatest human migration in all history. Per was one of nearly forty millions who came in one century.

After making very slow progress most of the day, Per was able to show his contract, tickets, and $12 in American money. That seemed to answer a lot of important questions. After giving some other correct answers, with the help of an interpreter, he was allowed through the line.

As he sat in the rotunda of Castle Gardens waiting for his westbound train, Per marveled at the colorful sights around him. Many of the girls and young women had worn their best native costumes for the landing. These were rich in reds and blues and other bright colors. Some costumes, he recognized from his homeland. Men and boys loafed around wearing the more drab colors of homespun cloth or dark store bought suits. Most wore small brimmed caps or hats in somber tones to match.

Soon Per was joined by Gustav. The two sat and watched the other immigrants, as they speculated on the train trip to Chicago. Towards evening the two boys were joined by their friends, Torjus and Andreas. Both looked exhausted.

"We just tried to help a countryman who was cheated," said Andreas.

"The money changer gave him only half as much as he had coming," explained Torjus, looking angry.

"We couldn't find the scoundrel anywhere."

"Now the poor fellow doesn't have enough left for his train ticket."

At that point, the railroad agent came to sort out the immigrants and to tag them for loading onto the railroad cars. Reluctantly, Per and Gustav said goodbye to their friends, and went with the many who were bound for Chicago. That was a main point of distribution Per had been told.

The two men found the immigrant car to be an old remodeled box car. Fine sleepers, diners, and soft cushions were not for them. Instead, theirs were hard wooden benches both for sitting and sleeping. They carried their own food. As the immigrants prepared to eat, the pungent odors of sauerkraut, garlic, and other national foods mixed with stale tobacco smoke and strong body odors, reminding Per once again of the ship's steerage.

By the time the train began its laborious journey, daylight had disappeared into night. As the immigrant car crept along the tracks, some of the people snored in sound sleep, while others dozed fitfully now and then. No one realized the great distance between New York and Chicago.

Since the train stopped to switch freight cars in every village and city, Per and Gustav were able to get off every now and then. They found the fresh air invigorating and the earth good and solid.

Time stretched on. Night came once and then again, and time began to hang heavy for Per and Gustav. Everyone grew tired and listless. To keep up their spirits, the boys often talked of their plans in the New Land. Some times when they passed large and well kept farms. Per daydreamed again of being a *stor bonde* and of marrying Sigrid.

Late on the third day, the train stopped outside the depot at Chicago.

"It looks like more health inspectors," suggested Gustav.

Sure enough, the doctors were from the National Board of Health. They came to check on small pox vaccinations. In due time, the officials seemed satisfied and the train was allowed to resume its tedious journey. Shortly thereafter, the young men found themselves in the great depot at Chicago.

A relative had come to meet Gustav and Per found himself alone again. However, the tag system seemed to work very well, and Per had no difficulty getting on the right train bound for Madison, Wisconsin.

Nearly two days later, Per reached the depot at Prairie du Chien. A man who spoke Norwegian gave Per directions.

"Take the ferry across the river to McGregor, and then you can take the train right into Decorah."

"Many thanks," said Per, setting out once again.

1881 was a wet spring, and the mighty Mississippi was high. Although Per had just crossed the Atlantic Ocean, he was impressed with the Father of Waters. Never had he seen anything to compare with this river. Crossing on the ferryboat proved such an adventure that Per lost some of the lethargy he developed riding the train.

Only hours later, Per heard the locomotive began a gradual descent into a large valley. Big bluffs stood out on both sides, and at the bottom lay a town. He figured it must be Decorah. Tired as he was, Per found the sight a beautiful one, not unlike some scenes in his own district of Hadeland.

At the depot, Per got off carrying his iron bound wooden chest. Several people were in the building, but none looked to him like Norwegians. He tried his best to say a few words in English, but he was unable to make himself understood. He tried Norwegian. Then he saw a man smile and walk up to him.

"Are you Norwegian?" the man asked in Per's own language.

"Yes, yes, I am!" exclaimed Per, much relieved.

"Are you looking for someone?"

"I want to find Anton and Anne Rocksvold."

"Rocksvold? Yes, I know them. They live east of town."

"Can you tell me how to get to their place?"

"One of Anton's neighbors was in town a while ago. I think he might give you a ride out there."

No more than a half hour later, Per was sitting on the front of a wagon beside the driver. The team of horses left the town at a brisk trot, as they took a well traveled road to the south east. For a mile or so they followed the low ground of the valley, then they began the steep climb up the road. Gradually they wound around the bluff to its top. Up above, the countryside settled down to rolling hills, large fields, and patches of wood.

Every now and then, Per could see a farmstead. Most of the buildings were made of logs, perhaps eight inches to a foot in diameter. The roofs were of wood shingles or shakes.

"This is the old stage road from Lansing to Decorah," explained the driver, speaking Norwegian.

"Does this road go past Anton and Anne's place?" asked Per.

"No, but we follow it a few more miles."

The April day was sunny in northeastern Iowa, and the grass was turning lush and green. After breathing stale air for many days, Per liked to fill his lungs with good fresh country air.

Per found the driver very curious about Norway and about his trip. He asked many questions in some detail, which Per answered the best he could. In return, Per learned that the man's name was Hans. Also that he had emmigrated from the district of Toten, which lay next to Hadeland, some twenty years earlier.

The time passed quickly for Per, and soon the driver brought the horses to a stop. They looked across the field to a farmstead, as Hans pointed toward the house.

"There is the place," he said. "Anton and Anne live there."

Per climbed down from the wagon. "A thousand thank yous for the lift," he said, shaking hands with the driver.

For the last time, Per picked up his wooden chest and lifted it to his shoulder. He set out on foot the remaining distance to the farm buildings. The house was a good sized log cabin with a loft above, standing on the high ground. Near it were several other log buildings, including a low stable. Per hurried toward the house.

This was the place his aunt, Anne Elvestuen Rocksvold, lived. Per had finally come to the end of his journey.

CHAPTER THREE

Winneshiek County, Iowa

Per was met at the door by a woman, whom he found vaguely familiar. She was a comely young woman in her early thirties. Although at first she did not recognize him, this had to be his Aunt Anne.

"I am your nephew, Per Elvestuen," he said in his most polite manner. "I have come here from Norway."

"Per? Is it really you?" she asked. "Why of course! My, how you have grown up. Amund said you would come this spring."

Anne had last seen Per when he was five. Was it already thirteen years since she had left Elvestuen? Now here he was, a fully grown young man, and a fine fellow to be sure. Suddenly she became aware that he was still standing outside the door.

"Come in, come in," she said quickly. "Supper will soon be ready. You must be tired out from traveling."

In just a few minutes, Per had met the other members of the family. Anton was a tall, pleasant looking man with a mustache. He didn't look especially strong or robust, Per reflected. Anton and Anne had four lively children: Peter, Clara, Emma, and Albert. All seemed interested in their new cousin and helped to make him feel at home. Albert, who was only two, was shy at first but not for very long.

During the meal, the family asked Per about his trip. They were much impressed with the speed of his crossing. A sailing vessel had been much different. In 1868, for example, it had taken Anne seven weeks to reach Quebec. From there they had travel-ed a great many days by canal boat, immigration train, and final-ly by wagon before reaching Decorah.

Later in the evening, Per lay on a good corn husk mattress in the loft with Peter, who had already fallen asleep. Per was feel-ing strangely content. It had been so good to come to his Aunt Anne's after traveling such a long way. He had eaten his best meal since leaving home. His kinfolk had acted in a most cordial way, and had spoken to him only in Norwegian. His mind went back to the rolling hills, the trees, and the streams he had seen east of Decorah. The sun had been bright and the air pure, not so different from his own district of Hadeland. Soon he would see his brother. As Per grew drowsy, his being in a new and strange land did not seem so bad.

The next day, Anne was again anxious to talk with him. She asked dozens of questions about Erik and his family, and about friends and neighbors. She spoke of the countryside around Elvestuen, and Per was surprised at the detail of her memory. He realized that she thought of Norway often.

"My, how nice it is to talk with you, Per," she smiled.

"You are so kind," he answered. "It was good to come here."

"You are welcome, Per. Talking to you is almost as good as a trip back to Hadeland."

Per tried to make himself useful. He helped Anton and Peter milk the cows and feed the stock. Then he split a lot of wood and carried water from the well for Anne. He had been taught to earn his keep.

Anton and his brother Ole had come from Toten, Norway. They had two specialties, besides farming, from which they made extra cash income. One was making yokes for oxen, and the other splitting shingles. Both of these products were in con-siderable demand.

Late in the day, his Aunt Kari and her husband, Iver Berge, stopped. Kari had been the first of the Elvestuens to sail for America. That was in 1861, two years before Per was born. Iver had been on the same ship, and the two were married shortly after they reached Iowa. Kari reminded Per of Erik, as the likeness was unmistakable. She greeted Per warmly.

"So you are Erik's boy, Per," she said several times. "How nice it is to see you! I do believe you take after your mother, Petronilla." She sounded very Norwegian, Per thought.

Once again, Per was obliged to tell of his trip and family back home. After twenty years, Kari and Iver's interest in the homeland was still strong.

Per grew excited when he visited with the menfolk. He learned Winneshiek County was named for an Indian chief. Also that it was not an early settled part of Iowa. Further south, pioneers had entered the Black Hawk purchase in the early 1830's; but here in Glenwood Township, settlers did not come until twenty years later. Anton was an early arrival. By the time Iver came no open land remained, but he was able to buy 80 acres from one neighbor and 40 from another.

Anne's youngsters took to Per, and he to them. The two older ones reminded him of Engebret and sister Kari. Both had been to school and could speak English well. When they laughed at Per's first attempts to speak English, Anne scolded them.

The following evening Per met his brother, Amund. The two men shook hands. A year had passed since they had last seen each other, and they had a great deal to talk about. Amund confided to Per that he planned to leave Iowa near the first of the month.

"Wages are high and workers in big demand in Dakota," he said.

"I hoped we could be together," Per replied.

"There is still free land to homestead in that country. You can come with me," suggested Amund.

"I would like to stay here a while first," said Per thoughtfully. "After I get used to everything, I'll come there too."

"You can have my job at Nordbraatens. Later you can come to Dakota."

Per was disappointed that his brother planned to leave so soon, but he was thankful at the prospect of a steady job. He liked to think that the two of them would be together again before long. Per had always looked up to his brother, who was four years older than he.

The next morning was Sunday. The sun rose bright and clear. Since it was such a good day, the family decided to walk the two and a half miles to the church. Per walked with them. He had noticed the church, with its great spire, since the day he arrived. In the distance, it looked much like the state church at Brandbu.

"Our church was started 12 years ago," said Anne. "Building it was such a big undertaking for the pioneers that it took several years to finish."

"Much of the limestone came from our farm. We often hauled stone with our oxen and wagons early in the morning before we began our own fieldwork," explained Anton.

"The people were still poor and lived in log cabins and sod huts. The church cost nearly $12,000 in cash, besides all the donated work and materials. The settlers sacrificed to have a church," added his Aunt.

"Was it built without taxes?" asked Per in surprise.

As they neared the church, he could plainly see that the state church at Brandbu could not come close to the majesty of this one.

"The stone walls are two and a half feet thick and 70 feet high," Anton went on. "The main part of the church is 40 feet wide and 90 feet long."

Per did not answer. He was looking at the church in awe. The 140 foot spiral pointed loftily toward the heavens. Little shivers ran up his spine. As he looked again at the beautiful limestone walls, he thought they would surely stand for all eternity. Suddenly Per was filled with pride for his Norwegian countrymen, who had settled here.

"When they came to a new land, they took their God with them," thought Per. This thought comforted Per. He had found a safe harbor on American soil. Out here in Iowa his people had built a temple in His name and created a second homeland near the center of a new country.

As they walked toward the high ground on which the church was built, Per could see the people congregating. Some, like themselves, were walking. Others were driving oxen or horses. People were standing in small clusters visiting. Among them he recognized his grandfather, Amund Kjos Elvestuen, who was now coming toward them. Per could still remember sitting on his lap as a small boy. Now his grandfather was close to eighty.

"I greet you from father and mother and all from Elvestuen," he said putting on his very best manners, as he shook hands with his grandfather.

"God bless you, my boy," answered the old man. "My how you have grown since we left Elvestuen. Now you are a man. Welcome to America."

Inside the church, Per felt at home again. The altar and the benches were the same, and he could see the pastor was dressed the same. Per's gaze went to the big picture above the altar. It was of Christ, the risen Savior, on the road to Emmaus. Yes, surely everything was the same.

The church at Glenwood began to have meaning for Per. His mother had been loyal to the state church at Brandbu, but his father had been cool, even indifferent. Per had taken confirmation seriously, but since his enthusiasm for the Brandbu church had waned.

Pastor Vilhelm Koren's words stirred him, and he listened intently.

After the service Per went with his kinfolk across the road to look at the graveyard. Already many people were buried there.

"Many strangers are buried here," explained Anne. "In early days, a good many wagons passed by on the old stage road. Some would ask to bury their dead in our cemetery. These had died along the way, as they traveled westward."

"The travelers were never turned down," added Anton. "They felt better after their loved ones were buried in a church cemetery."

Per enjoyed that Sunday and the limelight among his relatives. Besides the Berge's, another uncle, Anders Amundson, and his wife Ingeborg came with their five children. Per found it confusing that his name wasn't Elvestuen. He was not used to so many relatives. Erik was the only Elvestuen to remain in Norway; his brothers and sisters emigrated to America.

Later in the week Per went to see Amund. While there he met Ola Nordbraaten, who was a strong man of about forty. Amund explained that Ola was a hard worker, and expected as much of his hired men. But he was also a fair man, who expected no more of his hired help than of himself. Ola's wife seemed a kindly women, several years younger than her husband. She looked very pregnant.

Nordbraaten farmed 240 acres. 120 of these were in crops, while the rest provided pasture, hayland, and woodlot. Ola was in the process of clearing another 40 of stumps and trees for additional cropland. Most of his neighbors still used oxen, but Nordbraaten drove four first class horses. In addition he had a large amount of livestock and needed a hired man to help him. After looking Per over, he offered him a job on the condition he would stay one full year at the least.

"I'll pay you $15 a month for eight months, and board and room for doing chores in the winter," he said. "For extra winter work I'll pay 50ᶜ a stump for grubbing, and 75ᶜ a cord for cutting cordwood."

To Per this sounded like a lot of money, as wages were only one-fifth that amount in Norway. Besides Amund had coached him as to what to expect.

"That sounds fair," he agreed. "I'll try to be a good hired man."

On the last Saturday night before Amund left the brothers decided to walk the six miles to town. The time passed quickly in talk and anticipation. In town they found people in goodly numbers, and many teams of oxen and horses hitched to the rails.

"Let's go in and have a drink," suggested Amund.

"Yes, let's do that," agreed Per. "It's the last chance we have together for some time."

Because of Erik's intemperance neither of the boys drank much. They walked in quietly and ordered two glasses of beer at five cents a mug.

The brothers were immediately recognized as recent immigrants. No sooner had they come in than they were spotted by a big, loud voiced man, who was several mugs ahead of them. Intending to make sport of them, he sauntered over. At first they tried to ignore him, but that was a mistake. He was not to be denied his fun, and this only made things worse. The men at the bar stopped talking to watch the heckler goad them.

"We don't want you dumb Norskies around here. You take jobs away from us good Americans and keep wages down for a working man."

He moved closer, jutting out his jaw and looking at them

balefully.

"Why don't you pack up and go right back where you came from?"

Per looked around quietly trying to keep his composure, although his stomach was doing somersaults. He didn't understand the words, but he did understand the tone. Not everyone in the place was sympathetic with the heckler, but Per sensed that no one would come to their rescue. The tormentor understood this also, but he misjudged the brothers. Because they did not try to respond with force, he believed them to be cowards.

"Ya Shur," he mocked. "You newcomer, immigrant sons-of-bitches! You smell yust like *lutefisk* and pickled herring!"

As the man finished his verbal abuse, he lunged forward and gave Amund, who was the nearest, a violent shove. Little did he realize that Amund had spent the winter doing the hardest kind of physical labor, nor that he was descended from a Viking and as strong as an ox.

As the anger surged through him, Amund grabbed the harasser around the waist pinning his arms tightly to his sides. Then carrying him across the room as if he were a bundle of straw, he set him down on a chair with such force that the man went straight through to the floor. There the heckler stopped with a jarring crash. For a minute the room was quiet; then the men at the bar began to talk again. The man arose slowly from the floor.

Later when they began their homeward walk, Per looked at Amund with admiration. He realized that he was lucky not to have been alone.

"My, but you're strong," he said. "He was big and mean too."

"I didn't mean to set him down so hard," explained Amund modestly, "but he went right through the chair to the floor."

"Lucky for me that you were there," said Per quietly.

On the way back the two walked mostly in silence. Per understood well that they had been singled out as immigrants, because they looked and acted different from the others. Not all Americans welcomed newcomers. Per made a silent vow that he would lose no time in learning to dress, talk, and act like

Americans. He had learned a lesson and did not want to be singled out and badgered again.

In a few days the time came for Amund to leave for Dakota Territory, and so the two brothers parted again. Per promised to come later. He sensed that he needed more time with his own kind. That way he hoped the shock of being uprooted from his old country and transplanted into this new world would not be nearly so great.

Working for Nordbraaten was a good experience for Per. Since he was used to having his father for a boss, he found Ola less of a perfectionist and easier to please. His new boss was an excellent farmer and a superb horseman. At first Per aroused Ola's displeasure several times by his ineptness at driving the horses. When he slacked the leather lines and let one slip under a single tree, his teacher lost his temper. In the long run, however, Per turned out to be an intelligent pupil and eventually handled the teams very much like Ola himself.

The variety of work on the farm was great, but the first major task was to cultivate corn. There were 40 acres to be cultivated three times. For this job, Per used a walking 2-horse single row cultivator. As the horses moved down the corn row, he grasped the two wooden handles to steer the gangs so as not to plow down the corn. The reins were fastened together at the back of his neck. Per came to like driving the horses, and didn't mind the walking except during hot weather. Between each cultivation, Per was kept busy hauling manure, fixing fence, and doing dozens of minor jobs.

Per liked the outdoors. During the many days of good weather, he enjoyed the sun and fresh air. Nature abounded in a variety of birds, insects, animals, and butterflies. The blue sky and green plants, contrasting with the dark colors of the earth, made a soothing combination of colors. Per often saw the sun rise and set.

The second big job on the farm was putting up hay. Riding up and down the field on the seat of a mower or hayrake, with the good smell of new mown hay, was fine; but Per soon found that haying was not all fun, since the weather turned hot as they were ready to stack. At first Per could not get used to the hot Iowa summer. As the sun blazed down from a clear sky, the last gentle breeze failed completely. The temperature broke the one hundred mark. Sweat and dirt combined to form tiny black rivulets down his face and neck. In the morning his shirt was caked with salt and grime.

First they pitched the hay into the hayrack with a fork, and then Per forked it into the stack. Ola made a waterproof haystack that resembled a huge loaf of bread. By the time they had completed the second stack, Per was getting more accustomed to the heat.

"You're a pretty tough Norskie at that," chuckled Ola. "It took a lot of Norwegian steam to get all that hay up in this heat."

During the hot summer, Per discovered that taking a quick splash in the creek behind the barn was most refreshing. He bathed in the nude, having no swim suit. Although nearby trees offered scant cover, he willingly took the risk. After dark when all the work was finished, he sometimes took more leisurely swims.

The harvest proved to be another Herculean task. Since it took three men to operate the McCormick hand tying reaper, Ola had to hire another man. Two of them stood on the side platform tying every other bundle with a wisp of straw, as the grain moved through the machine. By the end of the two full weeks of work, Per had grown dexterous at tying the bundles.

Shocking Ola's 80 acres of heavy grain proved to be the hardest work of all. The two hired men worked very hard for four days since the bundles were long and lay heavy on the field. Again Per's shirt dried stiff with sweat and grime overnight.

Since everyone in the neighborhood stack threshed, stacking the grain was the next job. With the help of a neighbor, whose grain they had harvested, the four men finished fourteen cone shaped stacks from Ola's fields in just over a week of steady work.

Per disliked the chores each morning and evening, especially when the weather was so hot. It was then that the milking was especially disagreeable. Per was glad that Ola bred his cows at such times that most of them freshened in the fall. The morning milking was tolerable, but in the evening the cows gave off an unbearable heat. Their tails switched unmercifully, and one might kick or put her foot in the pail. Worst of all was when the cow stepped on the milker's foot while fighting flies. Per was sure the animal turned her foot a full turn before releasing her weight from his foot.

"I'll sure be glad when the kids are old enough to do the milking before we come in from the field," Ola was often heard to say. Per agreed heartily, but decided that keeping his thoughts to himself was best.

The threshing was done with a 1878 J. T. Case thresher made in Racine, Wisconsin. The separator was made of wood with steel teeth and wagon type wheels. The machine was operated by means of a horse power and tumbling rod pulled by four teams of horses.

"We tried oxen, but they got dizzy after a while," chuckled Ola.

"Got dizzy?" questioned Per.

"From going around in a circle, guess that's why they call it horse power. Going around doesn't seem to bother them."

Since the machine had no feeder, blower, or device to measure and weigh grain, men were necessary for band cutters, straw stackers, and for weighing and sacking grain. These sacks were then hauled to the granary in farm wagons pulled by oxen. There the men emptied them into bins.

Per found threshing in Iowa the most interesting of all farm work. A crew of a dozen men was necessary to stack thresh. He was amazed to see four to six big stacks disappear daily, unless very hot weather necessitated slowing the work. The regular threshing run was finished in three weeks. After that the crew did custom threshing for another week.

During threshing Per became good friends with one of his cousins, Amund Berge, who was just one year younger than Per. Because there were several Amunds named for the grandfather, Per began to call him "Berge". Since young Berge was born in America and had attended school, he could speak both English and Norwegian very well. From him Per began to learn the English language.

After threshing came the fall plowing. Driving four horses, Per followed a sixteen inch walking plow for about twenty miles each day. To plow 80 acres took a full month. With his hands on the wooden plow handles, Per found that walking in the furrow wasn't all that bad. The northeastern Iowa weather stayed mild and nice during the early fall.

Per continued his efforts to Americanize himself. However, learning English was difficult. Sometimes he played games with the Nordbraaten children, who had been to school. Other times Per spoke his very best American to horses in the field. Gradually he began to improve.

"You say the words in English, but they still sound Norwegian," laughed Bertha, the oldest of the Nordbraaten children.

"Well, I'm trying hard," Per replied. "Say it again."

Per still had thoughts of home, and he often dreamed of Sigrid. Sometimes he had grave doubts that she would wait for him. He was saving money but could not own land until he was of age.

That fall he wrote two letters to Norway. The first was to Sigrid, explaining that he would need more time. He promised to write again as soon as he was able to obtain land. The other was his second letter to Elvestuen. Writing made him nostalgic, but not homesick in the way he had been when last he wrote.

The same fall, Per had a letter from Amund telling of the great bumper crop in eastern Dakota. Because of the great demand for labor Amund had been able to earn $2.00 a day during harvest and $2.50 a day for threshing. He went on to say that he expected to go into northern Minnesota to work in the lumber camps during the winter months.

Soon after the first hard frosts it was time to husk the corn. Husking corn by hand was an entirely new experience for Per, Since there was no such crop grown in norther Europe. Again Ola proved competent as a teacher and Per learned to fill the high wagon box twice a day. Mornings were often chilly and white with frost, but afternoons were usually sunny and mild.

On the first of December Per began to grub out tree stumps. Good sized first growth had been cut earlier for wood, but the tough old tree stumps still remained. "Piece work" turned out better than working by the month. Grubbing did take a lot of Norwegian steam as Ola would say, but the cold was invigorating. By sharpening his grubbing hoe often, Per found he could take out two stumps in a good day.

Shortly before Christmas the weather turned bitterly cold. First came a raw biting northwest wind and then a rapid drop in temperature, until one morning the mercury dropped to twenty below zero. The snow cracked under Per's feet, and the woods echoed every sound. By working vigorously in the protection of the trees he found that he could stay warm.

Dressing warm was important. Per wore heavy woolen underwear, wool trousers under duck pants, and a knit wool sweater under his coat. His cap had warm earlaps, and his mittens wool liners. Heavy knit wool socks and boots completed the outfit, allowing Per to work outside in the coldest weather.

Doing chores became difficult. The manure froze inside the stable. Ice formed almost instantly from water pumped into the tank. Per split a hickory fork handle lifting a good sized forkful of hay in the frigid barn loft. The cows didn't want to go out to drink cold water, but the horses acted frisky.

"Damn it but it's chilly!" exclaimed Ola.

"America is full of surprises," agreed Per. Actually he found the cold weather a little bit exhilarating.

Per continued his habit of attending church at Glenwood and seldom missed for any reason. Since it was also a meeting place for friends and neighbors, the church served a social as well as religious purpose. Sometimes after the church service, his Aunt Anne or Kari invited him for Sunday dinner.

During Christmas his relatives and their neighbors celebrated the holiday for twelve days in the traditional Norwegian fashion. Per thoroughly enjoyed the *lefse, rull, fatiman, lutefisk,* and *kjötboller* that the women prepared, as well as the *krumkage, fatiman,* and other delicacies that they baked. These dishes were already becoming more truly American-Norwegian than native Norwegian, as the immigrants clung to their native dishes and special foods for the holidays.

During Christmas, Amund Berge and Per began to talk about cutting cordwood together.

"Why don't we chip in to buy a good crosscut saw and work jointly?" asked Berge.

Per readily agreed. "Sounds like a good idea."

"We can make more money working together than

separately."

"I've heard that expert woodsmen usually work in pairs."

Nearly everyone in the Decorah area burned wood during the 1880's, and so there was a good market for cordwood. Wood was hauled to town for cash. A cord measured 4' wide by 4' high by 8' long, and was cut and stacked in four foot lengths. By cooperation the two men were able to increase their output by nearly half again as much.

Working together proved of benefit in other ways too. Per told his cousin a great deal about Norway. In turn he learned much more about America. In confiding their plans to each other, the two found a mutual interest: both were interested in going further west to the new frontier.

Over a period of time Per met more of his relatives in Iowa. Another Elvestuen aunt named Ingebor was married to Ole Kjorlien, who lived north of Decorah. They had a flock of seven children. His youngest aunt, Elina was married to a man named Gulbrand Tangen. They too lived in the area.

Per learned to like big gatherings of relatives. When the men spoke of politics or history, he listened intently. Another of his interests was the frontier and free land.

"Is there really a Homestead Law?" he asked one Sunday.

"Yes, there is," answered Anton.

"Abraham Lincoln signed the Homestead Act in 1862," explained Iver. "I can remember because it happened soon after we got to America."

"Is it true that the land is free?"

"Yes, except for a filing fee of $14 on a quarter section, and another fee of $4 for proving up the land," answered Iver.

"The settler must work his claim and improve it. He must also live on the land for five years," added Anton.

"How can a country give land to everyone? Can any be left?"

"Yes, millions of acres remain," said Anton, "but the best is taken first."

Per knew each of his relatives had a large tract of land. Now he reaffirmed the idea that he too would have his own quarter section of land.

* * * * * * * * * * *

The second year in Iowa was an especially good one for Per. He grew in confidence and ability to speak English. His dress and actions became less like those of an immigrant. Furthermore, his earnings and savings were greater. As the seasons changed, he was now familiar with the work and knew just what to expect. From Ola he learned to handle and to love horses, and also a lot about farming.

In the fall, Per had another letter from his brother, Amund, who was at Kindred near Fargo, in Dakota Territory. Amund was enthusiastic about renting land. He also told of filing a claim on a homestead some distance west of Kindred. Amund ended his letter by urging Per to come in the spring.

As he and Berge worked in the woods together they often spoke of going to the Red River Valley. It became a habit for them to clip out articles and editorials about that part of the country from newspapers. They read much about the Great Dakota Boom. Some extravagant claims were made for the area, and one enthusiastic editor called it the Garden of Eden.

Early in the spring Berge said, "Per, I think we should make plans to go to Dakota when the weather warms up."

"I'm glad to hear you say that," agreed Per. "I've already made up my mind to go, and I'd hoped we could go together."

"When do you want to go?"

"Around the first of May. How does that sound to you?"

Berge nodded. "Sounds like a good time to me."

"Then we're agreed!" exclaimed Per. "The first of May we'll head for Dakota Territory!"

CHAPTER FOUR

On to Dakota Territory

By March of 1883, Per and Berge's decision to go to Dakota was final. They had several reasons for going. Both were lured by newspaper accounts and advertisements. Posters put out by the Northern Pacific Railroad painted a rosy picture of the area. Besides, Per knew his brother had been paid high wages in the Red River Valley, and that he had filed on a homestead south of Valley City.

"In March of 1884 I'll be twenty one, then I'll file on a claim too," Per told his young friend.

Each Sunday, the two cousins talked about and planned their trip. They found rail fares expensive and connections complicated. Since going by rail would cost more than a month's wages, they decided to travel on foot. In their planning, they underestimated the miles between Decorah and Kindred.

As the time for departure neared, Per grew more and more impatient to get started. However, had he known all that was to happen in Dakota Territory, perhaps he would not have been quite so eager.

On the last Sunday in April, relatives gathered at the Iver Lien home after church services. This was a farewell party for the two young men.

After two years, Per felt close to his Iowa kinfolks. He understood that they had welcomed and taken him in, when he first came. His adjustment to the new country had been made easier. Had he been thrust among strangers as a newcomer, the shock of change might have been much greater. From them he had gained knowledge and confidence to take with him to a new frontier.

His grandfather presented Per with a five dollar gold piece. The gift was a most generous one.

"Good luck, Per," he said. "May God go with you."

Per's eyes brimmed with tears. He had a premonition that he would never see his old grandfather again. He thought the gift a splendid one, but most of all he was grateful for the kindness shown him.

"Many thousand thanks," he replied. "You have been wonderfully kind."

"You are welcome."

However, all was not seriousness that Sunday. The menfolks bantered jovially with the young men, who were setting out to find their fortunes.

"I hear that money grows on trees up in Dakota Territory," declared Iver, with a broad smile.

"No doubt you'll be millionaires in no time," added Anders.

"You'll probably turn into 'bonanza' farmers with thousands of acres," agreed Anton.

"Stay out of the brush," joked another, "they tell me it's full of Dakota Indian Maids!"

Saying goodbye to his Aunt Anne and Anton was especially difficult for Per. Leaving their family was almost like leaving his own all over again. They had invited him to stay when he had nowhere else to go.

On the first morning of the journey Per and Berge got off to a good start. Iver gave them a lift into Decorah on his wagon.

"Goodbye now," he said gravely, shaking hands. "You must write home, Amund."

"I will. Goodbye."

The two started westward with great enthusiasm, as it seemed like a great adventure. They were on foot and traveling light. In their packs, they had an old army canteen of water, beef jerky from Nordbraatens, and cheese from the Berges. Each had a jacket, extra underwear, a blanket, personal articles, and a few of the most necessary items for camping. Both realized that their packs would be heavy enough before nightfall.

Since the boys were used to walking near twenty miles a day behind a harrow or plow, they were well accustomed to being on foot. The man who rode behind his horses was often suspected of being lazy. The boys were not hesitant to walk, and they hoped for a ride every now and then.

Berge and Per were dressed in good work clothes. They kept themselves well groomed, since they did not want to be taken for hoboes. Subsequently they found most of the people along the way friendly and helpful.

Late in the afternoon of the fourth day they were given a ride with a man driving a team of horses. Near Lake Mills, Iowa he gave them directions to the home of Ole Elvestuen Kjos, Per's uncle. As the boys came to the house, a woman met them at the door. She did not recognize Berge.

"Is this the place of Ole Elvestuen Kjos?" he asked.

"Yes, that it is," she answered, looking curious. A man appeared at her side that Per took to be Ole.

"Well, don't you know me? I'm your nephew, Amund Berge."

"Yes, now I can see you are Amund," declared his Aunt Anna.

"And this is your nephew, Per Elvestuen," he went on, turning to Ole.

"You are Erik's son?"

"Yes, I came from Norway two years ago."

"I remember. My sister Anne wrote to us."

Their expressions became friendly. As Per had hoped, Anna promptly invited them in for supper. By this time, all five of the children had appeared. They scrutinized their newly found cousins with much interest.

Like the other immigrants, Ole and Anna listened spellbound to news from Hadeland. In like manner, they were interested in their brothers and sisters near Decorah. Ole asked about his father, old Amund. It was many years since. Ole and Anna had left Decorah for Lake Mills.

As was the custom among Norwegian-Americans, the conversation was held in the native tongue. The time passed pleasantly until it was discovered that bedtime was long overdue. Since neither of the hosts would hear of them leaving, a bed was fixed on the floor for the night. The men found this an improvement over sleeping on the ground as they had done for three nights.

After an early morning breakfast and lengthy "goodbyes", the two were back on the trail. Now they turned in a more northerly direction toward Mankato. Twice that day, they were offered rides and at nightfall Berge calculated that they had traveled thirty miles. That was an unusually good day.

By this time Per and Berge settled down to a routine. As their muscles toughened for walking, the two came to spend ten hours on the road each day. Typically, they walked for two hours and rested for a half hour except for a longer break at midday. They planned to travel twenty miles a day on foot. Any rides they could catch, would be to the good. Rides with oxen were slow, but at the end they were refreshed for walking.

Eating proved to be a necessary task, yet a vexing bother on the trip. Both had young and ravenous appetites. Sometimes they were able to buy bread, milk or eggs from a farmwife. Other times they were satisfied to eat raw potatoes. Every now and then they exchanged heavy work for a good cooked meal. Both thought it a good exchange. Even when they had to buy food at a general store, a few cents a day went a long way in the spring of 1883.

Berge and Per made good time to Mankato. Luckily they caught several rides. About noon of the seventh day, they crossed the river into town.

Mankato proved to be larger than they had expected. The city was bustling with horses, oxen, and people. Business was brisk. The two boys were tired and bored with walking by this time, so they decided to spend the rest of the day looking around.

Later they met a German farmer at the livery barn who was setting out toward New Ulm in the morning. He agreed to give them a ride in exchange for help to unload and load his wagon again in the morning. The farmer drove a superb team of horses, and Per established a camaraderie by joining him in this admiration. The two hit it off well despite a language barrier. The driver spoke German mixed with broken English.

It was late afternoon before they reached the man's farm. That evening Berge and Per worked for a meal. Between them, they sawed and split a huge pile of firewood for the kitchen stove. By the time they had eaten, rain had begun to fall. After making sure neither one smoked, the German let them sleep in his barn loft. Per slept soundly except for being awakend occasionally by mice scampering over his blanket and bed of hay.

In the morning a slow drizzle was falling. Both of them were reluctant to resume their travels, but they knew that New Ulm was only a few miles down the trail.

"I sure hate to start out this morning," gumbled Per. "It's wet."

"We were spoiled yesterday by riding. Today will be no fun at all," agreed Berge.

"It looks like a miserable day."

"Don't remind me. Let's go."

The travelers made poor headway that day. As rain was still falling when they came to New Ulm, the boys waited until the drizzle stopped. However, as they went on the rain continued off and on throughout the day. By late afternoon, both were damp to their skin, and it was becoming more and more difficult for them to keep up their spirits.

"Do you see that old log hut over there?" asked Per.

"Yeah, lets stop. It has to be better than outside."

The sod roof of the abandoned cabin leaked, but the boys found dry wood near the old iron stove. With it, they started a fire and dried out more firewood. Meanwhile, they entertained each other with depreciative humor.

"Talk about dumb Norwegians!" scoffed Berge. "We really should have our heads looked at."

"True. We hardly knew enough to come in from the rain," agreed Per.

It's not easy to laugh when you're wet to the bone."

"No, nor when you are walking in mud."

"Anyway things can only get better and not worse."

"You want to bet?"

The next morning the sun shone bright and clear. As the day warmed, the river began to look inviting. The boys had not had a bath since leaving home. During mid-afternoon, they ventured into the river. At first the water felt icy cold.

The Minnesota River was not in flood stage, but the water was still high. Neither had much experience with a river of this size, and before they realized the danger the current swept them downstream. Per was a good swimmer from boyhood, yet he needed every ounce of strength he could muster to grab a stout limb at the river's edge. As he hung on with both hands, his thoughts went to his friend.

"Berge!" he yelled. "Are you here?"

"I'm over here," came an answer from a nearby tree.

They crawled out and lay panting, completely naked, on the riverbank. "That was a close shave," said Berge, quietly.

An hour later, the boys were pleased when a well dressed man stopped by the side of the trail. He drove a lively team hitched to a surrey. As the horses trotted along Berge seemed lost in thought.

"Wasn't it along here that the Sioux Uprising took place?" he asked.

"Yes, it was. The raids started suddenly, taking settlers by surprise," said the driver with sudden interest. "Young braves under Little Crow and Shakopee, eager to fight the whites, began a bloody six week massacre, killing several hundred whites. Some of the victims were women and children.

"Didn't they attack New Ulm too?" continued Berge.

"Yes, several hundred Sioux laid seige to it. They burned most of the buildings and killed many of the defenders, but they were not able to capture the town itself."

"How could they hold it against several hundred Indians?"

"Much credit for defending New Ulm goes to Charles Flandrau and his men, who arrived from St. Peter in time to help hold the town."

"What did the Sioux do next, when they couldn't take New Ulm?"

"They attacked Fort Ridgely. Had they done so earlier, the fort would have fallen, since it was defended only by Lt. Sheenan and a few soldiers. Instead the young braves wanted to plunder first. Later more soldiers and many settlers came to the fort. Actually the cannon, expertly handled, stopped the attacks. After losing perhaps 300 braves, the Indians withdrew."

"How did the uprising end?" asked Per, eagerly.

"A young soldier names Sturgis rode 125 miles to Ft. Snelling for help. Governor Ramsey sent General Sibley up the Minnesota River with troops. About a month later they defeated the Sioux at Wood Lake. About 300 prisoners were rescued and large numbers of Indians were captured, mostly women and children.

"What happened to those who took part in the massacre?"

"Many of the chiefs and braves, who had taken part in the massacre, escaped to Dakota."

The two travelers looked at the driver with a new respect. He certainly knew a lot. They leaned forward attentively. Both wanted to hear more.

"Of those captured and tried, 38 were later hanged at Mankato. The rest were pardoned by Abraham Lincoln. Even though twenty counties were involved, most of the Sioux remained friendly. Out of about five thousand Indians on the reservation only hot headed young men, that could be numbered in hundreds, took part in the hostilities.

"Why did the Indians start the fight in the first place?" asked Per.

"There is no doubt that the Indians were being cheated and mistreated by the traders and other whites at the Indian Agency. According to the treaty, the Sioux were to receive annual payments in food and gold for the lands given up. Chiefs unable to read and write, and often influenced by fire water, signed these treaties. Also the white traders kept books on Indian purchases while the red man did not, consequently the greedy traders always ended up with all the gold. The Indian knew he was being cheated, but he couldn't prove or dispute it.

Per was surprised. Usually he had heard that Indians were blood thirsty, plundering savages who attacked for no reason.

"In 1862 the gold shipment was a month late, but still the traders refused to distribute food to the hungry Sioux until the money came. When the Indians asked for their supplies, one trader sneeringly told them that they could eat grass. After the uprising started, he was found with a hayscythe through his stomach and a wad of grass stuffed into his mouth."

"Did they ever catch the Indians who escaped?"

"The settlers demanded revenge. General Sibley and General

Sully were sent to Dakota to punish the Sioux who had fled. Since the soldiers could not identify the guilty, all Indians were attacked. Hundreds of them were killed, including many women and children, and the troops destroyed their homes and winter food supplies.

"It's really too bad so many Indians had to suffer for what a few of them had done," reflected Per, thoughtfully.

"Yes, that's right. The uprising was caused by insensitive whites, greedy for gold; and by hot headed young braves anxious to fight and plunder. Very few of the guilty ones suffered. Instead innocent people on both sides, often women and children, paid the price for the misdeeds of others."

"Were there any big battles around here?" asked Berge.

"Yes, Ft. Ridgely is just a few miles ahead. As long as I'm headed that way, I'll take you to the site of the old fort."

As Per looked at the old stone buildings and frame barracks, he found the sight strange and exciting. He did not find it difficult to imagine an Indian attack with defending soldiers and settlers. The driver pointed to the pock marks from bullets on the walls.

"What became of the friendly Sioux?" asked Per.

"They are living on reservations here, along the Minnesota River. One is across the river near Redwood Falls and the other near Granite Falls."

Once more the two travelers looked at the well dressed stranger with a great deal of admiration.

"Thank you," said Per, "you surely know a lot about history."

"I should," replied the stranger. "I'm a history professor."

The young men took their leave from the driver near Morton. At that point they left the river trail. Both would have denied it had anything to do with the massacres, but they turned to the north and took the most direct course possible toward Willmar.

The next two days were slow and tough ones. Late on the second day they were within sight of Willmar before they were offered a ride by a Norwegian farmer. That night they stayed in town.

A day later, on the trail toward Benson, the boys were called on to put out a fire. As they approached a farmstead, a

Norwegian woman ran out of the house crying, "Fire!" "Fire!"
They ran the rest of the way and looked to see flames inside the
house.

"Have you any water?" yelled Per.

"No!" answered the woman, in great agitation.

"Do you have any milk or buttermilk?"

"Yes!" she cried, pointing. "Inside!"

Per stormed into the house and picked up a big pan of buttermilk. This he threw directly into the flames. The fire sizzled and
slowed but did not go out. He grabbed up a blanket and tried to
smother the remaining flames, but the blanket caught fire instead. He had to stamp it out. Suddenly Berge appeared in the
doorway with a bucket of water brought from a distant well.

"Here let me soak the blanket first!" yelled Per.

After Berge had sloshed the water on the blaze, Per easily
beat out the remaining flames with the wet blanket. The fire was
out!

The housewife could not thank them enough. She fully realized that her home would undoubtedly have gone up in smoke
and flames without their help. When her husband returned from
town, she explained the episode to him in detail. Berge and Per
found themselves heroes for one evening, as the couple treated
them to the best they had: a glass of wine, a good meal, and a
bed for night.

The next days passed without incident. The two men walked
doggedly towards the northwest, persistently following the trail
to Dakota. Very seldom did they ride, even for a short distance.

At last one day Per and Berge had their first glimpse of the
Red River Valley of the North. The land flattened out until it was
nearly as level as a floor. They could see for miles. Trees were
visible only along the river and near the farmsteads dotting the
landscape. The soil that had been plowed was black and heavy
and looked unusually rich. Per thought the old lake bottom
might be a farmers paradise; in fact he had never seen anything
that compared.

Early the next day the two walkers saw Breckenridge in the
distance. Before the end of the day they reached the town.
Shortly thereafter, they crossed the bridge to Wahpeton and
walked into Dakota Territory.

One of their earliest experiences in Dakota was unpleasant. They picked a spot for the night near the trees and river separating Breckenridge and Wahpeton. As they were about to roll out their blankets for the night, several hoboes sauntered into the area. Per thought them to be unsavory looking characters. Right away they spotted Berge and Per, and were looking toward the two and talking in low tones. This was enough to arouse the suspicions of the young men.

"I think we better move out of here," said Berge softly. "I just don't like the looks of those fellows."

"They're too many for us," agreed Per. "Let's pick up our packs and start walking toward Wahpeton. If they come after us, we can outrun them."

Simultaneously the two picked up their belongings and strode briskly toward the town, which was perhaps forty rods away. A few times they glanced back fleetingly, to see if they were being followed. The tramps watched closely but stood their ground. The boys continued on beyond town, stopping only when darkness came. Neither felt quite sure what intentions the hoboes may have had, but both felt better that they had moved from the river.

As usual the boys were up at sunrise and soon back on the trail. Now that they had reached Dakota, they knew it could not be far to Kindred. They expected to reach their destination some time the next day. Per found himself anxious to see his brother again.

The day was destined to be a good one for travel. Soon they had their first ride with a man who drove a fast horse and a light buggy. Six miles down the road they were back on foot again.

On that same forenoon the two young men had their first introduction to bonanza farming in the Red River Valley. In one field they counted 12 gang plows with five horses on each. They were just finishing a square mile section. Along the outer rim of the same field, five 4-horse harrows were taking a combined swath of nearly 100 feet as they moved in formation down the field.

Per and Berge stopped to stare at the operation which seemed quite unreal to them. They could not have imagined farming on such a scale unless they had seen it with their own eyes. So this was what was called bonanza farming!

"Wouldn't it be great to work on a farm like that!" exclaimed Berge.

"Maybe it would," admitted Per, "but I'd rather have my own land."

After walking for another hour, the boys came to a different field being planted. Ten 2-horse seeders were sowing grain. From another direction came a man with a team and wagon directly toward them on his way to the field. The wagon carried a load of grain sacks. The man stopped to talk briefly.

"It's near the end of planting season," he explained, " and this is barley on spring plowing."

"Who owns this farm?" asked Berge.

"It's part of the Dwight Farms. They have over 25,000 acres here."

Per could scarcely comprehend what he had seen and heard. In Norway a ten acre field would be a large one. Most farmers had one or two horses. Even a *stor bonde* didn't farm much by comparison. In Iowa, Nordbraaten's 240 acre farm was considered a large one, and seldom did one see more than four horses in the same field at one time.

The two travelers got two more rides in rapid succession. Both of the drivers were busy and traveled along at a brisk trot. The miles faded rapidly. When the second driver informed them that Kindred was only 20 miles away, they were pleased and surprised. The sun was still high in the sky.

The two resumed walking again. They had not gone many miles before yet another man in a buggy stopped to talk with them. He explained that he was a foreman for J. B. Powers, who owned the large Helendale farm to the west. The man went on to explain that he had just discharged several men for drinking on the job. He could use some men, if Berge and Per were looking for work.

Berge was eager to accept and said as much; Per, on the other hand, wanted to push on to Kindred. In just a minute or two, they decided to part ways. Berge accepted the foreman's offer, and Per went on to meet his brother.

"We shall see each other again soon," promised Per.

"Yes, I hope it won't be too long," agreed his cousin.

Amund Berge stepped up into the buggy, as the foreman turned the horse to the west and Helendale. Berge looked back and
waved at Per.

For a minute Per stood alone on the trail that led to Kindred.
Berge had been a good friend, and Per would surely miss him.
They had shared a lot since leaving Decorah. He could not help
feeling lonely as he walked northwest. For some reason the flat
landscape looked much more desolate than it had a few minutes
earlier.

"We had different plans and so we had to part," reasoned Per,
talking to himself in his native tongue. "I must get some land of
my own."

For the next two hours he trudged on alone. Then another
driver with a horse and buggy stopped to talk. He was headed
for Kindred and asked Per if he wanted a ride. The lonely
traveler gladly climbed into the buggy. With any luck at all, he
thought he would get to Kindred by nightfall.

"Where did you come from?" asked the driver.

"From Decorah," Per explained. "My friend and I walked."

"You walked from Decorah?"

"Yes, except for a ride now and then. My friend and I just
separated this afternoon.

"When did you leave Decorah?"

"The first of May."

Again the driver was surprised when he learned that Per was a
recent immigrant from Norway.

"You don't act or speak like an immigrant," he said. "Are you
by any chance looking for a job?"

"No, I'm looking for my brother, Amund Elvestuen,"
answered Per. "Do you know him?"

"No, I'm sorry but I don't," said the man looking thoughtful.

"He is working on a farm near Kindred," said Per.

Per found that the driver had come from Abercrombe that
afternoon. The willing mare brought them the last ten miles in
about an hour, and the sun was just setting as they entered the
main street of Kindred.

"Many thanks," said Per as he climbed down from the buggy.

The driver smiled and waved as he drove off to the livery barn.

Once more Per stood alone, looking at the nearly deserted

main street of Kindred. A feeling of being alone in the world came back again. If you had a relative, it wasn't so bad. And he did have a brother, if he could find him.

Several times he stopped to ask a stranger if he knew Amund Elvestuen. Each time the answer was the same: no one knew a man by that name. Soon Per quit asking.

Per felt a great need to get cleaned up after his long trip, and so he decided to go to a hotel. So far he had spent very little on the trip. The man at the desk said he could have a single room with a cot for 25^c. When Per found he could have hot water with it, he agreed to take the room. The cot looked inviting to a man who had slept on the ground for many nights. But the room was small indeed. However, Per decided he was satisfied with his deal.

"Tonight I'm going to live like a king!" he promised himself, as he prepared to shave and bathe with warm water. "Too bad Berge isn't here."

Later that night, as Per lay in the luxury of a bed, sleep did not come easily. Too many thoughts filled his mind. From Decorah to Kindred in 18 days, that must be some kind of record! He figured they had walked well over 300 miles, besides the rides that would add up to at least another hundred.

"We must have traveled close to 425 miles in all," he thought. "That's further than we figured."

After dark, Per felt keenly alone again. For the first time in a long time he lay awake thinking about family and home back in Hadeland. He wished that he could go back for a visit, but that seemed entirely out of the question.

"I wonder how it goes with Mor," he mused aloud. "If only father would stop his drinking."

Per felt guilty. Perhaps he should have stayed home and helped her.

Lastly, Per's mind turned to Sigrid. He was still thinking about her when he fell asleep. During the night, he thought he saw his mother's sad face, and later on he dreamed of Sigrid. It seemed as if he were trying to take her in his arms but, for some reason or another, she eluded him.

CHAPTER FIVE

Red River Land

The following morning, Per set out once again to find his brother. Business places were just opening their doors for the day. At first he was disappointed in his quest, but later he talked with the blacksmith.

"Yes, I know Amund Elvestuen," he replied. "Worked for me two years ago this spring. Sharpening plowshares."

"Can you tell me how to find him?"

"Nope. Sorry but I can't."

"You said he worked here?"

"Yes. He was a damn good worker too, Wish he was here to help me with that big stack of plowshares over there."

"Amund is my brother," said Per, with a smile. "Maybe I could help you with the plowshares."

"Are you a blacksmith?"

"I was an apprentice in the same blacksmith shop he was. Could I help you a few days until I find him?"

"The blacksmith grinned and spat on the ground. "The pay is a dollar a day plus board and room. The work is damn hard."

So it was that Per came to work in the blacksmith shop. Soon he began to get the feel of the work again. As he heated the plowshares to a cherry red and pounded them out on the anvil with the big hammer, he had a sense of being back at Elvestuen. However, his new boss was less critical than Erik had been.

Per continued to check around for information concerning his brother. During the noon hour, he asked the clerk at the general store about Amund.

"Sure I know him," he replied. "He comes in every Saturday night for a plug of tobacco."

"Do you know where I can find him?"

"No, but he works around here."

Since there were plenty of plowshares to last, Per decided to work in the blacksmith shop until the weekend. Amund would probably be busy anyway Per decided, and he could use the money.

It was near quitting time on Saturday evening, when Per saw Amund's big frame practically fill the doorway.

"Jorgen said I would find you here," said Amund in Norwegian, smiling.

"You're a sight for sore eyes," replied Per, offering his hand. He felt it gripped in a solid handshake. No flowery words were exchanged but it was evident that the two brothers were happy to be together again. It was already two years since they had parted in Iowa.

Amund could scarcely wait to speak again of the chance to rent a quarter section of land. Excitement and urgency was in his voice when he spoke, which Per found contagious. Lars Henrickson, the owner, had already broken about fifty acres, but he wanted the land further improved. In a few years his own growing sons could help him farm the land, but for the time being he would give them a good deal if they would break at least 40 acres a year. Lars was willing to pay them $2.50 an acre for breaking sod, but the backsetting would be their part of the work. Further he would advance them seed for planting and oats for feed until the first harvest. If necessary they could exchange work for the use of his machinery the first year. Since he owned a share in a threshing rig, they could exchange work for that also at threshing. In short, they would need very little cash to get a start in farming.

"Since there's little money from unimproved land the first years, we can farm here while we open up our own homesteads," explained Amund.

"I think it worth a try," agreed Per. "We can do better than by working for wages.

He was interested from the beginning. If there was anything Per wanted it was a chance to get ahead in life. The proposition looked like an excellent idea to him, and so he agreed to go into partnership with Amund.

The very first consideration for working the land was the purchase of either oxen or horses. The two brothers spent the entire Sunday looking around and talking to various people. Because this was a period of great demand, both oxen and horses were costly. A team of horses would cost about $400, while a yoke of oxen would bring about $200. That was the going price for good young stock. At first Amund favored the oxen, but Per stoutly held out for horses. He had learned to love horses at Nordbraaten's and felt that it would be demeaning to settle for oxen.

The brothers had heard the arguments of oxen versus horses before, since every man seemed to have a strong opinion on the subject. Now they listened again as Amund's boss, John Kjos, and his neighbor Justin Svensen, summed it up for them.

"A good yoke of oxen costs only half as much in the first place, and you don't have to buy expensive harness," claimed Justin, who drove oxen. "You can find plenty of grass all around, so you don't have to feed them grain."

"That may be, but they are worthless for traveling, as you can go faster on foot," countered John, who drove horses. "They're so slow you can't get any work done in a day, besides an ox can't work as many years as a horse."

"Well, oxen seldom get sick, besides you can butcher them when they get too old. It just makes good sense to buy oxen."

"You can argue all you want to, but when it's all said and done what can possibly be more stupid and cantankerous than an ox when he is thirsty, hungry, or just plain tuckered out?"

Since it was nearly 60 miles to Amund's homestead, he agreed with Per that horses would be best. Traveling back and forth with oxen would simply take too much time. As for Per, he had not been convinced by any of the ox arguments and would have favored horses even if it hadn't made such good sense.

Because a considerable outlay of money was involved, buying

horses became a matter of much concern to the two Elvestuens. They determined not to hurry. Since there were shysters trading horses, they were thankful to have learned something of judging good horseflesh from Nordbraaten. This knowledge would serve them well now.

On the third day of scouting, Per found his horses. He seemed certain that minute he set eyes on them. The pair he picked were young buckskin colored animals. The gelding was named Charlie and the mare Nellie. With a good set of collars and harness Per thought them well worth the $400 he agreed to pay.

Before closing the deal, Per looked them over carefully. He noticed they were clear-eyed and smooth skinned, with unblemished knees and legs. They both stood firmly on all four legs with heads up, and when he drove them, he found they were sure footed and lively. The horses were of medium build, and each one weighed a good 1300 lbs. Just about right, Per thought, for his needs. Furthermore, it was a case of love at first sight.

Since Per did not have enought money to pay cash, he had to get a loan of $100 at the bank. He had little trouble getting the loan, as he found horses were most acceptable collateral. The interest was 12%. After paying for the team and a second hand spring wagon, Per found very little money left in his pocket. However, this did not trouble Per.

The next day, Per was pleased to be offered a job by a Kindred merchant. He was to receive $2.50 per trip for freighting between Kindred and Leonard, a distance of about twelve miles. The trip took him a ten hour day, including loading and unloading. This gave him some time for leisure.

By the following Sunday, Amund had his team also. They were a pair of young blacks with white markings. Per helped check them out and agreed that they were indeed sound and true. He was as excited about the team as Amund.

That same Sunday, the brothers hitched both teams to the breaking plow. Per drove the horses, while Amund handled the plow. Before beginning, they set a long stake, with a red handkerchief tied to it, at each end of the field. This is what Per sighted at as they struck up the first furrow. As soon as two furrows were completed, the brothers moved the stakes five rods up the field and repeated the process. Striking up the land was really a two man job. After that one of the horses had a furrow to follow and so one man could work alone.

The two teams worked well together under Per's guidance. The 12" breaking plow slashed through the tough virgin sod and turned it rich and black. Per felt positively elated as he looked at the fresh straight furrows. His mind pictured two giant hands reaching down to pick up the two ends of sod and stretching it out like a great black ribbon, a foot wide and a half mile long. Never had the sun seemed quite so bright or the air so fresh as it did in Dakota that day in late May.

"What a great four horse rig!" exclaimed Per, as they stopped to rest.

"The four can pull that heavy plow like nothing," agreed Amund, smiling.

"We've made several rounds, and they show no sign of being winded."

"I don't think we could have picked better."

The two agreed that Amund would continue his job and that Per would break sod with both teams. The cost of oats, food, expenses and Per's wages would come from the $2.50 an acre their landlord paid for breaking sod. Per was delighted with this arrangement. Even though he would have to bach it, he would be driving their new horses!

What was left of the original homesteader's shacks still remained on the land. The small buildings were in poor condition but much better than none at all. Per did his best to repair them, but the roofs still leaked.

He began his work each day with enthusiasm. Along with breaking the sod, many other jobs had to be done. The horses had to be cared for and fed, water pulled up from the well, ground oats and hay provided for feed, and a primitive form of housekeeping performed. Their three plowshares had to be sharpened twice every week, since a sharp blade lasted only one day. Per had very little spare time.

Breaking sod day after day was a hard job on both man and horse. Luckily all were young and easily restored with rest. No stones or stumps impeded the progress of the plow, and the weather continued to be nearly perfect into early June. The rain that fell was needed or the sod would have become too stubborn to turn over.

Lars explained carefully to Per the exact process of breaking the land. The plow was to be set about three inches deep, and the sod was to be broken during late spring or early summer.

"The hot weather will rot the sod so it can be crossplowed in the fall," he explained. "For backsetting, the plow is to be set two inches deeper than the breaking. That makes the soil airtight so it will cure."

Per listened attentively. He tried to do everything right, because he was most anxious to succeed.

Usually on Sunday the two brothers got together. Amund gave Per moral support and they planned the future together.

Towards the end of June there came a hot spell. Per began working mornings and evenings in the field, taking a long break during the hottest part of the day. This saved on the horses and on himself and allowed them to accomplish more work each day. At the end of five weeks Per had broken 50 acres of sod besides doing the other necessary work.

As Per worked alone with the horses and plow, he often talked to himself and daydreamed about Sigrid. Her laughing eyes and her smile were imprinted indelibly on his mind. If he could only get a homestead of his own, everything would work out. Then he could send for her.

"If I could only see her again," he thought, "waiting wouldn't be so bad."

By July, Amund finished his job. He was impatient to get back to his claim to dig a well and do some breaking. So far he had not met the time requirement for residence, either.

"Why don't you go with me, Per?" he suggested.

"I'd like to see your land," Per agreed.

"You can look at the country at the same time."

"I should look for land. I'll soon be twenty one."

It was just past noon when they left. The day was hot but not unpleasantly so. As they followed the wagon trail almost directly westward, Per felt it a good change from breaking sod. The flatness of the Red River Valley disappeared so gradually that Per was scarcely aware of the change.

Late in the day the trail turned a little to the south to avoid the

Maple River. Amund stopped for the night at the southernmost bend. Here was knee high grass on the bank and water for the horses. The animals were put out on picket chains. When dusk came, the men crawled under the wagon to sleep.

"Tomorrow, I have something to show you," said Amund sleepily. "I think you'll be surprised."

Per did not respond. Already his breathing was deep and regular.

At sunrise they were up and soon on their way. The day was clear and sunny. By midmorning they had reached the east bluffs of the Sheyenne River almost directly west of their campsite on the Maple River. As they stopped, Amund walked out and pointed down into the great valley below.

"Here is what I wanted to show you," he said, gesturing down and across to the other side. There was something near reverence in his voice as he spoke.

The men gazed down into the gigantic depression, formed centuries ago by the melting glacier, as its torrential waters rushed towards the 700 mile long Lake Agassiz. The bright eastern sun at their backs shimmered down on the trees and the river in the green valley below. Across to the west, perhaps two miles away, was another set of mighty bluffs. The beauty and grandeur of the scene held Per motionless. Finally he spoke.

"Surely the hand of God was here, Amund."

"Yes, Per, it is a miracle to find such beauty out here on the flat Dakota prairie."

Before beginning the descent, Per and Amund chopped two stout poles and placed them under the wagon between the spokes of the two hind wheels. They secured these posts to the wheels with halter ropes. This device braked the wagon as they followed the winding trail to the bottom. There they untied the poles and crossed the river on a shallow sand bar. For a ways, they went along at the bottom of the valley before they began the steep climb around the bluff and to the level ground to the west.

On the other side of the valley, they turned to the southwest through the Indian grass that stood as high as the bellies of the horses. The northwest wind made ripples like waves in the thick grass. The landscape itself continued quite flat except for an occasional knoll or low spot. They saw a few sloughs with coarse rushes and grasses. Some larger ones contained water.

The hot sun was nearly straight south in the sky by the time they reached Amund's claim shack. As they came nearer, Per examined his brother's property with great interest. The main improvement was the 12 by 14 tar paper house. Two or three rods away stood another outhouse. He saw no other improvements. However, it was the land that excited Per's imagination. By now he knew something of the size of a quarter of land, that it measured a half mile square. Surely now Amund more than qualified as a *stor bonde*. Per wondered if he too might be fortunate enought to own 160 acres some time soon.

"What do you think they would say at Elvestuen, if they could see your land," he asked.

"They would never believe I have so much," answered Amund, smiling.

The same evening the brothers visited some neighbors that had also been their neighbors in Brandbu Parish in Hadeland. The two Smedshammer brothers had brought their brides from Norway. Amund accompanied them when the three came to file on homesteads in 1882.

The Smedshammers greeted the Elvestuens as long lost brothers. Here in the New World close kinships developed between people who came from the same section of their country. Norwegian immigrants seemed especially loyal to this concept. Because the Elvestuens and the Smedshammers had been neighbors in the same parish in the Old Country, a bond developed between them in America much as if they had been blood brothers. The strength of such a relationship was enough to last a lifetime.

"Why don't you find a homestead here near the rest of us, Per," suggested Christ. "Then we can all be neighbors."

"Yes, why don't you?" agreed Bent. "There must be a city man around here who is willing to sell his land."

"I'll try to do that," promised Per, hoping it would be that easy.

He did spend the following day looking for land. In his search, he found a claim that caught his attention. Per thought it looked more lush with growth than any other in the neighborhood. This land was located three miles from his brother's homestead and even nearer Christ and Bent's claims. The more Per thought about this quarter, the more ideal he felt it would be for him.

Per knew this land had been settled the year before. He also knew that one requirement of the homestead Act was that 10 acres of sod must be broken each year. Nearly all the claims around had a small field of crop or some sod broken, but Per could see none on this land. A homesteader's shack stood near the southwest corner. He hoped that this might be owned by a man from town, who had no intention of making his home on the land. Per decided he would try to buy this land as soon as he was of age, which would be the following March.

Per spent a week in the area. During that time he helped Amund break a few acres of sod and dig a well.

Breaking sod was more difficult here than in the Red River Valley. The glacier had left stones in the soil. Since the horses were not accustomed to this, the driver had to try to train them to ease up when the plow hit a stone. If not, the evener might splinter or the plowshare crack. Between them, they managed quite well without major mishap.

"We've already broken up more than all the fields on Elvestuen," said Per, as they stopped to rest the horses.

"Yes, that is true."

"Now you are a *stor bonde*."

Amund smiled, but he did not answer.

As soon as the well was finished and the breaking near completion, Per grew restless to be on his way again. Amund had plenty of work to keep him busy until harvest.

After Per returned to Kindred, he did a variety of work. Three days a week, he again hauled freight. He also helped Lars stack hay in return for the use of his mower and hayrake. As a result he had hay ready to stack when Amund returned. Horse hay was worth $4 a ton. Per figured they had stacked enough to last two seasons.

During this time, Per also applied for his first papers of citizenship. This declared his intention to become a citizen. These papers were needed if he were to homestead land. He had no reservations about being naturalized, but he did tend to be nervous when dealing with officials.

Citizenship was to be taken seriously, if one wanted to become an American. Per had brought this dream with him from Norway. Now it seemed within his reach, although he could not get final papers for another five years. In the meantime, he realized that he had a lot to learn about his new country and its government.

From time to time, Amund and Per had discussed changing their names. For a while they considered "Erikson". Elvestuen sounded just too Norwegian, and both wanted something a little more American.

"I think the name 'Rocksvold' would be a good one," suggested Per.

"Well, it's not a common name, yet it has a good sound," agreed Amund.

Later both of them agreed on the name and eventually adopted it as their own. To the brothers, the change of name did not seem strange or unusual. As late as the 19th century in Norway, surnames were commonly changed from one generation to the next. Yet news of this change was not readily accepted by the Elvestuens in Norway, and attempts by Per and Amund to explain proved to be of no avail.

One Sunday before harvest Per went to find his cousin, Berge, at Helendale. He was directed southwest toward the sand hills. Since the place looked like a small town from a distance, he had no trouble locating the farm.

He found his cousin near the bunkhouse. Berge greeted him with a grin.

"My, but you've gotten rich and fancy, driving buckskin horses," he remarked with a twinkle in his eye.

"If I didn't have such a big bankloan on them, it wouldn't be so bad," answered Per, trying his best to keep the pride from his voice. "Do you want to go for a ride?"

"I can remember when we were poor and had to walk when we wanted to go someplace."

After two months of separation, they were like brothers. Now there was news to share and much to talk about. Both thought it was like old times again.

"Why don't you come with me this fall to look for a homestead?" asked Per. "Maybe we can find one near each other and be neighbors."

"You forget I'm only 19 and happy right here at Helendale," said Berge.

"Well, it would be nice if we could be together."

"I heard the foreman say Helendale needs men and teams for harvest and threshing. If you haven't hired out, why don't you come here and work?"

"Amund and I may think about that."

"It's a good place to work. The food is the best I've ever eaten."

"After eating my own cooking, that's something to think about. I'll speak to Amund about this."

"Good! Harvest will soon begin."

A week later, Per found himself sitting on a harvester on the bonanza. Twelve 3-horse binders moved down the field in a row, with eighteen shockers following behind. A foreman watched the work from a horse and buggy. A mechanic carried spare parts for the binders, and another man supplied twine to the self tying binders from his wagon. Per was instructed to pull out of the line if his machine failed. He was forbidden to try to fix it himself.

The brothers found that the operation could cut, bind, and shock a 640 acre section in about four days. Each received $2.50 a day for man and team. The harvest lasted almost 20 days.

As soon as harvest was finished, threshing began. Per noticed a few important differences from threshing in Iowa. A steam engine powered the separator, but it had to be pulled by a team to be moved. The engine was unable to pull itself from one place to another. The new type straw burning engine required an engineer, a fireman, and a man to haul water. Bundle haulers brought shocks directly from the fields to the machine with hayracks and teams. With his team, Per hired out to buck straw from the machine for $2.75 a day.

Bent and Christ Smedshammer, each with their yoke of oxen, arrived just in time for threshing. They were hired to haul bundles. Per was surprised to find that they had worked at Helendale the year before to earn cash for winter. He was delighted to find five men from Hadeland on the crew.

Per found working on a bonanza much to his liking. Including lunches, they were fed five times a day, and he found the food excellent. Hot water was provided for baths. The rules were strict and the men orderly; anyone caught drinking or fighting was fired on the spot. The threshing machine ran twelve hours a day, but Per appreciated not having to do chores. Caring for his own horses was no hardship. Except for some chaff and dirt, the job was most agreeable.

"Wouldn't it be great to thresh the year around!" exclaimed Per on a beautiful September day.

"That's the truth," agreed Berge. "Good money, good food, nothing like hanging around a steam rig in the fall."

Per was surprised to find men from nearly every walk of life among the thirty or so in the threshing crew. Some worked as lumber jacks in the pine woods of Minnesota during the winters. Others had jobs in town such as bookkeeping, clerking, or teaching for most of the year. A couple were college students; and a few could be classified as hoboes. The largest number were homesteaders, who came to make enough cash to carry them through the first lean years.

With so many young men around, some horseplay and practical jokes were inevitable. Per and Berge were among the first to join in anything that promised fun. Greenhorns were taken on snipe or rabbit hunts after dark, and left in some meadow or field holding the bag and lantern. While they waited hopefully for game, the pranksters fanned out and went home. Hours later the greenhorns usually came to the realization that they had been tricked. Just a little imagination on the part of each one kept things lively, but Per and Berge were careful not to go too far. They didn't want to be fired.

The threshing lasted 31 days. With the money Per had before, he found that after being paid off, he had well over $150. He felt rich again, until he decided to pay off the loan on his horses. Another $20 went for boots and winter clothes. That left him with only $27 and some change, but he expected to make another month's wages plowing. Best of all, his team was now free and clear of all debt.

"Shall we go into town and celebrate tonight?" suggested Per.

"Do you want to go into the saloon?" queried Amund, with a smile.

When Per and Amund got into town, that is just what they did. It was now more than two years since their unpleasant experience as newcomers. The saloon was crowded with men. Now that threshing was finished, workingmen were spending hard earned money freely, and the saloon was the busiest place in the town. Most men drank in 1883, but Per felt that most laborers considered it a necessity.

No one in the saloon recognized them as immigrants. By now they were both "Americanized" enough to pass as natives.

"Tonight you didn't have to set anyone down in a chair," jested Per.

"No, I didn't," agreed Amund.

"I'll never forget the night you did."

"I won't either. He acted so mean that I lost my temper."

"I wonder if he has picked on any more newcomers."

With threshing completed, it was time for fall plowing and backsetting. Again, Per agreed to do the plowing, while Amund worked for wages. As before, Per was to take his wages and expenses out of the payment for breaking sod. There remained just enough to cover the fall plowing, they figured.

Per used a 16" walking plow and four horses to do the backsetting and the fall plowing. Making twenty miles a day, he could plow a little over three acres a day. Only a few days remained in October, when he completed the last of the 100 acres.

While plowing, Per had a lot of time to think. Sigrid was having too long a wait, he decided. Getting land was taking much too long. Now was the time to look for a Homestead. He simply could wait no longer!

Per's thoughts went back to the land he had seen while visiting Amund. The soil had looked unusually rich. If possible, he should live near Amund, so that they could share machinery and costly tools. Furthermore he knew some of the neighbors. They were good Norwegians from Hadeland.

"Just think, if I could get the very land I looked at, near Amunds . . ." mused Per to himself. That was a pregnant idea.

When Per finished the fall plowing, he immediately headed westward.

CHAPTER SIX

Ever The Land

Per was impatient as he drove westward. Although the pace of the horses was good, the miles passed too slowly for him. In the spring wagon he carried a breaking plow, a few supplies, and some utensils. Since Amund would not finish his job until the last day of the month, the two had agreed that Per should take both teams west. That way he could do some breaking while he looked for land. It was nearly the end of October, and winter could not be far away. Now was the time to act.

His thoughts went back again to the quarter section that had caught his eye on his last trip. If only the owner was someone who didn't care to live on the land. It was worth looking into.

"There wasn't any breaking done," he said aloud. "With winter coming up, this might be the right time to make him an offer."

Early on the following day Per drove up to the lonesome tar paper shack. It stood by itself on the prairie, except for a smaller outhouse and garden. The man who came to the door reminded Per of a French-Canadian he had come to know during threshing. Their conversation was less than perfect, but each made himself understood without difficulty. Per learned the settler was indeed a French-Canadian, also that he was a jeweler by trade. He had filed on the claim the previous year and spent the winter on the homestead.

In turn Per volunteered some information about himself. He was new in the area but his brother had a homestead nearby. Finally, he broached on the real purpose of his visit.

"Do you know of any open land around here?" he asked.

"No, all the land has been homesteaded except for a few tree claims," the squatter replied.

"Tree Claims?" Per had never before heard of the Timber Culture Act, and the settler went on to explain.

"A homesteader can file on a second quarter, but he has to plant 10 acres of trees on it."

"How does he get to own the land?"

"After eight years he must have 675 trees growing per acre."

Per wanted to ask him outright if he had any intentions of selling his land, but he decided to try being a little more crafty about his approach.

"Do you know of anyone around here, who might want to sell his rights to a homestead?" he asked instead.

"With winter coming, I might sell my rights for the right price."

Per threw caution to the wind. "What is your price?" he asked eagerly.

"Eighty dollars. Fifty cents an acre is cheap for good farm land like this."

"I don't have that much." Sadly, Per began to turn to his team.

"Wait a minute! How much do you have?"

"I only have about $40," Per answered truthfully.

"If that's all you have, I'll make a deal for that much."

So they quickly agreed between them that Per should buy the rights to the homestead and the improvements for $40 in cash. To close the deal they would have to go to the land office. Earlier that would have been at Fargo, but now there was an office at LaMoure, only twenty miles away. Per had heard the Fargo-Southwestern had reached that point by midsummer, and as if by magic a town of some 300 people had sprung up in no time at all. The two men agreed that Per would come back in the morning and they would make the trip together.

Per was elated. Acquiring the land would leave him short of money, but he would borrow if necessary. He simply had to have this land now. There might never be a second chance.

Per paced the floor of Amund's shack until very late. What if the deal fell through! This was hard to believe, surely it could not be that easy.

He was up before the first crack of dawn. By the first direct rays of the sun above the eastern horizon, he was on his way to the homesteader's shack. At first Per was afraid the settler might have changed his mind overnight, but apparently the French-Canadian considered the deal already made.

As usual, Per was in a hurry. In his impatience to get to LaMoure he often urged Charlie and Nellie into a trot. Mostly the two men were absorbed in their own thoughts, but now and then they engaged in bits of conversation.

"Where will you go when you leave here?" asked Per.

"Back to Valley City," answered the settler.

"What do you plan to do there?"

"Find a job in a jewelry store."

At the land office in LaMoure, the official in charge soon discovered that the homesteader had not fulfilled all the requirements for the first year. First he asked about the improvements and then about the agreed price.

"No, you can't charge more than the value of actual improvements," he informed them. "Those are govenment regulations."

The second man in the office, whom Per decided might be Norwegian, began to question the settler further. In due time the two officials determined that the price could be $20, but no more. They also informed the seller that if he didn't make certain improvements, including breaking ten acres of land, he would not be able to hold his homestead.

Since the settler had no horses or oxen, Per knew the breaking would cost him at least $25, even if he could find someone willing to do the job. This was an unexpected turn of events, and Per was worried about its outcome. The homesteader seemed to be thinking things over carefully.

As might be expected, the buyer and seller reacted differently. The French-Canadian looked disappointed at this turn of events. He had not expected to sell his rights so cheaply. Per, on the other hand, was overjoyed at his possible good fortune and was trying to hide that fact from the others. Finally he heard the settler agree to the terms.

Per still had another hurdle to cross. He was able to show his Intent to Become a Citizen paper, and he had the necessary $20 in his pocketbook. Then they asked his age. Per was only twenty!

"What is the date of your birthday?"

"March 8th."

A short conference was held between the two officials. Per held his breath, as he felt his destiny hang in the balance.

"Since you will be 21 in less than six months, I will certify the sale," he heard the clerk say. Per felt as if he could jump at least six feet into the air.

The documents were drawn up and duly signed and sealed. Per was greatly relieved to realize the homestead rights had been passed on to him. The entire episode had worked out almost too well to be true.

Upon their return from LaMoure Per agreed to purchase several items from the seller. The old stove, an iron kettle, a large stone crock, an old table with two backless chairs, and a muzzle loading shotgun was his for six dollars. He also agreed to give the French-Canadian a ride to Valley City. Now Per could afford to be generous.

As Per drove away from the settler's shack on his way back to Amund's claim, he stopped near the middle of his quarter section to look at his land. It was flat, unimproved, and covered with prairie and slough grasses. So far the land stood, as it had for centuries, untouched by mower or plow. The tar paper shack was its main improvement, and yet Per thought his new domain most beautiful.

'How lucky I am!" he exclaimed out loud. "It's the land I wanted from the very first."

Per's thoughts turned to Sigrid. If only she were here to share this good fortune with him. At that moment, all his dreams seemed certain of fulfillment. He would transform this land into great big fields and pastures. Cattle would roam about, and he would buy more horses. Soon he would build a big house and barns. He would indeed become a *stor bonde*.

"I'll write to Sigrid. She must know about this land," he thought.

The next weeks Per worked like a demon. His ambition knew

no bounds. He well realized how much there was to accomplish and how little time remained before freezeup. The jobs were endless: break sod to meet the requirements, cut and haul wood for winter, stack hay for the horses, bank up the shack with sod blocks, dig a well, and build a stable.

Two men were needed to dig the well. One worked down in the ground with a spade, while the other hauled up buckets of earth with a borrowed windlass. The work progressed well, except when they struck a good sized stone. At twenty feet water flowed from a vein. The two men curbed the well with rough lumber purchased for that purpose. After the water settled, Per could draw it up with a bucket, a simple frame, and a pulley and rope. He was pleased to find the water good to drink, although very hard indeed.

Luckily Amund owed Per work and the use of his team. As they struck up the first new furrow of earth on Per's land, a tear rolled down his cheek, as the pride and joy swelled up inside him. Good black earth! Per had broken sod before, but this was different. It was his own land!

Per grew discouraged with the haying. This he did without benefit of mower or rake, but rather the hard way, with scythe and fork. He learned to hay, a little at the time, whenever his horses needed a good rest.

"I've got to chop wood before winter comes upon me," Per told himself.

Because he needed wood cut for heating and cooking, and poles for building a stable, Per had to make two trips to the Sheyenne Valley. There he cut wood, hauled it to the top in small loads, and reloaded the wagon to take a big load home. Fuel for heating proved to be a real headache on the Dakota Plains. He learned not to be too proud to pick up buffalo chips, or to burn twisted hay whenever he could to save on wood. However, he sorely missed the woods of Hadeland or even of Decorah country.

Building a stable for the horses turned out to be a tedious job in itself. Per was too busy to work at it steadily, and instead worked a few hours now and then. First he plowed strips of sod three or four inches deep by twelve inches wide. These he cut into three foot strips to use as building blocks for the walls. He laid the blocks around a framework made of poles. The new stable was small, yet took a great many building blocks. When the walls were high enough, Per laid a sturdy ridge pole across the middle of the top. From that he laid many smaller poles and branches to make a framework for the roof. Over these he placed coarse slough hay and blocks of sod. When finished, the new barn had two large stalls, one for the horses and another for hay.

The prairie wolves came on a cold bleak day in the middle of November. It turned out to be the last day Per broke sod that fall. He counted five of the shadowy forms as they watched from a safe distance. Whenever Per looked they seemed to be watching, and this gave him an eerie feeling. The horses seemed very nervous. Normally he would have continued breaking until dusk, but on this day Per quit earlier. The wolves did not follow him home.

Before dark, Per fastened the door of the stable securely and dropped the wooden bar into place on the door of his shack. On second thought he loaded up the old muzzle loading shotgun. After darkness fell, he could hear their plaintive howls in the distance. Per shuddered. He ought to get a rifle, he thought.

Per did not finish banking the house before freezeup. In the last days the sod strips were frozen until noon, even on the warmest days. He had just too many jobs to finish at one time.

For nearly a full month, Per worked seven days a week without letup. The Norwegian Lutheran Church was specific and strict about keeping the sabbath, but Per could see no other way to get all his work done.

The first substantial snowfall and final freezeup came during the last days of November. With the new snow came a brisk northwest wind and cold weather. Per was pleased that winter had held off that long. Finally he took time to look around. He found the pure white landscape quite beautiful.

Per thought often of writing to Sigrid, but he was undecided what he would say. His homestead was not a fit place for her to live. Furthermore he didn't have money for her passage. He simply could not ask her to come by steerage, since she was used to better than that. Yes, he could see there were problems with her being the daughter of a *stor bonde*. A letter was something he had to think about carefully.

The fact was that Per was almost out of money. He had spent what he had for such things as curbing for the well, firewood and poles, oats for the horses and a 100 pound sack of flour. He simply had to find a way to make enough money to see him through the winter. Per discussed his plight with Amund.

"I must find a way to make a little money. I'm nearly broke."

"Maybe we can cut cordwood for wages," suggested his brother.

Suddenly Per had an idea. "The buffalo bones! That's it, Amund. I'll sell the buffalo bones."

He had uncovered buffalo bones while he was breaking sod. The bones had not been visible in the grass until he had come right upon them. After that he kept his eyes open, and in time he had collected several piles. He knew that in railroad towns buyers paid good money for buffalo bones.

Per often wondered how these bones came to be on his land. Had they been killed by Indians? Not likely, or they would have taken the bones with the meat. What then, wolves? Hunters? Berge had once explained to him that millions of buffalo were being slaughtered simply for their hides and perhaps a few choice bits of meat, such as tongues or humps. Such hunting had recently taken place in Dakota as well in other plains areas. Per had been told that now, few of the buffalo remained.

"What a terrible waste it is when so many people in the world are hungry," declared Per aloud. "The Indians hunted them for food for hundreds of years, but the white man killed them off in just a few years."

After the freezeup, Per borrowed a wagon from Bent and loaded it with bones high above the sides. Surely there must be a couple of tons, he thought; but when he sold them at $6 a ton, he was paid $9 and some change. Well, it wasn't much but it would pay for his winter's groceries.

After the first snowfall Per learned to be a hunter. With him it was a necessity rather than a sport. A fair number of prairie chickens and some jack rabbits inhabited the prairie lands. Quite often, he managed to shoot one or the other. This was the only fresh meat he had. A little salt pork and a few pounds of dried cod supplimented the game.

Since Per did not have a cow for dairy products, his food often became monotonous. Sometimes he bought a gallon syrup pail full of milk from a neighbor. Less often he also bought butter. When he had milk, Per often made a milk mush that he called *gröt*. This he made simply from milk, salt and flour. Other times he made corn meal mush. Early in the winter, he had potatoes buried under the floor. Later on they froze. After that they were not as good, and soon after, they thawed out. In a short time, the potatoes were spoiled.

During December Per made his first trip to Fort Ransom. He knew that his flour sack could not last through the winter, and so he purchased three bushels of wheat from Christ Smedshammer. He informed Per that the wheat could be exchanged for 100 pounds of flour at T. J. Walker's mill. Per estimated the distance to the old fort to be about 14 miles.

Along the way, Per met another settler along the trail. He stopped to talk with the man and found him to be another Norwegian.

"The Sheyenne Valley is settled solidly by Norwegians," his new acquaintance informed him.

"Is that right?"

"Yes, in fact every settler between here and the Red River Valley is a Norwegian."

Per did not presume to question the truth of that statement. Instead he felt impressed and grateful that there should be so many of his own countrymen here in the eastern part of Dakota Territory.

As Per came to the western edge of the bluffs near Fort Ransom, he stopped his horses and stood up in the spring wagon for a better view. Again the beauty of the Sheyenne Valley held him. This scene was not as spectacular as the one of his first crossing with Amund, but he found this much like his own district of Hadeland in Norway. The entire valley was covered with a blanket of pure white snow. Through the naked trees Per could plainly see the frozen river, like a silver ribbon winding its way along the bottom, until finally it meandered out of sight in the distance.

Seeing such a sight again, reminded Per how much he missed the sights of his boyhood home. A melancholy feeling came over him, as he stood lost in thought. His own neighborhood had looked like this during the winter.

Some time later, he found T. J. Walker's mill on the flat above the river bank. After a short wait the men emptied his sacks and began to grind the wheat into flour. Per's imagination was aroused when he noticed the words, "Hold That Fort" printed on the sacks. His interest in his new territory and its history prompted a question.

"When was the fort built here?"

"Fort Ransom was built by Major Crossman and his men during the summer of 1867," answered Walker.

"Where was it? Was it big?"

"The fort was big enough to accomodate 200 men. They built it right on top of Bear's Den Hill."

"Why did they build the fort right here?"

"The fort was built to guard military supply trails from Fort Abercrombe to Devils Lake and the Missouri River. There weren't any settlers here that early, to protect."

"Were there any Indian wars around the fort?"

"No, but there were plenty of skirmishes and running fights. In the early years, the Sioux often tried to stop messengers and supply trains from reaching their destinations."

"When was the fort closed? When did the soldiers leave?" persisted Per.

"After a few years the Sioux were all pushed back across the Missouri and the fort wasn't needed here. When the railroad came to Jamestown in 1872, the government moved the fort there, instead. Ox carts carried the equipment and supplies overland to Ft. Seward. From that time, this was no longer a military post defended by soldiers."

All of this was most interesting to Per. When he asked directions to the old fort, they were clear enough and not far out of his way.

Fifteen minutes later, after a hard climb, Per stood viewing the remains of old Fort Ransom. He could see stone buildings much as they might have looked when the fort was in use. However, the log buildings had many logs missing, and the sod houses were crumpled to the ground. Yet taken altogether, Per found himself able to imagine how the fort must have looked eleven years earlier. Looking at the remains of the breastwork and buildings, Per could almost see the blue uniformed soldiers.

* * * * * * * * * *

The coming of winter did not mean that work stopped for the two brothers. Endless tasks kept them busy during the cold season. One constant aggravation was cutting wood for fuel and hauling it home. Since a cord of wood measuring 4' x 4' x 8' sold for about $3.50 in town, few settlers could afford to buy wood already cut. Most homesteaders chopped their own on the river-bank and paid the owner 50ᶜ a wagon box for what they took.

Amund and Per also paid at first, but later they cut extra wood to pay for their wood. For nearly two weeks, they were hired to cut cordwood at $1 for each cord. The price included stacking it in the owner's yard.

Because they had previous experience cutting cordwood, the two were able to make a reasonable wage at the job. Even those few dollars were welcome, since living without any money was most difficult. During these days the brothers were able to haul home a good supply for each, as well.

On one of the trips to the Sheyenne for wood, Per discoverd there were a goodly number of fish in the river. The two Norwegians immediately made plans to catch some. Fish had always been an important part of their diet. Now they missed fresh fish.

Fishhooks, lines, and sinkers were soon purchased at Fort Ransom. The men began to carry frozen bait with them, until conditions should be just right for fishing. One evening conditions seemed ideal, and so they decided to stay and try their luck. The night was clear and moonlit so that they could drive home later without difficulty.

Each one cut a hole in the ice with an ax and scooped out the broken ice. The lantern was set between the holes, and the men baited their hooks in anticipation. After a ten minute wait, Amund had his first fish. After that both began to catch fish almost as fast as they could rebait the hook and get it back into the water.

"I've got another one," called Amund.

"This is the most fun I've had in a long time," chortled Per.

"The fish are almost jumping up out of the water! We must have caught 25 or 30 good ones by now."

"Just like being back on Randsfjord!"

After a while the fish biting petered out until it stopped, much as it had started. However, on the ice lay fresh frozen fish, enough for many a meal. The brothers thought the fish to be a kind of pike or pickerel. Most of them weighed from one to two pounds, although a few were larger. The two men divided the catch fairly and placed the fish in two separate sacks.

By the time they reached Amund's claim shack, the time was already 8:30, but the men took time to fix themselves a fresh fish meal. Per decided the fish was very good tasting later on when he was consuming huge quantities of boiled potatoes and fried fish. They agreed that this must not be unlike a Viking feast after having gone so long without the taste of fresh fish.

"We must do this often," suggested Per, leaning back in his chair. "We still have many meals left from this one time."

"Next time our luck may not be as good," warned Amund, "then we will have to put a little *snus* on the hook!"

Per placed his fish into his large stone crock and set it in the snow on the north side of his shack. A good sized stone served to hold down the cover and keep it securely in place. During the cold winter this served very well as a refrigerator, and fresh frozen fish continued to provide a welcome change in Per's normally tiresome diet.

His stomach acted up considerably before Per finally got a letter written to Sigrid. How could a man know how to write to her? She was used to having everything so fine and nice at home, because she was after all descended from landed Norwegian nobility.

"If only she weren't used to having things quite so fine," agonized Per, thinking of his humble shack, "Then I could send for her as soon as I have the money for passage."

He wrote quite an elaborate letter to Sigrid. Per said that he was in possession of quite a large amount of land in Dakota Territory, and that he and his brother were renting much additional land near Fargo. Since all this land was very rich and fertile, he would have a great deal of money in a short time. However, first he would have to raise some crops. It would take more time. He needed to make improvements and build a new home for her. Perhaps in another year he would be able to send for her. Per went on to explain that he could scarcely wait for the day when she would come. He closed by saying he was sorry it was taking so long, but that he hoped she would understand and be willing to wait. When the time came he would write again and send money for her passage to America.

He double sealed the letter with dark red wax. The match flickered before he blew it out. Since he had done his best, Per was satisfied with what he had written.

"There. Now I've finally written," he thought. "Now I must go to the post office."

CHAPTER SEVEN

The First Dakota Winter

The early part of the winter was not severe, and snow scarcely covered the ground. During December no genuine Dakota blizzards came. There were chill winds and crisp frigid mornings, but Per was able to travel about and do winter work with little difficulty. Since he had not encountered severe weather by the beginning of January, Per did not get an accurate perspective of Dakota winters. His faulty impression was soon to be corrected.

Thoughts of Sigrid and the letter filled Per's mind. His thoughts brought both happiness and worry and sometimes carried him from emotional lows to peaks.

"Will Sigrid be glad to get my letter? Did I do right to write as I did? Will she be willing to wait for me? Will Herre Kjos see me as a *stor bonde* now that I have so much land? Did I overstep the bounds of my station in life?" These were only a few of the questions Per asked himself.

Usually Per ended by thinking of Sigrid's look and her touch. That was a good note, one he could not forget. He was certain she too would remember.

Amund and Per celebrated Christmas together. They didn't attend church or exchange gifts, but they did prepare a special holiday meal. Instead of traditional Norwegian foods they feasted on roast Jack rabbit. With thawed out vegetables and a fresh apple, each thought the festive meal complete.

On days following the holiday both Kari and Kjersti in turn invited them for a Christmas meal. Then they did eat potato *lefsa* and *lutefisk*, homemade of dried codfish. The Smedshammers could not celebrate Christmas for 12 days as had been their custom at home; but their gatherings were festive and no one spoke in anything except Norwegian. Per came to value highly these times with his friends.

Because of his isolation, Per came to depend heavily on his neighbors. The Homestead Act, in a sense, dictated that each man live upon his own claim rather than in a village, as did most European landowners. In Dakota a neighbor could be found in nearly every direction within a mile. Those who lived next to each other became important to one's life and survival.

During the holidays, Per met several of his neighbors. He found that most of them were from Trondhjem and spoke a dialect different from his. They proved to be friendly and outgoing, although not as close in kinship with Per as others from Hadeland. Understandably they had their own feelings of brotherhood with the others, who were also from Trondhjem. Nevertheless Per was glad to be living near his countrymen.

In fact he soon found that only a small minority were not Norwegians. Among them was a neighbor to the west, who was French-Canadian. Beyond him lived a Swede, who had been a carpenter in Chicago before coming to Dakota Territory. West beyond Griswold was a settlement of Germans. Per had heard that there were a great many Germans in the western part of the county.

One day Per had occasion to visit with the Swedish carpenter. Among other things he told of experiences that he had the first year of homesteading. He spoke of carrying a sack of flour from Valley City 30 miles to his claim shack. Sven also told Per that his Danish wife had Indian visitors, while she was alone at home with the children. Several braves, riding through, asked her for food. Being terrified of them, she brought out everything she had to eat. The Indians greedily accepted the food and seemed satisfied to ride off to the northwest.

"I believe they were Sioux on the old Indian trail to Jamestown," her husband informed Per.

"Probably none too friendly either," added Per remembering what he had heard of the Sibley and Sully expeditions into Dakota.

Per was greatly impressed with the story. He wondered if Indians would ever stop at his place.

Another neighbor was a bachelor like himself. True, Anders was not from Hadeland, but he was still a good Norwegian. He was short of stature but well built. His spirit appealed to Per. The two began a close friendship.

When cutting wood in the Sheyenne Valley, Per normally hauled up only a half load at the time. The first half was laid on top of the bank to await the other half to make a full load. One day, Per came to the top of the bank with the second half load just in time to see one of his neighbors sneaking off with his first half load. He easily recognized both the man and his team of horses. As his anger mounted, Per swore under his breath.

"Why you damn old sneak thief, you!" Per shouted loudly after him, as the man drove off at a furious pace. "You bastard you!"

Per's first impulse was to give chase after the man so as to confront him. He would teach the damn thief a lesson! But as his anger cooled and Per's calm reason returned, he was certain the man knew he had been seen and recognized. In fact he may even have heard Per shout. That would have to do for now. But as Per stomped around with some remaining anger, he was certain that in the future he would see this man as a sneak thief.

During January, the weather grew colder, and there were occasional squalls of snow and wind. Artic blasts sometimes dropped the temperature as much as forty degrees overnight. Still there was no major blizzard.

One of the main expenses for Per that winter was the care of his horses. Twice during the winter, he had to buy ten bushels of oats. Since one could not let sweaty horses stand out uncovered in the cold, he also purchased a pair of lined duck horse blankets. Horses were valuable property and were to be properly cared for. Besides Per wanted only the best for his new team.

Charlie and Nellie grazed outside when they were not being worked. During the work season, they were put out on picket chains. But for the winter months, they were turned loose to graze. Since Per gave them a small half-measure of oats every evening, they soon formed the habit of standing near the door of the stable nickering when it was time to come in for the night. He curried and petted each one in turn, to which they often responded by nickering or nuzzling. Often he spoke to them as if they were human.

"Come on, Charlie! Come Nellie! Time to come in the stable. We sure wouldn't want the wolves to get you, now would we? You'd probably wander off so someone could steal you. Some fellows would probably like to get their hands on a fine pair of buckskins like you!"

Per never grew tired of his horses. Much of his spare time was spent caring for them during the winter, as well as during the working season. Charlie and Nellie came to be his friends. For that reason, living alone was not quite so lonesome.

* * * * * * * * * *

Nearly a third of the way around the world Sigrid examined her reflection in the mirror. She slowly combed her hair as she appraised herself. Yes, there was some reassurance in what she saw, a grown woman in full bloom. For yet another time, her thoughts went back to Per. She found him a very difficult man to forget.

"Why doesn't he ever write to me?" she asked her image. "He was so serious, so sure, before he left for America. I can't believe he's forgotten me. . . Still it's been two years since I heard from him."

Sigrid frowned. What if Per actually did write and ask her to come to America as he had promised. She had often wondered about her decision. It was true that she did enjoy the advantages of being Herre Kjos's daughter. Still her feelings for Per were stronger and more disturbing than those she had for anyone else.

Downstairs, Herre Kjos stood lost in thought. For a third time he took the letter from his pocket to read it again. Yes, of course he remembered Per. He was the son of Erik, the blacksmith. Per had been on the Kjos farm several times, including twice for the harvest. Sigrid had taken to him, no doubt about that. Her attraction had been a matter of concern at the time, since Per was not a suitable match for Sigrid. When the ambitious *husmand* left for America, the question seemed to have been resolved.

Perhaps the young man might go far at that. He might well end up a *store bonde* in America. Was it fair to keep the letter from Sigrid? Should he speak to her about it? What if her decision was to go to Dakota . . . ?

"No, I simply cannot let her go off to this God-forsaken place called Dakota Territory, to live with Indians and buffalo. My daughter will have a better life here in Norway," he reasoned with himself.

Herre Kjos took the letter between his fingers and tore it into strips. The fire flared briefly each time he dropped a piece into the flames. He found no joy, and only a little self rightousness in what he did.

"A man does what he must when it concerns his only daughter," he muttered under his breath.

Herre Kjos blew out the light and found his way to the bedroom by the flickering embers of the fireplace.

* * * * * * * * *

After the next moderate snowfall, Per decided to build a sleigh. His experience in the blacksmith shop gave him confidence to go ahead with the project. However, he was concerned with his lack of tools.

Because he thought the runners the most important part of the sleigh, he carefully selected two pieces of oak, well seasoned, and about ten feet long. Per hewed these out roughly two inches by three inches in size, and worked tediously to get them fairly smooth and even. In order to get a bend or curve at the front end of the runners, he put them in a large kettle of boiling water. Each time they came to a boil, he applied pressure to make a curve. After repeated tries, he eventually worked out a pretty good bend in each. The two were not exactly alike, but close enough to work he thought.

The rest of the framework was easier to make. Per was able to do the work with the few simple tools that he had on hand.

Before the sleigh could be completed, Per had to go to town. He needed strap iron for the runners, carriage bolts and screws, and boards to make a box and floor. In town, he willingly paid 10¢ a pound for nails, one cent for each bolt, and a half cent per screw, but he balked at paying three cents a board foot for planed boards. Instead he bought rough lumber at half the price. In this way, he was able to complete his sleigh for less than $2.00 in cash.

Since he had made it from scratch, Per looked at his sleigh with some pride. True, it was not as nice as a factory made one, but it could carry a few sacks of grain or some supplies easily. Per was satisfied.

The next day, he made a special trip to his brother's claim, anxious to show off his new creation.

"Mighty fancy sled you have there," observed Amund, with a slow smile.

"Well, it's not the prettiest sleigh in the world."

"Do you suppose I could borrow it for the winter?"

Per had to smile. "No, but you can borrow it now and then."

Later in January Per discovered the difference between the weather in Norway or Eastern Iowa and that of the open prairie. The first day was unusually mild, and a soft breeze blew out of the southwest. The snow was thawing a little. Per had no conscious idea that a blizzard might be due.

Gradually the skies became overcast, and by afternoon clouds hung low and heavy. Towards evening snow began to fall. Snowflakes swirled gently around the buildings. In the morning a coating of three or four inches of new snow lay on the ground pretty much as it had fallen. A little more accumulated during the forenoon. Still Per had no warning.

In the afternoon, the weather continued to be mild. Later when Per put the horses into the barn for the night, he noticed the wind had shifted to the northwest. It was picking up rapidly. As he curried the snow from their backs and carefully divided the oats between them, he talked to each horse by name.

"Hello, Charlie Old Boy. How are you tonight?" Per prattled as he patted the gelding on the rump.

"Do you want some oats too, Nellie Girl?" he went on, as she nickered in anticipation of oats and attention.

Per regarded horses as having human understanding. Plainly, they showed their appreciation of being talked to and petted.

As he drew water from the well, Per noticed a definite increase in the wind. This prompted him to bring in some extra wood chunks. He packed an armful of hay into the manger, and decided to bring another into the shanty for fuel. As he went into his little house for the last time, he also picked up the shovel and carried it with him. He heard the wind gusting. Visibility was near zero.

"Sure glad I don't have to be out on a night like this," Per mumbled, going into the warmth and shelter of his one room home.

With almost a gallon of milk on hand, Per decided on milk *gröt* for his supper. When it thickened, he spooned it out on a large plate and sprinkled it with brown sugar and cinnamon. Last of all, he dabbed a spoonful of butter into the middle. Per relished his meal. Thus his body accumulated no fat.

Before bedtime he recognized a blizzard in full progress. He saw nothing when he tried looking out the door or window. Most of the snow that had fallen earlier now seemed suspended in the air, as the wind howled fiercely across the flats of the open plain.

As usual, Per prepared to sleep in his heavy underwear. The mattress ticking was filled deep with prairie hay. A bull buffalo robe and a wool blanket that were purchased after threshing served as covers. Generally, he let the fire go out at night, but on this evening he filled the woodburner and closed off the draft.

Per hurried into bed and rolled up in the heavy covers. As the chill wind cut through the uninsulated shack, the bed in the corner was cold despite its position only half a dozen feet from the stove. For a few minutes he shivered and then he grew warm and sleepy.

The next morning, Per decided there had been no letup in the wind. He had been up to add wood to the fire during the night, but the cabin was icy, despite some fire still burning. After he perked up the fire, the temperature grew warmer near the stove, but not in the the rest of the room.

Per dressed warm for the snowstorm. Over thick woolen trousers, he pulled on bib overalls. With this, he wore a flannel shirt, thick knit socks, and a sweater. Normally he didn't wear this much clothes inside with a fire burning, but on this day the flimsy house served as little more than a windbreak.

The water pail was frozen over with ice. As Per opened the door to get fresh snow to melt, he saw the opening nearly covered with drifting snow. Because the door opened in to the lee of the wind, he opened it wide. As he threw the snow into the air with his shovel, the gusting wind carried it away as if it had wings.

"Whee! The snow's headed for Minnesota!" he chuckled to himself. "Maybe it'll go clear on down to Iowa."

He shivered as he swung the door shut and replaced the heavy wooden bar. Cold air had come in, but it didn't matter that much. In spite of the small size of the shack, it remained cold except very near the fire.

For breakfast Per measured water into a kettle and brought it to a boil. Then he added salt and corn meal, stirring as he did so. When the mush had boiled and thickened, he ate it with a little brown sugar and milk. The cold weather gave Per a very good appetite.

Per tried to look out of the window, but found it covered with frost. When he thawed out a spot with his hand, he still could see nothing. Instead he drew on his sheepskin coat, pulled down the earlaps on his cap, and put on wool lined leather mittens.

"Time to tend the horses," he said, making a habit of speaking to himself. "Surely it can't be that tough to get out to the stable."

Per opened the door and stepped out into the storm with confidence. As he lost the protection of the building, the frigid wind lashed snow against his eyes and face, blinding him for a moment. He responded by putting a mittened hand over his upper face to shield his eyes. In this manner, he stumbled forward into the storm for some distance. When he looked up, expecting to see the barn, he saw nothing except foggy whiteness. Puzzled, he took a few more steps forward. Still no stable! Now the unprotected part of his face was taking the full brunt of the vicious storm.

Slowly the thought dawned on Per that he had lost his way. Impossible! How could it happen on such a short distance? Looking around, he saw nothing except snowy whiteness in every direction. For a moment, Per hadn't the slightest idea where he was!

A feeling of panic caught him, and then his thinking settled down. One thing was sure: he must get back to the house. It couldn't be more than fifty steps away. As Per turned his back directly to the storm for protection, he noticed his own footsteps in the snow. He lost no time retracing his path, bending low to watch the ground intently, but the blowing snow made the tracks dimmer until they were erased completely. For a moment he stood stockstill. Then he took a few calculated steps directly with the wind. There, barely visible, was the faint outline of his claim shack.

With great relief Per found his way back inside. Later he might try the weather again, but not now. A North Dakota blizzard was nothing to fool around with. He had learned his lesson. Per had heard of people walking in a circle, lost in a storm, but he never dreamed that this might ever happen to him. The consequences of wandering away from the buildings were too dramatic to shrug off. In his mind a new respect was forming for the raging blizzard outside.

For the remainder of the day, Per stayed indoors except to shovel the gathering snowdrift from the doorframe. The vigorous action helped to relieve the tensions and restlessness that built up within him. Time passed slowly, since he was not used to being inactive. Several times he checked out the storm, but since it seemed as violent as ever, he made no more attempts to go out.

"Hope Amund doesn't try anything foolish," Per said suddenly out loud. "He's not one to sit around indoors."

Per also thought of his new friends and neighbors. He hoped that they were all safe and sound at home.

"Most of them were here last winter. Maybe they have better sense than I had," he reasoned with himself.

Evening and darkness came early. Per cut cubes of salt pork and fried them in a pan. When the pork was done, he poured off most of the fat and added pancake batter to the pan. After the huge pancake had browned on both sides, Per ate it with a spoonful of corn syrup. The meal was delicious.

Sleep did not come easily the second night of the storm. Per had a feeling of nostalgia that would not pass. His thoughts went back to his family and especially Mor. For the first time, he questioned the wisdom of coming to Dakota Territory. As for himself, he could endure these hardships, but what about Sigrid? He would have to build a better and warmer home, that much was very certain.

Because Per was an optimist by nature, these thoughts eventually passed. He felt equal to any hardship for the promise of the future. His dream was here in America. After all, wasn't that the reason he had left Norway in the first place? Per determined to make a better life, not only for himself but for the children who would come after him.

Warm in bed, Per let his imagination go. Soon he had his crops harvested and threshed, both on his own claim and the land in the Red River Valley. Why in the fall there would be so much grain, he would be rich! Then he would improve the farm, buy more stock, and build a new house and barn.

"This will be such a fine place, Sigrid will be proud to live here!" he told himself with conviction. "She will be proud of me too."

He didn't question that she would come to him. His optimism was a good and peaceful note. Shortly, Per fell asleep.

The following morning, the storm continued as violently as ever. Per busied himself with trivial chores to prevent cabin fever. He was worried about his horses, as they had not been fed or watered in more than two days. Time dragged on. His only release was the exercise of occasionally clearing the doorway of snow. By afternoon, he still had not been to the stable.

Late in the day, Per thought he sensed a difference in the wind. He rushed to the door. Yes, the storm seemed to be dying down. Now perhaps he might be able to get out to the horses.

Quickly he dressed into his outer clothing and grabbed up his shovel. He took time to tie a towel about his face. As he rushed through the door, he was conscious of great white drifts of snow. There was the outline of the stable, vaguely visible through the blizzard. A big drift carried his weight as he climbed over it. At the stable he found the door buried by a large snowdrift. Per worried lest his team was lacking for air inside.

"Nellie! Charlie!' he called out. "Are you all right in there?"

Answering nickers came from the two horses inside. They were alive! With renewed enthusiasm, he dug away at the snow bank covering the doorway. Darkness wasn't too far off. He had to get the door opened soon.

When Per first looked inside, he could see nothing but darkness. As his eyes became accustomed to the inside of the barn, he could see that his horses had eaten away enough coarse slough hay from the ceiling to form a small opening to the outside. Through this hole, a drift of snow had formed. He could see his horses had taken big bites to appease their thirst. The animals looked to be in good condition.

"My Lord, but you are smart horses," he laughed in delight. "I sure didn't have to worry about you two."

Per carried two armfuls of hay into the manger. He didn't try to open the well, as he knew the horses would get along with the snow. He carried a good armful of hay back to the house. Twisting hay would give him something to do, besides saving on the precious wood.

Back inside the shack, Per checked the calendar. Saturday night. Time to take a bath and change underwear. This schedule was typical of pioneers he knew, if indeed they bathed that often during winter. The cabin had warmed as the wind diminished, but Per's teeth chattered before he reached the warmth of his bedcovers.

The following morning dawned cold and clear; the air was sunny, crisp and still. The sub-zero temperature penetrated the little claim shack as if it were a cardboard box.

Outside, Per's breath came in great clouds of steam. The wind-swept snow lay in enormous banks across the landscape like so many great dunes of white sand. He could see the stable door was pretty well covered again. Except for the leeward side, the buildings all had bare spaces of several feet around them.

The cold bit sharply at his exposed nose and face. Per shuddered, then grabbed up his shovel. Time and work would soon clear away the snow from the doors and well. He decided to bank up his house with snow to make it warmer. All this was a small matter. He would soon dig himself out.

He looked up again to see the storm was over and the sun was shining clear. Suddenly, Per felt exultant! It was good to be alive! He had survived the blizzard!

CHAPTER EIGHT

A Bumper Crop

Spring finally came to Dakota Territory. March did not give up easily, but came and went with characteristic fickleness. Chill winds and snow showers persisted until the very end . At last the sun began to win. As the days grew longer the rays more direct, Per saw the last of the snow melt and warmth return. The earth and all living things were ready to perk. Soon it would be time to plant.

Per, tired of winter, had long looked for signs of spring. Now they began to appear. First came the great Canadian honkers, flying in strict "V" formation as they winged their way to northern nesting grounds. Next came the wild ducks. Per could not see the prairie chickens, but he heard the booming sound of the male, as he began his mating rituals.

Another newcomer, who sang in a melodious flute-like way, surprised him. The meadow bird was quite a large one with a brown streaked back and a distinct V in black, on his yellow breast.

"What in the world do you have to be so cheerful about?" grumbled Per, smiling in spite of himself.

In early April, Per and Amund decided the time had come to migrate to the Red River Valley again. The Sheyenne River was still high and dangerous, and so the brothers went an extra five miles north to make a safer crossing than the usual one. Travel went best during the morning hours, when the ground was still frozen. Later in the day, the wagon wheels cut deep ruts in the soft ground. As they came to the sticky clay soil of the Red River country, travel became especially irksome.

"Two years ago this spring, the mud was so sticky after the snow melted that I saw wagon wheels so gummed up, they wouldn't turn around any more," declared Amund.

"Well, it isn't that bad this year," observed Per.

"No, spring's work is not far away the way it's drying."

"With sun and wind like today, it will not be long."

On the trip, the brothers discussed taking out a loan since their cash reserves were next to none. They needed machinery and tools, money for food and expenses, and for their own homesteads seed and oats.

During the late winter, they had made a harrow for two horses. This too had been done almost without cost, except for the purchase of four dozen harrow teeth at 40ᶜ a dozen and two boxes of rivets. All the rest was labor. They choose hardwood limbs about the size of a man's forearm for the framework. Small holes were made for the harrow teeth which were driven in with a hammer. A rivet was then put in on either side of the harrow tooth. The two sections were hooked up to a hardwood beam, and the doubletrees attached with a log chain.

By watching the bonanzas and other large farms, Per and Amund learned that they needed machinery if they were going to grow large acreages of wheat or flax cash crops. For the spring's work they needed a seeder, and for harvest they would need a grain binder. If necessary, the two agreed they would go in debt to get the money for these purchases.

The two had pondered about just how the machinery could be transported. Now the idea of transporting machinery on a flatbed hayrack began to form in their minds. This mobility would enable them to raise crops both on their homesteads and rented land near Kindred.

At the bank, the brothers found their credit was good. Furthermore a team of young horses was still good security for a loan. Interest was 12% as usual, but they were glad to get the money. Cash was scarce on the frontier, and they could not operate without credit.

The young men were fussy about selecting a seeder. After looking at many different makes, they chose an 8 foot 2-horse "Buckeye", made by the P. P. Mast Company of Springfield, Ohio. Normally a man walked behind this seeder in the field. The seller claimed that it would conserve seed and produce a greater yield than one could by broadcasting seeds by hand.

"We can sow 15 to 20 acres a day with this," boasted Per, who felt he was coming up in the world.

"That's right," agreed Amund. "Our biggest trouble will be to keep up with a two horse harrow."

"If we get too far behind, we can change teams every few hours and put in a long day with the harrow."

"We could do that."

The new seeder worked well except on fresh sod. There the shoes caught and brought up chunks of sod that hindered other farm operations. The land that had been broken during the summer and crossplowed in the fall, presented no problem for the seeder.

By the time Amund and Per had finished planting 100 acres on their rented quarter, the first of May had passed. Since the time was now late for planting wheat, they decided flax might do better on the homesteads. Another advantage of the flax was that it would mature later at harvest. Thus one crop would be earlier than the other, simplifying their operation in two places.

Per could use neither harrow or seeder on his own land. The sod, broken in the fall, had not decayed sufficiently. He would have to find another way.

"Try green branches," advised Amund.

"Green branches? For a drag?"

"I've seen it done. That's what I aim to do."

"I will try it. Seeding by hand isn't so bad."

Mulching up the ground by dragging the field with tree branches proved to be a workable plan. Per went one way and then the other. After broadcasting the flax seed, he repeated the dragging process to cover it over. Per thought it important the the field be smooth enough for a binder at harvest, since it was too large to reap with a scythe and cradle.

By the end of May, Per broke up another 4 or 5 acres of land. Most of it he sowed to flax, but a small part he planted to potatoes and root crops. Vegetables would be welcome, especially during the winter.

After the spring planting was finished, Per took time to measure his fields. He was surprised and pleased to find he had 16 acres of flax. In addition, he had a good sized garden. Besides, this was his own land and his own crops, not to be shared with anyone.

Few insects were in the area when Per first came to his new homestead. The mosquito was one notable exception. 1884 was a wet year, providing the insects with an abundance of pot holes and other stagnant water for breeding grounds. Soon the pests appeared by the millions, relentlessly seeking the warm blood of man or beast like vampires in the night. Only the midday sun or a brisk wind could drive them to the protection of the tall grass. Even there, they were easily disturbed as one walked through the prairie grass.

"Charlie you're absolutely crazy tonight. No wonder with all these mosquitoes!" called Per. "Wonder if I can't build you a smudge fire."

He had seen it done. First he built a fire of dry hay, which he later covered with green grass. The result was great billows of smoke. The two horses soon discovered that standing in the line of smoke meant relief from their tormentors.

Per had his own troubles with them. During the day, he had ceased trying to kill them, as they were far too numerous. Nightfall was another matter. Then they seemed larger and were more aggressive than ever, and his patience was sorely tried. They found their way into his shack (screens were not yet in general use) and Per had no mosquito netting. Either he had to sleep entirely covered, with only a very small hole for breathing; or else he had to close the door and window and suffer summer heat that way. In either case, a few wiley devils were sure to find their way to warm human flesh.

Almost immediately after spring's work the sod busting began again in the valley. Again cooperation proved more productive than if each man worked his own team. Besides, this left the other man free to accomplish other work. During the four to five weeks of breaking, they also put up hay to last through the next year.

Early in July the operation moved back to the homesteads. There the two men continued the same work, except that they could not borrow haying equipment. The scythe and fork were ever slow and tedious. As the weather grew hot, both operations became laborious. Frequent rains helped the breaking but hindered the hay making.

Once in a while Per walked to Griswold for provisions to save on the horses. On such a trip he first heard about the territorial governor being tried by a jury at Yankton (the capitol of the early territory). Also that he was removed and replaced by the president, Chester Arthur.

"Have you ever heard of Jeremiah Ordway?" Per asked his brother.

"Isn't he the territorial governor?"

"Did you know he was investigated by a grand jury?"

"Is he a crook?"

"I don't know. He held such a high office. Do you think he can be one?"

"Don't be too sure. You know what Erik would say."

"Well, the president did kick him out. He put in another governor."

"That just about proves it, doesn't it?"

As July progressed, the weather continued near ideal. Mother Nature seemed to smile on Dakota and the soil responded with abundance. The fields stood tall and thick with grain, and the heads were forming long and heavy. The flax on Per's homestead rippled in the wind, like a blue-purple sea.

"Have you heard talk of a bumper crop?" asked Amund.

"Yes, it looks like 1884 could be a banner year!" exclaimed Per.

"The crop does look good."

"What if we can hit it big the first year?"

"We had better get back to Kindred. We have to buy a binder."

"What if they should be sold out? You're right. We better go."

"All right, let us get ready and go."

"What shall we do for money?" Get another bank loan?"

"Dealers are anxious to sell machinery. Maybe we can find one who is willing to give us credit until fall."

Since a binder was a major purchase, the brothers again proceeded with caution. They wanted the right machine and a good deal, and they were not about to be hoodwinked. Buying a wire-tying binder was a temptation, since they were so much cheaper, but Amund's old boss cautioned against it.

"Those who bought wire-tying binders want to get rid of them. The wire troubles the livestock. Better get a twine-tying machine," he advised.

Several brands of twine-tying binders were for sale, but all of them were high priced machines.

"The new Johnson or the Wood look the best, but they are expensive," declared Per, with conviction.

"We'll use a binder for many years. We don't want trouble during the harvest," counseled Amund.

"No, a crop lost is worth more than a few dollars saved now," agreed Per.

By making inquiries, they found that the Dalrymple farms near Cassleton used Walter A. Wood binders. Per was impressed. Word of mouth said this was the largest of all bonanza operations. When the dealer agreed to take $50 and the balance interest free until October, the brothers bought a Wood binder.

Their new six foot 3-horse binder could cut and bind from 12 to 15 acres of heavy wheat each day. By sharing the shocking half days, the men found they could keep up with the binder most of the time.

Both young men were keyed up to a fever pitch. Getting the big crop harvested without mishap was most urgent. The sight of thousands of shocks standing in neat rows, like army tents, spurred them on to greater efforts. Hard work and optimism seemed about to pay off.

As soon as harvest was completed at Kindred, they loaded the binder on the flatbed and hurried back to their homesteads. Finding the flax a little green, they arranged to help Bent and Christ finish their harvest with the new binder. In return, the Smedshammers agreed to help them stack grain.

The brothers found flax more difficult to harvest than wheat. Moisture caused flax straw to twist around rollers and gum up the machinery. They soon learned to wait for sunshine. Shocking was easier and so they finished at the same time.

As agreed, Christ and Bent came with oxen and hayracks to stack flax. With one man in the stack and three hauling, the four men finished Per's two big stacks in one day.

"We had better hurry to get back or threshing will begin without us," predicted Amund.

"With a bumper crop, they will wait for no man," agreed Per. "Lucky for us Lars owns part of a threshing rig. Some settlers will wait a long time this fall."

"The bonanzas will thresh all theirs first."

"Yes, with the help of the small farmers, before any threshing is done for homesteaders."

"Are you saying it's the same here as with the *stor bonders* back in Norway?" asked Per with a twinkle in his eye. "America may not be as different as we thought."

Amund smiled, then grew serious. "Yes, things are better here in America, but some things are the same the world over," he said.

The brothers only reflected the feelings of the small farmers toward the bonanzas. Even though large farm operations provided the homesteaders with much needed work, the settlers never identified with the absentee landlords.

Amund and Per could afford to be smug, since their landlord owned part interest in a threshing machine with several neighbors. The brothers would exchange work to get their threshing done. After that, good money would undoubtedly be offered for custom threshing. Because of big crops, small famers would have to compete for threshing crews or be passed by for a time.

"Threshing our flax may be another matter," observed Per. "We will be lucky to get that done before snowfall."

"It will be a big job to do by flail," answered Amund.

After the regular threshing run was finished, Per was pleased to find his share of the crop to be 700 bushels of wheat, after taking out enough for seed. For a little while he felt rich again. Money didn't grow on trees, but he was getting a good start.

Rumors said the abundance of wheat was lowering the price. Per heard the settlers say the price was down 25^c a bushel, and they gumbled about working only for the railroads and millers. Per did not take these rumors seriously. He was only beginning to learn something about the tribulations of being a small farmer in Dakota Territory.

Per liked the feeling of success and did not want to lose it. He chose to remain an optimist, because he wanted to feel that he had done well.

"Now I must write to Sigrid," he thought. "I'll ask her to come and share my good fortune with me."

One the following Sunday, Per wrote to Sigrid. Again, he told her of his land and crops. He asked her to come in the spring, if she was willing, and promised to send her money for a second class passage. Expressing his feelings and affection was more difficult, but he hoped she would understand and come as soon as possible.

As threshing continued on through September, Amund and Per realized they could not get their fall plowing done with only one team each. Yet, at $3.50 a day for man and team, they could not afford to quit. Several times the two discussed buying another team of horses, but $400 was just too much money.

"We might be able to get an older team for less," suggested Amund.

Though the idea was not to Per's liking, it was a practical one. He wanted to send Sigrid money, build a new home, and pay up his debts and his share of the machinery. He didn't relish paying out high interest rates.

"Well, lets look around to see what we can find," he agreed.

After 40 days of continuous threshing, the owners decided they had threshed enough. Now was the time to plow and do fall work. Per was satisfied to receive $77 from Lars, after his threshing expenses had been paid.

On the same day, Amund had good news and wasted no time telling Per.

"John Kjos has a team he is willing to sell reasonable. I have driven them and they are not bad."

"How old are they?" asked Per with sudden interest.

"About sixteen."

"What does he want for them?"

"$125, spot cash!"

"That's a lot of money for an old team. If they have a quarter of their work years left, it surely must be the poorest quarter."

The team proved to be somewhat rawboned, but they looked sturdy enough. Per noted that their stance and appearance was sound. After driving the horses he was satisfied. They would have a hard time doing any better, he thought.

"You're getting a bargain, because I know you'll treat them well," John assured them.

Even with another team and a second plow, it took the brothers a solid month to finish the plowing and backsetting on 150 acres. During the same time, they sold enough wheat to pay up their debts. The rest of the grain they held, hoping for a better price.

By the time Per got back to his own homestead, it was early November. Winter could come at any time. He had 28 acres to plow or backset before the freezeup, if possible. His flax was not yet threshed. Besides, he wanted to get his house enclosed and haul wood and coal for winter.

During the summer, Per had dug a small cellar and framed it with posts. He also built a better floor, with a new trap door to the cellar. This is where he put his potatoes, rutabagas, and carrots for winter use.

Soon the ground was frozen on cold mornings, and Per did his plowing whenever he could. He was persistent, since it was so important that he get it done.

"It sure doesn't look like the threshers are going to get here," Per remarked. "They must be doing only the big jobs this fall."

"Maybe it's just as well. I hear they are asking 15ᶜ a bushel for wheat," answered Amund. "Flax is probably twice as much."

"15ᶜ a bushel for threshing 45ᶜ wheat?" countered Per, in disbelief.

"The settler doesn't have much left for his work."

The cost of threshing would be nearly equal to the cost of lumber and materials for his new home. Per decided to start his new home instead. During the coming winter he could use it as a granary to thresh his flax a little at a time. On cold days he could burn the flax straw in the stove.

Small farmers often told Per that line elevators were owned and controlled by milling companies. Also, they told him that these enterprises were forcing independent elevators out of business. Per had heard that one should not sell grain to a line elevator where there were no competitors as they were likely to weigh short, dock high, and grade low. However, Per had not paid strict attention to these words of caution, because he had no grain to sell at the time. Besides, he had no first hand experiences with intentional fraud, and so he proceeded to do the very thing he had been warned against.

Because Per had sold several loads earlier in the fall, he knew his wheat was a full 60 pound weight per bushel and that it graded number one hard wheat. Since the grain had been raised on new ground, it contained practically no weed seeds or other dockage.

Imagine Per's surprise when he received a #2 grade on his wheat at the elevator. He was further astounded to find the dockage 11% and the weight at 3290 pounds for a full 60 bushels. The sacks were carefully measured out to four half bushels each, as usual.

Per understood immediately that he had been cheated, but the wheat sacks had already been dumped into the pit. He wished that Amund were there with him. Maybe between the two of them they could do something. Per knew that the other two men working in the elevator could not take his part.

"Do you mean to say that this is right," he asked, his anger mounting to impotent rage.

"Sure, that's correct."

"You must be mistaken. I've sold to other elevators this fall. The grade was #1 hard wheat, the weight 60 pounds, and the dockage about 2%!"

The manager shrugged his shoulders. "You are the one who is mistaken," he said blandly. "We have made no mistake here."

"This is the last damn wheat you will ever get from me!" grated Per, tersely.

He jumped up on the wagon seat, and gave Charlie a sharp slap with the reins. The surprised horse pranced excitedly, pulling hard on the lines, as the wagon rumbled down the wooden plank ramp.

Per seethed. He understood only too well. The homesteader was at the complete mercy of the elevator operator. If a manager chose to be dishonest, the settler could do nothing except take what he was given. Banding together was the only way they could hope to protect themselves. Per figured about one-fifth of his load of wheat had been stolen. This was a lesson he would not soon forget.

Per was still angry when he told Amund about the incident. "A dozen farmers should bring their loads in together and watch the operator weigh and grade. In case of monkey business, they could all face him at once."

"In that case, he would probably have to be honest."

"I am never going to sell him any more grain!"

"That is about all we can do. That will hurt their business."

"I will hurt their business, by telling everybody they are crooks!"

As early winter came, Per brought home the lumber for his new home. The dimensions would be 14' x 20'. Per's idea of a house did not include pretentious size. He figured he needed one larger room and a sleeping room as long as a bed, if he should chose to divide the space this way. In the meantime, the total space made a very large room.

With the help of a carpenter neighbor, Per soon had his house enclosed for the winter. He would finish the inside later.

One of Per's main projects was to thresh his flax. In several days he threshed out ten bushels. In the following months, he made at least one trip to town with sacks filled with flax, usually what he could haul by sleigh or spring wagon. In five months, Per reckoned he had threshed out nearly a hundred and fifty bushels from his crop.

The winter of 1884-85 was an average one in Dakota, better than most during the 1880's. Per traveled about quite well with either the spring wagon or his sleigh throughout the winter. The brothers cut their own wood and hauled it home from the banks of the Sheyenne. A ton of coal, saved for the coldest weather, added greatly to his comfort.

Per's diet was a good deal better the second winter. His small cellar was filled with potatoes and other vegetables. When cold weather threatened to freeze his goods, he hung his kerosine lantern in the cellar over night. Fresh game meat was still supplemented by salt pork and dried codfish, but for a special treat he had pickled herring. Besides his regular staples, he now also bought dried fruits, corn syrup, and cheese.

Since he still lacked either a cow or laying hens, Per had to depend on his neighbors for eggs and milk products. However, since money was not as hard to come by the second winter in Dakota, he was able to have these items on hand much of the time.

The first part of the winter passed rapidly for Per, as he planned and prepared for Sigrid's arrival. Eventually he began to look for an answer to his letter. When he did not get one, he began to worry.

"I just can't believe that Sigrid wouldn't even answer my letter," he told himself. "Something must have happened so that she never received it."

Per thought seriously about sending another letter to make sure. He must be certain that she heard from him.

February was halfway gone before an answer came from Norway. The letter came from the Kjos Estate, but Sigrid had not sent it. Herre Kjos had written it himself. The letter was short and to the point, written in good book Norwegian.

"I wish to inform you that Sigrid was married before Christmas. We will appreciate it if you do not bother us with any further letters. I am sorry about this, but that is the situation."

Herre Kjos

Chapter Nine

From Dreams to Reality

When Per first read the message from Herre Kjos, he was stunned. He sat for a time, seemingly drained and devoid of all emotion. No, it could not be true. He looked at the letter again and re-read the stinging words, ''Sigrid was married. . .'' No, not his Sigrid. There must be some mistake!

As the full realization of what he had read began to penetrate his mind, Per experienced a sickening feeling that expanded throughout his being. Yes, it was true! Herre Kjos had written the letter himself.

For a few moments, Per seemed to lose all control. First he wept bitterly; then he cursed like a madman. He pounded his fists on the table until they were numb. This must be a nightmare, only he was fully awake! Finally he broke into sobs that shook his entire body.

Per had no sleep that night. He was out of bed a dozen times, his mind racing over everything that had happened. Inside he felt a great void. By morning his head ached and his body hurt.

The first days following the letter from Kjos continued like a bad dream. Sigrid had been a part of him so long that letting go was like an amputation. Unaware of mealtimes he went without food. At night he tossed and turned until very late. Early in the morning he awoke with a start, wide awake. Sometimes wet with sweat.

"Why didn't I write to her oftener? If I had, maybe she might have waited," agonized Per. He blamed himself, not Sigrid.

There were times when he was angry at God. If God was good, why did he allow something like this to happen?

Amund was immediately aware something was wrong the moment he saw Per. At first Per did not want to tell him, but then in his misery, he confessed to his brother. Amund's reaction was swift and forcible.

"Have you taken leave of your senses? Didn't I warn you a long time ago?" his brother demanded. "Herre Kjos would never let her marry you. Can't you get it through your head, that she is the daughter of a *stor bonde?*"

The harsh words stung. They were small comfort to Per, but their reality may have been the beginning of his recovery. He could see how ridiculous it must seem to someone else. Perhaps it had never been real, only something to dream about. He must have been a simple minded fool to think Sigrid could ever actually marry him.

His brother's look was kinder than his words. For the next several days, he kept Per company and he kept him busy. With spring's work coming up, there was no lack of work in preparation.

"First we have to make two more harrow sections," Amund reminded him. "We have two more horses this spring."

"We'd never get done with a two horse harrow this year," admitted Per.

"Do you want to go along to the store? We have to pick up harrow teeth, some rivets and groceries."

"Yes, I'll go."

Per welcomed hard work. It relieved his tensions. Constantly, he caught himself thinking or daydreaming of Sigrid. Try as he might, at first he could not get her out of his mind.

The volume of work increased in proportion to the number of acres farmed. Now the brothers had 150 acres of cropland on Lar's quarter near Kindred, besides their own homesteads in the North LaMoure area.

Before the end of May, Per had sowed near 40 acres of flax on his own land.

This was almost equal to the amount Amund had on his. Per

had a competitive spirit, and did not want to take a back seat for his brother.

More than ever, Per turned to his land and to his horses for comfort and companionship. Whenever he could find time, he looked over his fields. Forty acres! What a big beautiful field! Best of all, this was his own. There was something so solid and enduring about the land.

"The land stands forever!" asserted Per, as if he had an audience. "It can be handed down from one generation to the next."

However, that was not a happy thought because it brought Sigrid back to mind. As far as he was concerned, future generations seemed highly unlikely.

But because Per was healthy in body and mind, he gradually adjusted and began to mend. Each month was better than the last.

As always, late spring and early summer was the time to break sod. For all pioneers this became a redundant task that seemed to have no end. Breaking sod became a true test of tenacity and persistence that often spelled the difference between ultimate success or failure.

Sod busting for an extended period of time was hard on horses. The work eventually wore them down, even if they were given the finest care. Per fed his horses six quarts of oats and a manger full of hay three times a day. In addition to this, he carefully curried and watered the animals and allowed them to roll on the ground at the end of the day.

Taking care of horse collars was a job in itself. Unless the collars were kept soft and pliable, the horses would get sore shoulders from continued work. Per wiped them clean each day, and sometimes added a fine film of harness oil to the surface. Occasionally he pounded them with a heavy stick or hammer handle to help keep the collars soft.

As haying season approached, Per began to think of machinery that would make the job easier. He planned to get a cow before winter and he knew a cow couldn't forage well outside in cold weather. She would need to be kept inside the stable and fed hay.

"Have you thought about a mower and rake?" he asked

Amund. "We will need much more hay if we are to have cows."

"Yes, if we are to have cattle, we must buy a mower and rake," His brother agreed immediately.

Haying machinery wasn't such a large purchase. Both a mower and a rake cost less than half as much as a grain binder. Yet, the brothers decided to get credit for the investment, and to buy very carefully to get the best possible machines for the money.

After due process, they came to an agreement. Their selection was a "Standard" 2 horse mower made by Emerson and Talcott, and a "Buckeye" hand dump rake manufactured by P. P. Mast & Co. The hayrake was an 1885 model, just received by the dealer. Per was pleased to think that they could put aside the old scythe and rake for the latest equipment on the market.

Even if new machinery took some of the drudgery out of haying, much hard labor still remained before the hay was stacked. The men still pitched hay into the hayrack and stack with a fork. Like others of their time, Per and Amund expected hard manual labor.

"That was quick," commented Amund, as they completed a second stack.

"We have put up more hay in a week than we did all last year."

"Do you remember putting up hay in the Old Country?"

"Yes, it took all summer."

"We sure are up to date here."

The two men tied down the stack with binder twine, which was thrown over every two or three feet. These strings were in turn weighed down by tying a stone to each end. This device kept the top from blowing off the stack, so that it remained watertight to keep the hay from spoiling before winter. A good, tied down stack would shed water.

Shortly after Kjos's letter came from Norway, Per began to "bum" a chew of tabacco from Amund every now and then. Out of sympathy, Amund was good natured about this at first, but soon grew tired of the imposition.

"If you're going to chew tabacco," he said curtly, "you better start buying your own."

Tobacco chewing was a common habit. Per knew smoking was considered more dangerous, as the men worked around hay, bundles, or dry grass. Prairie fires were still a danger. Finding a place to spit was not a problem out of doors, besides public places provided spitoons. At home Per could use the coal hod or stove. Few considered chewing tobacco uncouth, and Per gradually formed the habit. He did not realize it might be harmful to his health.

During the summer, Per made up his mind to continue using his old shack as a house. Since he banked it and fixed up a cellar, he found it wasn't so bad for a bachelor. That decision would also enable him to continue to use his new building as a granary. By his own calculations, it should hold 1500 bushels of grain. He thought that would do for some time.

The building had to be remodeled before it could be used as a granary. Per needed three bins, one each for flax, oats, and wheat. He also cut small doors under the rake of the roof at each end, so sacks could be dumped into the bins at threshing time. He saved off a small space near the door for sacking the grain.

Just before the harvest, his friend Anders stopped by with the good news.

"Johan is going to have a party tonight," he said. "Be sure you don't miss it, Per. We're gonna have a big time."

Had this happened earlier, Per might have decided against going to the party. Now he thought it a good idea. Such a get together would break up the tedious humdrum of the daily work.

Per, like many others, felt the work monotonous on the frontier. Few had either the time or means for usual kinds of recreation such as those enjoyed by townspeople. As a result settlers often let off steam in wild and exhuberant ways. Excessive use of liquor usually played a part, and its use was common among some of Per's neighbors.

This was the first party Per had attended in the neighborhood. He had never seen anything quite like it, either in Hadeland or in Iowa. Generally, the men came to let their hair down, and after a few drinks many lost their usual inhibitions. Per had a few sorrows of his own to drown, and after a while, he began to find the event very entertaining.

"God kveld, kjäre venn!" Per's friend, Anders greeted him loudly in Norwegian. He was already a little unsteady in his gait.

Inside the house, a dance was going in full swing. The fiddler sat on a chair on top of a table pulled into one corner. Obviously, he was feeling good, as he fiddled and called the dances. With flushed face and drooping mustache, he bobbed his head and stamped his feet in time to the music. Per could hear the scraping and stamping of feet on the rough lumber floor. Now and then several of the men stamped their feet hard in approved Norwegian fashion.

Except when they were dancing, the men stayed on one side of the room and the women on the other. Everyone was dressed in his or her best. The women's long dresses were all gathered tightly at the waist, and Per thought them quite similar except that some were more frilly than others. Some of the men wore store bought suits, while others wore gray homespun brought from Norway. A few wore their best work clothes.

Since the men greatly outnumbered the women, there were no wallflowers. Bachelors were many and single girls few, and so some young men danced with other young men. They didn't want to be left out.

Outside again, Per found much drinking and loud voices. Some of the men had bolstered their egos with alcohol. Others did their best to impress a friend or neighbor with boasting or bragging. A few tempers ran short and several fights took place. Anders was becoming a problem and had already been in two fights. They were short, since he promptly lost both.

Per was becoming worried about his friend, who already had one black eye and other marks of battle on his face. Anders did not seem concerned in the least, as he went right on with his celebrating.

Now Per heard shouts again, and heard the word "fight" several times. As he came around the house a loud argument was taking place, and shortly the two men squared off with each other. One swung wildly. The other connected with a haymaker, and friend Anders collapsed on the ground.

"Get up now and fight like a man!" the other exhorted. But it was of no use. Anders was out cold.

Per decided he couldn't leave his friend there on the ground. Anders had been beaten up three times and needed to be rescued from further injuries. Per picked him up with effort and slung him over his shoulder. Anders, in his limp form, was a good heavy load. Several of the men were reluctant to let Per take the unconscious man away.

"Wait a minute Per. Let me hit him just one more time!" one implored.

"You wouldn't hit a man, who can't stand up, now would you?" asked Per, with a smile. He thought it best to get Anders out of there.

After carrying Anders a short distance to safety, Per tried to revive him. At first his friend turned quarrelsome, but when he understood what had happened, his attitude changed. In a few minutes, Anders was able to walk on his own power. At first he wanted to go back to the party, but Per eventually talked him into going home.

A few days later the harvest began with a rush. The brothers worked twelve hours a day in the fields. Whenever the weather was fit, they changed horses every three hours. When it was not, both men shocked. In this way, they completed cutting, binding, and shocking 230 acres of grain before threshing began. They were unable to get their flax stacked, but because the fall was reasonably dry, the crop did not spoil in the shocks.

After threshing, while the men exchanged work stacking grain, Christ and Kjerstie told about the big prairie fire that had swept through, during their first year in Dakota.

"The fire came when Bent and I were threshing at Kindred," said Christ. "The grass was terribly dry and burned like tinder. Kjerstie and Kari were home by themselves."

"When we first heard the big fire, it sounded like a train," explained Kjerstie. "Kari and I were both frightened out of our wits."

"Well, they did have the good sense to bring the cow and some other things into the sod house. It was a good thing. Everything outside burned up!"

Per soon learned that prairie fires were a constant threat on the frontier. A great deal of slough grass and prairie remained, since most homesteaders broke up only the minimum the first years. During the early spring and fall, the native grasses often became very dry, and fires could easily be started by accident.

During the same fire, Anders was caught out on the open

prairie. He felt it useless to try to outrun the fire, since it traveled much too fast. Attempting to burn off a spot ahead of the main fire, he started a back fire as fast as he could. By the time the big fire reached him, the burned off area was still small. Anders saved himself by hunching up close to the ground with his leather jacket pulled tightly about him. Although the heat was intense and terrifying, the fire soon passed by, and he survived with little damage.

"I was a little bit singed here and there," he confided to Per, "but before long, I was healed up just as good as new."

To the southeast, near Bear Creek, a group of people worked desperately to stop a fire thought to have been set by sparks from the Fargo-Southwestern. Neighbors carried water from the creek and fought the fire with brooms covered with rags, doused in water. They saved a man's home, but not his hay stacks. Luckily, he had already threshed his crops.

Per heard these and other stories when he first came to North LaMoure, and therefore was careful about his firebreaks. These he made by plowing furrows around the buildings. Several rods further out he made a second set of furrows. He picketed his horses on the land between and around the farmstead, so that the grass was cropped very close.

During the fall of 1885, another fire swept through to the south of the neighborhood. Per was worried about his grain stacks and hay, but the fire didn't come close to his buildings. He understood it to be next to impossible to stop a fire traveling with the wind, but beating out the flames as they crept back against the wind was not so difficult.

Later in the fall, after Per had grown quite impatient waiting, the custom threshing crew moved into the neighborhood. About a week later, they came to thresh Per's flax. Because he had many more acres, Per received even more grain the second year than he did from the bumper crop.

After threshing, he felt as if hard work had paid off. Part of his crop paid off his bills and debts. The rest he could afford to hold until late winter, when the price was generally 10-15ᶜ higher per bushel. Per also sold enough flax at home for improvements.

The same fall, Per made another trip to Helendale. The reasons for his trip were twofold: He planned to buy a high grade cow for winter at the Powers bonanza; and he also wanted to see his friend and cousin, Amund Berge. The distance was more than fifty miles from his homestead.

He was disappointed to find that Berge had left the bonanza only a short time earlier. The foreman informed Per that many of the men were laid off after plowing, and only a skeleton crew remained to care for the stock during the winter. He was not sure where Berge had gone, but expected him back in the spring.

His purchase of a cow proved more to his liking. He chose a partly blooded red poll that had already been bred to a full blooded bull. Per was pleased to think this would be the basis of a quality herd some time in the future.

Bringing the cow home was a lesson in patience for Per. For a few miles, she moved along briskly behind the wagon. Then she seemed to play out from walking. Stopping several times along the way, Per half led and half dragged the animal as far as Shelden. There, by means of coaxing, pushing, and some prodding, he managed to get her loaded into the wagon. After that his progress toward home became a little more tolerable.

Per also realized his ambition of setting up a modest blacksmith shop. First he built a small shed, about 10 feet square in size, and then he purchased the forge, anvil, drill press, and vise. Last he bought the necessary small tools and a leather apron. After that Per could do ordinary kinds of blacksmith work needed on the farm.

"Ever since we left Elvestuen, I've wanted to sharpen plow shares, shoe my own horses, and repair machinery without going to town," he explained to his brother.

"You have a good blacksmith shop here," complimented Amund, with just a tinge of envy in his voice.

"You can use it whenever you want," answered Per, liberally.

Working in the blacksmith shop again, brought Per's thoughts back to Elvestuen. There were times when he expected Erik to walk in the door. Now he was thankful his father had taught him so well.

Word soon spread around the neighborhood that Per could do blacksmith work. Most asked neighborly favors, and in return sought to repay him in kind. Only a few exceeded normal bounds. But one day he came from the field at noon to find two neighbor children waiting with a pair of plowshares.

"Papa said you should be prompt. He doesn't like to lose any time in the field," stated the older of the boys.

Per bit his tongue. He had come dangerously close to telling the boy just what his father could do with the plowshares, but that would have been as devoid of grace and manners as was his neighbor's request. A Norwegian had to work hard at this business of staying composed. It did not come naturally to Per.

Per lit the forge and tried to pump the bellows gently. By the time he finished sharpening the plowshares, most of the noon hour was gone. Per had not yet eaten. Now he would have to settle for something cold.

The two boys turned and walked toward home, carrying the plowshares. They had not even said, "Thank you."

As fall ended and winter began, Per became absorbed with working for his naturalization. In three years he could take his examination and apply for citizenship. When that time came, Per wanted to be ready.

From his friend Anders, he came into possession of a *History of the United States*. At first he found the book difficult, mainly about wars he knew nothing about. But as he studied, he found the history more interesting.

Lincoln had long been Per's hero. Now he found another in Washington. He warmed to the struggle of the thirteen colonies for independence. Norway too, had wanted complete independence. and so he could easily identify with his adopted country's desire as well.

That the country had grown from thirteen colonies to a great nation, stretching from the Atlantic to the Pacific, he found incredible. This great expansion was intertwined with sagas of pioneers, who settled and tamed the wilderness. Many of them were immigrants who came to the shores of America from Europe, by the tens of millions. Per thrilled when he realized that he was one of them.

"It's such a strange story, hard to believe it's true," said Per shaking his head. "Strangest of all, we are part of it."

American politics were difficult to understand at first, yet Per, and other Norwegians had an advantage over many immigrants. They had attended school from seven until confirmation at fourteen, while compulsory education had not yet come to many European countries. Some beginnings of self government had roots going back to the constitution of May 17, 1814 in Norway. Per had often heard his father speak of the struggle of the *bonders* against officialdom, back in the Old Country.

As Per began to read the newspapers, together with his study of history, he began to gain some small understanding of politics. But it was only a beginning.

One day when Per went to pick up his mail, he was handed a letter by the postmaster and general store manager. He could tell the letter was from Norway. It was addressed to both him and Amund.

"A letter from sister Anne!" exclaimed Per, as he carefully broke the red seal and opened the letter.

Dear Amund and Per:

"We are heartened by your good fortune in America. I have decided that I want to come too. If you will be so kind as to send me money for passage, I will work for you until the loan is paid in full. I will also need instructions. Please answer as soon as possible.

Father and Mother are well. Engebret and Kari are both fine too. They all look for a letter from you. A hearty greeting from all."

Sister Anne

"Anne must be 18," smiled Per. "She is grown up by now."

As Per drove toward Amund's claim, his home came to mind as it had a hundred times before. Engebret would be growing up too. Since he had been confirmed the past year, he was probably an apprentice in his father's blacksmith shop by now. Sister Kari was twelve, considerable help to her mother no doubt. Five years was a long time not to have seen them.

"So Anne wants to come to America!" Per chuckled to himself. "Well, she can't get ahead in Norway on five cents a day."

Norway could not compare to America in this way, Per thought. Poor folks could not get ahead there. In Norway working hard did not help, if your folks were not of a better class. In America, there was hard work, but for those who were willing there was also a future.

"Here we have a letter from Anne," he confided when he arrived at Amunds, "and she wants to come to America too."

Amund was pleased at the prospect of having Anne keep house for them. To be a settler in Dakota Territory was a hard life, but to be a bachelor besides, was a tough lot indeed.

The brothers agreed without words. Their sister would be coming to America. They would help Anne.

"I'll write to her," offered Per. "I still remember how helpful your letter was for me."

"Be sure she does not come by herself," cautioned Amund.

Both were pleased that Anne's letter had come at a time when they were able to send money for passage. Earlier, it might not have been possible. Per had recently heard that a ticket on a steamer from Liverpool to New York could be purchased for as little as $15 to $20. The tickets also provided boardinghouses in case of a stopover. The journey to Liverpool and the train fare from New York would, of course, be extra and have to be added on.

"Sixty dollars should take care of everything," suggested Per.

"Better send enough for ferry, the train, steamship, and immigrant train," answered Amund, with enough left over to clear immigration in New York."

"Anne won't think much of our homesteader shacks," smiled Per. We may have to fix up a little before she comes."

"Oh, she'll straighten out everything in no time," replied Amund. "Anne was a regular whirlwind when she was only twelve."

In a short time all the plans were completed. The letter was written. The money was sent. All the arrangements were finished for Anne to come to America some time in the spring.

Chapter Ten

Hardships of the Late 80's

"Ouch! Damn it anyway!" exclaimed Per, as he watched a widening spot of red ooze over the white shaving cream which still covered his face. The nick was of small consequence, unless he was delayed. He was in a hurry. Hastily, he tore a tiny piece from a newspaper and stuck it on the bloody spot. Then, holding the straight edge razor a little more carefully, he finished shaving with a few deft strokes.

"Just got to take time to hone and strop the razor," he mumbled to himself, wiping the rest of the soap from his face. "A dull razor nicks easy."

Just a month ago, he had sharpened his razor until he could cut a hair in two simply by touching it to the blade. Since spring had arrived he had been too busy to think about keeping his straight edge in shape.

"With some help, maybe I'll have time to tend to some of these little jobs," he thought, with a grin on his face. "Being a bachelor here on the frontier is no snap."

In just four hours, he had to be at LaMoure, twenty miles away. If nothing went wrong, his sister Anne would be on the Southwestern from Fargo. He mustn't be late! If he hurried, he could haul five sacks of flax to the elevator. That would save him 40 miles later.

As Per urged his buckskin team to the southwest, he had time to plan what he would buy in town. As it was five years since he had seen his sister, he was planning a little celebration for her coming. It simply would not do to feed her *gröt* or something ordinary like that for her first meal in the Dakota Territory.

Two hours later, he unloaded his sacks at the elevator, cashed his check at the bank, and hurried on to the depot. Per unhitched his horses on a spot of grass, and tied one to each back wheel of the spring wagon. He divided the eight quarts of oats, brought from home in a sack, between them. The faithful animals needed rest and sustenance before the long trip back home.

Per was on time. As the train came noisily in to the depot the engine belched great clouds of smoke and steam.

"It's a coalburner," said Per out loud. He could well remember Berge explaining the difference. A bulging smokestack indicated a woodburner, and a straight one meant a coalburning engine.

As the train screeched to a stop, it created some commotion at the depot. Several teams close by acted as if the iron monster was alive, but Per noticed the big old dray team stood solidly, waiting for express to be unloaded. The conductor swung out of the door and set out the step stool for the passengers. Several people stepped off the train. Some of the men wore black suits, white shirts, and patent leather shoes. Two of the women were dressed in ruffled hoop skirts. Per thought they acted mighty elegant. Last of all came Anne, carrying bundles and packages.

Anne had grown up. She was a handsome woman, perhaps a bit buxom, yet very attractive. Although Per could tell at a glance she was very tired from the long trip, she smiled brightly at him. A feeling of empathy surged through Per. He could remember, as if it were yesterday, the time he stepped off the train at Decorah.

"Hilse! Hilse!" he called, smiling broadly. "I am so glad to see you again, Anne."

Tears filled her eyes as she greeted him. Per could tell the trip had been a grueling one. Crossing to America was an experience to daunt the most stout hearted, if his memory served him well. She still smelled of ship. He was reminded again of the unpleasant odors of the steerage in the "Angelo".

Per's errands in town were brief. He purchased a few groceries at the general store, and stopped for a bottle of wine. Then he brought Anne in for a cup of hot coffee. After that Per hitched up the team and they headed for home in the spring wagon.

The hot beverage and the cool spring air refreshed Anne, and she became talkative. This time it was Per's turn to ask questions and to listen, while she told of her trip and the folks back home. Per especially enjoyed hearing of his family. Letters were fine, but they told so little.

"It is so good to talk with you, Anne," Per said. "You have told me more already of home than I have heard in five years."

"Amund went to Kindred to sell wheat, but he will be back tonight. We talked of being together this evening for your coming."

"Oh, that will be nice!" she smiled. "I haven't seen Amund in a long, long time."

"You have grown up into such a handsome woman that I suppose half the boys in Hadeland were after you. Did you come to America to get away from them?" teased Per, with a sidelong glance at his sister.

Anne did not reply. But she smiled and her face tinged with red. Per could see that she was pleased with his flattery.

Soon they left the valley of the James River behind, and drove out across the nearly flat land of the prairie. The landscape rolled sparingly here and there, but for the most part it was nearly level. Anne didn't react to the countryside, except to comment on the fresh air. She had been cooped up in the steerage and immigrant train for many days, and so Per was not surprised.

The three hour trip passed quickly for Per, and soon they approached his homestead. Proudly he showed Anne his land.

"Here we are at my homestead," he said waving his hand. "Here is many times as much land as on Elvestuen."

The sun was nearly set when Amund appeared on the northeast horizon. By that time, Per had two prairie chickens frying in the pan, and potatoes and rutabagas cooking in the pots. The brothers toasted their sister with a glass of wine, but Anne would not drink alcohol. As they sat down to the meal, a sauce of dried fruit, milk, and butter were added. Coffee with sugarlumps for a sweet, completed the meal.

The three talked until long past bedtime. Finally Anne's eyes began to droop. Amund decided the time had come to leave, and Per gave Anne his bed for the night. He made his own bed on the floor and crawled in the covers. Anne was already asleep.

During the following days, Amund and Per found life more pleasant with Anne to help. She was a most willing worker.

1886 was not to be a good year. Earlier, the crops looked good, but by July the weather turned hot. Scorching winds from the south swept across the Dakotas. The heavy soil of the Red River Valley held the moisture well, but new breaking produced only a half a crop.

Work did not stop or let up because the crop was hurt on the homesteads. The brothers now had nearly 300 acres in crop. Farming that much was a big job for two men. From spring's work until after plowing, Amund and Per never let up. Most of spring, summer, and fall was spent in the fields.

Anne made life a little more bearable. She worked on tirelessly and yet remained cheerful. Besides cooking the meals and doing the housework, milking, and gardening much of the time for both of them, she often walked the three miles between the homesteads. Sometimes she also walked to the general store at Griswold for groceries and supplies. Usually she would knit as she walked, so as not to waste time, since the nine mile trip took nearly three hours. Anne also insisted on supplying Amund and Per with starched white shirts for dress-up occasions. This was unusual among the pioneers.

Word that a new young woman was in the neighborhood spread quickly. With so many bachelors, Anne soon attracted considerable attention. As a rule, the men came calling on Sundays. Because they were so many, one ran interference for another.

The suitors were a rough-hewn lot, often with a singular approach. Apparently Anne did not take to any one of them, although she seemed to enjoy the collective attention of all the men.

"They look like so many love-sick calves," joked Per. "How in the world are you going to put them all out of their misery?"

Anne only laughed gaily. She saw nothing wrong with having many suitors at one time.

"I wouldn't want to be left alone with some of them," she confided.

The winter of 1886-87 proved to be one of the most severe in the late 1880's. Snow and cold came early, and by December the temperature was mostly below zero. By January, the snowdrifts nearly covered the little house, the stable and the nearby haystack. Forty below was recorded. The frigid weather did not let up until mid-February, and even then the winter was far from over.

Early in the winter, Anne was able to joke about the weather. "They would not believe me back in Norway if I told them about the weather here. We must be next to the north pole."

"If the cold snap goes on, you will have to climb up on the roof and cut the frozen smoke off the chimney so the fire doesn't go out," jested Per.

Anne's introduction to Dakota's winters was swift and complete the first year. After a while, she grew homesick and depressed. Had it been possible, she would gladly have returned to her home in Norway. The isolation was simply too much.

The winds blew incessantly. First they came from the southeast with snow, and then from the northwest with a blizzard. Even on a clear day, a neighbor's house was difficult to see since his buildings were buried in snow.

Per sought to cheer up Anne. At first he tried to teach her English, and later to instruct her in history. At first she responded but later she lost all interest. Luckily a few hardy suitors braved the elements to come courting. That was the only variety she found in an otherwise long, dreary, and lonesome Dakota winter.

As the days passed, Per watched his sister with concern. Winters could be hard on men, but he saw they could be worse for women. He could not help but wonder what would have happened had this been Sigrid rather than Anne.

"I've heard some women go crazy with cabin fever," Per remarked to Amund. "For those who expect a baby, it must be even worse."

"The ones who are born here don't seem to mind it so much."

That winter, Per learned to read a newspaper from beginning to end. He especially tried to bring home newspapers written in the Norwegian language so that Anne could read them too. She found the mother tongue comforting. Several of Per's neighbors took the "Decorah Pösten" and the "Ved Arnen". A few had others as well. Per often exchanged newspapers with others. It mattered little if they were a week or more old.

Since studying for citizenship, Per understood the editorials better. He gathered that the years following the Civil War were ones of great dishonesty and greed both in politics and business.

As the terrible winter came to an end, Per learned that thousands of cattle lay dead in the open range country of western Dakota. Editors agreed that it was a devastating blow to cattle ranching.

Finally spring and planting time came again. In 1887, for the first time, Per and Amund farmed only their own land. By now both had an impressive amount of sod broken for crops on their homesteads.

For a time, the summer of 1887 seemed to promise a good harvest. Moisture from the winter snow started the crops, and additional rains brought them close to harvest. As the grain began to fill, searing winds came again out of the south. Per stood by watching anxiously and hopelessly, as the winds cooked the grain. Again for another year, Per and his neighbors had to accept a greatly reduced yield.

"We can't get ahead on 9 bushel wheat and 4 bushel flax," grumbled Amund.

"Especially when the price is only 45ᶜ and 80ᶜ a bushel," agreed Per.

"There won't be money for improvements this year."

"We can't control the weather. It does no good to work hard."

On 90 acres of cash crop, Per would have to live frugally, if he wanted money left for expenses the following year. He agreed with Amund. It wasn't their fault. They had worked hard; now there was no reward. It didn't seem quite fair.

He was still thinking of what he had heard on the 4th of July. He had attended a celebration at Lisbon. There he had heard a Farmer's Alliance man speak. This speaker stated flatly that territorial politicians were mostly unprincipled men, who had come from the east to get rich off Dakota politics. Most were land speculators. They cared nothing for Dakotans, and many were on the payrolls of the railroads and milling companies. Their job was to help the corporations keep grain prices down and railroad rates up. Besides their fair share, the speaker said, they were also taking a good part of what rightfully belonged to the farmer. They did so by creating a monopoly in the free market place.

"They take 30ᶜ for handling and shipping while you, who grow the wheat, get only 45ᶜ a bushel," he declared. "We must join hands to vote out these rascals and elect men who will work for the farmers."

What he said made a lot of sense, Per thought. Everything he said seemed to be true.

Later in the year, Per joined the Dakota Farmer's Alliance. For the $1.50, he received a year's membership, a newspaper called the "Normanden" and another, the "Dakota Farmer". He found both papers supported the small farmer in Dakota Territory. They questioned the "hands off" policy wanted by big business, and called instead for ways to regulate graft and corruption in politics and business.

In the meantime the mundane life of the settler went on. Work was never finished on the homestead. One morning, Anne came to Per with a thoughtful look on her face.

"What can be wrong with Molly?" she asked.

"Molly? What are you talking about?" countered Per.

"She is acting so restless and so strange this morning."

For a minute Per looked puzzled, then he broke out in a broad smile.

"There is nothing wrong with the cow," he chuckled, "except that it's time to get her to a bull."

It was most important that the cow be bred promptly, so that she would be with calf without delay. She must freshen and continue to give precious milk products, with a minimum dry period. For these reasons, Per took time from his work to tie the cow behind the wagon and make a trip to his neighbors. Per didn't have a bull himself, but his neighbor, Lars, had a fine one.

Per had always found the peculiar nose wrinkling of the bull amusing. The animal's expression would turn to a grimace when he smelled of the cow's vulva, while she was in heat. The bull extended his neck with the nose and upper lip curled to expose the upper part of the mouth. To Per, this had always seemed to be a curious mixture of expression of extreme pleasure and agony at one time.

Like his neighbors, Per found the late 1880's hard years in Dakota Territory. Little laughter or diversion tempered a hard day's work. Consequently one might say that bringing one's cow to a neighbor's bull became a form of welcome relaxation or even recreation. First, it gave a man a chance to visit with his neighbor a bit, and then most settlers found a kind of humor in the situation. Per had never seen anyone so busy that he could not take off a few minutes to watch and make a few sage comments.

The year before, Per had been embarassed because the husband was not at home when he brought his cow. However, the housewife was not fazed a bit and handled the bull as expertly as her husband. From what Per could tell by her reaction, he decided the women found the action just as interesting as the men.

The same idea struck him again when he got home. Anne smirked as she looked at the posture of the cow, and then remarked much too innocently, "Poor Molly, I do hope you are feeling better now."

"Being you take such an interest, I'll send you with the cow the next time," Per declared.

Since her first winter had been such a difficult one, the brothers decided it might be better for Anne to find a job in town for the winter. The men would get along without her from October until April. In the spring, she would be back. Anne quickly found a job at the Ledia Hotel in LaMoure. When Per visited her, he found she had a new collection of suitors in town, and he decided she would not be lonesome.

The early winter of 1887-88 began as if it were apologizing for the past one, but before it ended new records had been set for storms and cold. By December, the weather resumed where it had left off the year before. The storms and cold continued with few letups until March. But on the 12th of January in 1888, came the grandfather of all winter blizzards. The morning dawned deceptively clear and bright, and the temperature was mild enough to thaw. Per, who had now experienced many blizzards, suspected something foreboding in the air. Consequently, he prepared for the worst. Late in the afternoon, the sky grew dark, and the storm struck out of the northwest with sudden and dramatic fury.

Per soon realized it was to be a terrible storm. The blinding snow and the chilling wind lashed out of the arctic, as if in pent up rage. As the polar blasts continued, the air turned icy cold. Per thought the Almighty must be showing his anger to the people. He was reminded also of the old tales of Odin and Thor, the Norse Gods of war and thunder.

After a while, Per began to worry about his animals. Now he had a clothes line strung from his house to his barn so he would not get lost in a storm. Even though Per had a scarf wrapped around his face, the air almost took his breath away as he first stepped out into the blizzard.

He quickly pitched hay and shoveled snow into the mangers. Then he milked his cow. So far everything seemed all right. Per was glad he had doubled the size of his stable, since it gave his stock much more air.

The following two days were a repetition of the first day of the blizzard. Mostly Per stayed close to the fire and studied his civics, and the great storm raged on with no thought of letup or decrease in intensity.

Toward evening on the third day, when the great storm finally began to subside, Per was truly thankful. He had never experienced such a storm. As the wind lessened, the evening air turned still, clear, and crisp with cold.

Several days later, when Per read of the storm in the newspaper, he found it was regarded as the greatest and worst blizzard in the area's recorded history. Its size had covered several states. More than two hundred persons had lost their lives, half of whom were school children and others in Dakota Territory, who had been caught in the storm.

Numerous cattle and horses were reported suffocated in small stables. For a second year in a row, the cattle of the open range country had suffered a stunning loss. The damage was crippling and beyond repair, as the poor animals lay scattered across the countryside by the thousands, frozen stiff and lifeless.

"If I never had any respect for winter storms before, then I most certainly do now," Per told himself grimly.

As if to make amends for the terrible winter, spring came early. The heavy snowfall disappeared into the ground as if by magic, and spring work began early.

The seeds germinated well from the spring moisture, but later frost hurt some of the crop. Near normal rains during the summer seemed to bring the grain back again, and for a time it looked as if there might be a normal yield. Then strong hot winds began to blow from the south and the temperature rose to 100 degrees. For the third time Per's stomach tossed and turned as he watched yet another crop wilt before his eyes. Without a drop in temperature and rain there would be little crop.

But the weather did not let up, and to add further insult, hordes of grasshoppers came to finish the job. They came like marauders to take what little remained, stripping everything green. When they were through, nothing remained of the crop of 1888.

Per cut a few potholes with the mower, to get a few bushels for flour.

In all, he got less than ten bushels of oats for his horses. He had no flax or wheat to sell.

Later that fall, Per noticed well dressed men in top buggies driving in the neighborhood. Soon he came to realize they were collectors, looking for interest from the settlers. Per knew his neighbors had no money to pay.

Times were tough for Per, yet he felt lucky to have a better start than some. He and Amund had paid for machinery with crops raised in the Red River Valley. Some of his neighbors were being forced to sell what little they had to satisfy bills and debts. Others were in danger of losing newly owned land because of mortages. A few simply abandoned their claims and left Dakota. Per, like most of the other immigrants, was determinded to hang on to his claim at all costs. The land was the last of his dreams, and he was not about to give it up easily.

A new kind of humor grew up, born of desperation and hopelessness of the times. Per heard settlers joking about it when he went to town.

"It sure does look like rain, don't it?" one remarked.

"Well, it don't matter to me. I've seen rain before in my day, but my boy here (nodding toward his 12 year old son) he ain't never seen no rain."

Not only did the Yankees tell jokes, but Per's neighbors began to talk of snow, cold, and blizzards in a humorous way. During the summer the stories turned to drought, wind, grasshoppers, and other calamities. Per figured it was a kind of safety valve, to keep people from going out of their minds.

For Per there was one highlight in 1888. That came in the fall of the year when he was at last sworn in as a naturalized citizen. He had studied civics and history from books, and from newspapers he had gained an interest in political matters. Per worked himself up into a sweat before the examination. He had visions of himself, standing before the official, unable to answer the questions.

Actually, when the time came, it was not so difficult. After a nervous beginning, Per calmed down and answered whatever was asked. Soon the examiner seemed satisfied.

Last of all came the hearing before the judge. Amund and Anders went along to vouch for Per's character. The examiner was also present. Per and five others stood before the judge. He heard the examiner say that they were ready for the oath, and should be given their final papers. The six of them took the oath, and the judge pronounced them citizens of the United States.

Outside the courthouse, Per thrilled to see the flag of the United States on the tall flagpole before the courthouse. Strange, he thought, that he had not even noticed it when they came in. Now it was his flag too.

Anders shook hands with Per. "Now you are an American," he said.

On the surface it was true, Per was an American. Except for his Norwegian accent, he had learned to speak, look, and act like one. Underneath were still differences from a natural born. Per had attended school, grown to manhood, and received his training in Norway. Being an immigrant was a vivid memory. His inner emotions were a product of America, the immigrant, and harking back to his homeland. Now he had exchanged his citizenship from his homeland to his new state.

Per could not define his feeling for America. His ambition and desire for land and better future had brought him there. He could appreciate government by the people, but sensed that democracy did not come to the undeserving. It was a blessing citizens had to earn. Actually, his feelings for his new country may have been stronger than that of most native born citizens.

Per's naturalization came in time for the presidential election of 1888. The two candidates were the incumbent Democrat, Grover Cleveland; and Ohio Senator, Benjamin Harrison, who introduced the statehood bill for Dakota. Later on, he supported another bill, allowing for two states from Dakota Territory.

Per voted Republican. It seemed the natural thing to do. Most Norwegians in Dakota were Republicans, and most newspapers had Republican editors. Per thought of it as Lincoln's party and the one that passed the Homestead Act. After the election results were in Benjamin Harrison was easily the winner. Per and his neighbors were gratified to have won the election.

After the total crop failure of 1888, Per went back to living much as he had the first winter in Dakota. One important difference was that he now had two cows and several hens. During the winter he was able to cut cordwood to pay for the wood he needed, but he was not able to find a job that paid in cash. Too many settlers were looking for that type of work. Hunting had become easier. Prairie chickens and jack rabbits flourished on a mixture of grain fields and grasslands. Per found tracking easy after a snow.

In the spring, Per had to borrow $100 for seed, oats, and operating expenses. But 1889 proved to be the driest year of all. The result was another crops failure. Towards fall, Per was obliged to borrow another $50 for fall and winter expenses. For the collateral he had, the banker was reluctant to lend him that much. In addition to his debts at the bank, Per also had other bills totaling about $50.

What if 1890 should be another failure? That question came to Per's mind often. It looked as if he would have to find a loan shark in the spring. If what Per had heard was true, few ever escaped such a man's clutches. His future was beginning to look very grim.

The hard times forced Per to think hard. Quite often his thoughts went back to the Glenwood church in Iowa. Gradually he began to believe that God was punishing him because he had turned his back on the church and his earlier Christian beliefs.

"I was much too busy making money and getting ahead," he thought shaking his head.

There had been no time to think of God or of church. Looking back, his neglect was not on purpose. There just seemed to be too much work.

"It must be the will of God," he admitted to himself. "This is my punishment for turning my back."

Life was becoming too hard. Blizzards and droughts could be endured. He could learn not to borrow except in desperation, but he could not face losing his land. He had lost Sigrid. Now he simply couldn't bear to lose his land.

Change did not come easily, but from then on Per talked more often with his Maker. He began going back to Scriptures from his confirmation. Strength to hang on came to him from somewhere. If anything, the struggle brought him even closer to his land.

Per knew a church had been organized at North LaMoure in 1883, and now church services were held at the school house, not many miles away. Rev. O. K. Anderson of Fort Ransom held services there on a regular basis when the weather permitted. As Per began to attend, he found the pastor sincere and very able.

* * * * * * * * *

An Omnibus Bill was passed on Washington's birthday in 1889, by Congress. Part of it provided for two states from Dakota Territory. The northern part was divided into 25 districts, each of which was to elect a delegate to a constitutional convention to meet in Bismarck.

Christ, Bent, Amund, and Per, now full fledged citizens, went to the polls to select a delegate from their district. They all voted for a Dakota Farmer's Alliance Man. All four followed newspaper accounts closely to learn what they could of events taking place at Bismarck. These accounts often disagreed, but they did tell the basic story that led to statehood.

Per and his friends often discussed politics and statehood. All found an interest in common around these events.

"I certainly hope the new state will be able to control the politicians better than the territory did," volunteered Christ.

"Good thing we are getting rid of that," agreed Amund. "I hear they ran us a million dollars in the hole!"

"Most of it went to make the shady politicians in the assembly rich," declared Per.

"Northern Dakota will have to pay half of that dept," added Bent.

"Maybe the new state will protect us from the men we elect to office," said Per, hopefully.

Newspapers reported the great pageantry in Bismarck. Great numbers of Indians and soldiers from nearby forts took part in the big parades on the opening day of the convention. That was also the 4th of July.

Later, Per and his friends were heartened to hear that Fred Fancher of Jamestown was elected president of the convention. Fancher was vice president of the Dakota Farmer's Alliance, and Per had heard him speak for the farmers.

Editorials claimed the convention reflected the reform ideas of the majority of delegates. Still, it seemed to Per as if the minority was able to block or defeat many of the reforms. The convention struggled with ideas of how to control the railroads and the milling companies. It also tried to curb the power of corrupt politicians. As the Norwegians watched, they felt an effort was made to keep control of the new state in the hands of the people. A secret ballot and prohibition was provided for, if ratified by the people of the state. By the time the delegates adjourned, Northern Dakota had a long and complicated constitution.

On October 1st in 1889, Per and other Dakotans went to the polls and approved the new state constitution. On the same day, they elected local officials, plus one representative to congress. The legislature would elect the senators.

Later in the fall, Per was to learn that on November 2, 1889, Benjamin Harrison, President of the United States, had proclaimed North Dakota a state.

Chapter Eleven

The Gay Nineties

In the spring of 1890, Per had no choice except to go to a loan shark for a loan. He simply had to buy seed for planting and feed for his horses. Because of the scarcity of money, he could not get money from a bank with the security he offered. The loan shark wanted everything Per still owned clear as collateral for a $100 loan. The interest was set at 25% and the property would be forfeited unless the note was paid within one year's time. Per was sick at the thought, but there was no other choice. He signed the paper agreeing to the terms and received the money.

* * * * * * * * * *

The new state of North Dakota was hard up. Since it was born during drought and depression, the government had barely enough money to function. The new state had inherited a huge debt from the territorial government, and the delegates had set limits on taxing power without voter approval. Per also learned that the politicians had promised a state institution to every section. Fourteen such institutions were authorized. Only a few could be funded.

The outlook for the new state continued bleak into late spring. Little rain fell in April and not enough in May to compensate for previous droughts. Another disastrous crop failure seemed inevitable. Were this to happen, Per knew he would lose everything. He now owed more than $300 in loans and bills, plus money he had borrowed from Anne to pay interest. Another crop failure would spell the end of his dream as a land owner.

"I've worked hard and scrimped and saved," complained Per aloud to himself; "yet I can do nothing to save my land if we have another drought."

It just didn't seem fair, he thought. Some were getting fat, taking a rakeoff from the farmers labors; yet he, who produced the food by sweat and toil, stood to lose his home and land. Had Per known where and how to fight for what was his, he would have done so physically, without any hesitation.

Per looked for a job. If he could find a job with his team, it wouldn't take long to pay off the main loans. However, it seemed as if every settler in the territory was looking for a similar job.

One day in town, Per was unnerved. As he walked down the boardwalk, he met the loanshark, who nodded curtly and smiled thinly as he passed. In Per's mind the tight smile soon became an evil leer. He visualized the villain coming to dispossess him of his property. As he drove homeward, Per's stomach felt as if it were churning butter.

During the next weeks, Per turned to his God in earnest. No longer was he as prideful as when events were going well, and he came to understand that he couldn't do everything by his own power. There was not the slightest doubt in his mind that God could intervene, if He so wished. Finally Per was ready to accept His will.

Per always believed that his prayers were answered. Whatever the reason, his luck took a definite turn for the better.

The first sign of this change was the birth of a beautiful, near perfect, black foal with white markings. A year earlier, a superb, dappled gray Percheron stallion had been brought into the neighborhood. Per had bred his mare, Nellie, to the stud and now about eleven months later, he had a frisky little filly. Per was delighted. The foal became his pet, and he named her "Fly".

Anne was also captivated by the new foal. Whenever the filly was around, Anne pampered her as much as Per did. Quite often she brought Fly a handful of oats, and once in a while she sneaked her a sugar lump.

During the month of June, good rains began to fall and growing conditions became ideal. The crops came back surprisingly well. As the summer progressed the weather held and more rains fell. By harvest time, Per's crops were looking better than they had for five years. Moreover, the heads were filling surprisingly well.

On the promise of a crop, Per was able to charge the necessary twine, oats, and supplies he needed for harvest.

At threshing time, Per's small granary was filled with wheat and flax. He built a small bin outside made of rails and hay for the oats. Earlier, he had borrowed money to buy oats, but now he had two year's supply. Furthermore repeated crop failures had brought up the market price of grain. Per sold no wheat that year for less than 75ᶜ a bushel.

1890 proved a good year for Per. He paid the loan shark, his other debts and interest, and his expenses as well. Nearly half of his grain remained in the bins. With some of the surplus he made overdue improvements and repairs, but he was careful to carry over enough for the next year's expenses.

During the same fall a significant event took place. Per had met all the requirements of the Homestead Act on his land. By paying the final fee of $4 for proof of title, he received a deed to his 160 acres of land. His patent for homestead was signed by Benjamin Harrison, president of the United States, on December 20, 1890. His dream of becoming a land owner had finally become a reality! Per had proved up his claim.

There were tears in Per's eyes as he looked at his land. He felt humble and thankful. How near he had been to losing the land, and yet here it was safely in his hands. God had been good to intervene for him, Per thought and he would not forget that so soon.

The following winter was a "snow winter." Great drifts covered the ground. Per found hauling grain to market or getting around most difficult. However, in the spring the snows melted slowly, soaking into the ground, and the soil regained much of the moisture it had lacked for several years. Per began to think the prospects for an excellent crop were good.

That spring another foal was born. This was another buckskin like his mother, Nellie. He was a sturdy fellow and as frisky as the first. Per soon names this colt "Dan." He took great interest in watching the two foals frolic about. Nothing was too good for them. Once again, Anne shared his delight.

Before harvest, Per purchased another horse. He knew prices for horses had dropped steadily during the depression of the late 1880's Now a good team could be bought for only half the price Per had paid for his team in 1883. Since Per's old horse, Adam, was no longer dependable for such a big harvest, Per decided to replace him with a younger horse. He found a nine year old brown gelding and after some dickering, he bought "Prince" for $75.

The growing season of 1891 was ideal. Before harvest, it was evident there would be another bumper crop. Since he had to have more room for grain, Per built a new 3000 bushel capacity granary. He did not borrow money to to this, but used his credit at the lumber yard, for which he gave a lien on his new crop.

Per was grateful for the outstanding harvest. When the new crops were in the bins, the new granary was filled.

"These last years, it wasn't easy to believe we would have wheat crops of twenty two bushels to the acre again." admitted Per.

"Exactly right," agreed Anne.

That same fall, Per reclaimed the old granary for a house. Over the door, he built a lean-to for wood and coal during the winter. Tar paper was placed between the double outside walls, and building paper and newspapers served as insulation between the studs before the inside wall was added. Last of all, a ceiling and loft floor were added. This house too, had a framed in cellar below a trap door. Per figured it would stay decently warm, if the house were banked up before winter.

After springwork the following year, Per built a new barn. The building was 28 feet by 32 feet in size, and there was room for several loads of hay in the haymow. The new stable was more than adequate for his horses, colts, and cattle. Later, he built a hayshed and dug a well inside the addition.

Per also made other improvements. First of all, he made another trip to Helendale to purchase a high grade heifer and a red poll bull calf. Then finding barbed wire reasonable in price, he set about building a much larger pasture fence for his stock. Herding cattle or picketing horses was irksome during the busy season. Lastly he bought new tools and machinery, including a new grain drill and a harvester-binder.

After considerable thinking, Per decided he could afford a new buggy and a fancy buggy harness. His friends ribbed him about this. A bachelor, who bought a buggy was thought to have courting in mind. He was not likely to spend that much money for farm purposes. Anne was excited about the new buggy. She found it shiny, sleek, and elegant.

"Now we can ride to church or to town in style," she said. "My, won't that be grand."

"So you are ready at last to go out courting," teased Amund with a grin.

Per just laughed at them both. He wasn't certain what he would do with the buggy, but he felt good to be able to buy something so luxurious. The Elvestuens would have made good aristocrats, he thought, as they did dearly love such finery.

Not all the years that followed were good ones. In 1892, the weather was drier again, and the price of grain dropped. The following year was worse, and the countrywide Panic of 1893 caused further collapse of wheat prices. Another period of hardship and depression for the settlers in North Dakota followed, causing many to sell out for what they could get. Bankers sold out others in order to satisfy mortgages.

"Only half the pioneers who were here when we first came are still here," observed Per.

"Yes, and almost all who remain are immigrants," agreed Amund.

"I think more settlers have left this year than in 1888 and 1889."

"And many who still live on their land have mortgages again."

Per never experienced quite the extreme poverty and hardship again that he did in the 1880's. Because he was unwilling to gamble with his land he never mortgaged his homestead. Had he been willing to take risks, he could have bought additional land cheaply. Some quarters sold for as little as $400, in cash.

"North Dakota will have more bumper crops and more failures," Per declared to Anne. "I am not going to get caught when the bad years come."

Gradually, he adapted to these extremes. After a good crop, he saved grain to carry over for an emergency. Per came to realize he could not rely entirely on wheat and flax as cash crops. By the time the panic came in 1893, Per was milking four cows. Anne soon gained a good reputation as a butter maker, which helped Per later. Housewives in town paid 50ᶜ for a five pound crock, which brought only 40ᶜ at the general store. Per averaged three crocks a week and had no trouble finding customers. During the poor years, he was usually ready to market a few good sized beef.

Per adapted also in other ways. He began to raise his own pigs to butcher in the fall. Enough hens for an egg supply and brood hens to supply meat was also part of his plan of economy.

Times remained hard. In Dakota there was no substitute for a cash wheat crop. Hanging on and getting ahead were two different things.

As drought and depression returned, the Dakota Farmer's Alliance gained in membership and strength. Regular meetings were held at the schoolhouse. Hardships created unity among farmers who were normally much too independent for organizing. Per and his friends and neighbors came. The women also came with their men to listen and to serve coffee for the social hour after the meetings.

Sometimes the Alliance leaders were able to get a speaker who understood the politics of Dakota. Per came slowly to an understanding of how men such as Nerhemiah Ordway and Alexander McKensie were on the payroll of the railroads, mills, and banks, while pretending to serve the public. These politicians and others like them knew how to take full advantage of the ignorance of the immigrants, while appearing most upright and sanctimonious in public. Behind closed doors they divided the spoils.

Per's information of these and other matters also grew from a faithful weekly reading of the "Normanden" and the "Dakota Farmer." These papers called for new state laws to regulate graft and corruption.

Per and his friends were especially bitter when they learned that politicians had caused feed and seed loans to be withheld from Dakota farmers after the terrible droughts of 1888 and 1889. Because so many politicians were land speculators, they withheld and suppressed this information from Congress and the east, for fear the news might hurt land values in Dakota.

"Most politicians don't know right from wrong, if it means money in their pockets," declared Per in disgust.

"Is there such a thing as an honest politician?" asked Amund.

As the brothers became more knowledgeable of Dakota politics, they discovered a struggle within the Republican party between McKensie and his followers, and the reform movement. Amund and Per, together with most Norwegian-Americans, came to support the reformers. Editors who received patronage in return, saloon keepers who opposed prohibition, and others who received political favors followed McKensie. Support for him also came from recent German-Russian and other immigrants, who were excellent farmers but lacked experience in self government. They voted for "Big Alex's" men because he was such a great fellow.

Reformers accused McKensie of running North Dakota from St. Paul, while on the payroll of Twin City Corporations, who wanted to keep the new state in a colonial status. They claimed that he established his residence in Bismarck only when there was a United States senator to be selected by the state legislature. Reform editors and speakers demanded that the power be taken away from St. Paul and brought back to the state capitol at Bismarck.

The reform mood was strong in 1892. At the polls Per and his friends helped elect a legislature and a governor sympathetic to the Farmer's Alliance. During the session that followed reform bills were passed to regulate the elevators, railroad rates, and usury charges. However, these reform bills all mysteriously disappeared before they reached the governor.

"How could they disappear?" questioned Per, in amazement. "Aren't we living in a democracy?"

"Governor Shortridge said in public that the reform bills were stolen," said Christ.

"We work hard for reform," said Bent angrily, "but the double dealing politicians make out that it's we who are the cranks!"

"The bastards are too smart for us! Even when we elect both the governor and the legislature, they outsmart us!" exclaimed Amund.

"Even when bills are passed, the wording is so tricky that they can't be enforced," added Per.

Per and his friends came to share attitudes common among Norwegians in eastern Dakota. They were suspicious of all politicians. The friends also came to fear great monopolies that could set their prices without competition, and were powerful enough to exert their great influence over government.

Both Per and Amund grew to be staunch Republicans. Most Norwegians were Republicans as they were also Lutherans. They simply voted for reform candidates except when they were duped into voting for an unknown McKensie man.

In 1893, an event took place that changed Per's relationship with his brother. That was the year Amund married Josephine. Per and Anne went to Fort Ransom for the simple ceremony performed by Rev. O. K. Anderson. Afterwards they ate a festive meal together. Then Per and Anne left the newlyweds to themselves.

The two younger ones did not go straight home, however. First they went to see Bent Smedshammer, and with him they found his brother, Christ. As these men were friends, there was often humor or banter between them.

"What calls for such a stiff white shirt today then?" inquired Bent, with a broad smile.

Per was not to be put off. "Did you know Amund and Josephine were married today?" he asked.

"No, Amund didn't say one word to us," answered Christ, looking puzzled.

"We better get something rigged up for tonight," suggested Per, with a bit of a glint in his eye.

The reaction to his suggestion was immediate. Kindred souls led to a meeting of minds with no further planning than a nod and a knowing look.

Before going home, Per made one more stop to alert his friend, Anders. With that he was satisfied that the news would get around.

That night the party-goers met at Bent and Kari's house, since their home was nearest the bride and groom. As dusk fell, the group stole silently northward, loitering along the way until well past dark. On coming near Amund and Josephine's place, they waited patiently until the lights went out in the house. A short while later, the visitors spread out around the house, and then suddenly the clamorous sounds began. Each person had some sort of noise maker, from a mixing spoon and dishpan, to a sawblade and hammer. At the same time the young folks yelled and whooped at the top of their lungs.

Before very long, a light went on in the house, and the young couple came to the door. The guests subjected Amund and Josphine to a good deal of good natured joshing and bantering. A while later, the two newlyweds were loaded in Amund's wagon, along with a dozen men, and taken for a ride. About a mile away Amund was dropped off the wagon, while all the other men brought Josephine back to the house. The groom appeared on foot later. All of these antics provided great fun for the visitors.

In the meantime, the women stayed home to cook coffee and to fix lunch for everyone. Because of the prohibition law, Amund brought out home made wine to treat the group in the customary fashion. Following that, the young folks played games, glad to get together for an evening of fun at a party. No one complained because the little house was too crowded, or because there weren't enough chairs.

It was near midnight before the party-goers were ready to leave. None spoke of getting up early. All knew they would be back at work soon enough.

In the fall of the same year, Anne left after the threshing was finished. She understood that times were hard, and that Per could not afford to hire her much as he might want to do so. Also, Anne was headed for Northwood, near Grand Forks. She planned to find her cousin Augusta Berge, who was married to Thor Lieberg, and lived near there. In a short while Anne expected to have a job in or near Northwood.

Anne and Per found parting difficult, as they had grown close during the past seven years together. Each one made an attempt at being light hearted.

"You'll probably marry some big strapping fellow, who is both handsome and rich, as soon as you get up to Northwood," Per smiled.

Anne laughed gaily at the suggestion. In turn she had a word of advice for Per.

"Now that you have such a nice buggy and new harness, you better find yourself a nice girl from Hadeland and marry her."

That set Per to thinking. Maybe he just hadn't met a nice girl from Hadeland yet!

During the winter a serious accident happened. As usual, Per's horses grazed out on the open range in winter. One night at dusk Nellie didn't come home as usual. He walked out to find her, calling out often but darkness came with no success. At daybreak, Per resumed the search. He soon found the poor animal lying on the ice, unable to get up from her fall. He could see that Nellie had struggled so hard without success, that she had severely crippled herself.

"Poor Nellie!" he said. "What a sad end for so faithful a mare!"

Reluctantly Per went home for his gun. When he returned, the horse nickered and seemed to look at him with pleading eyes. Per was unnerved. Then he steeled himself and pulled the trigger.

Afterwards Per wept. He felt as if he had killed his friend.

The rest of the winter passed rather uneventfully. Hauling grain to market was not hindered by great snowbanks in 1893-94, but the crops were poor and the prices poorer yet. In spite of his alertness, Per still experienced some unfair grading and dockage. He avoided the elevators that seemed to have tricky scales. By now, he did have a choice of bringing grain to market at Verona, LaMoure, or Grand Rapids without traveling more than 20 miles one way.

Another bountiful crop in 1895, helped to still the voices of revolting farmers of the fringes of marginal rainfall. The memories of most settlers were short lived, Per thought, when better times came. He felt that he had learned a lot during the tough years, and reform ideas did not die easily in him.

"Even when people are wised up, the politicians have their own way," Per grumbled to himself. "In good times people don't seem to care, so they can plot and plan and divide the spoils again."

By the mid-nineties both of Per's foals were fully grown, mature horses. He had cared for them superbly, and now they were splendid animals. Since they had been pets and friends, Per broke them to harness easily, yet he found them lively and high spirited. Since he could not praise them enough, Per began to build a legend of Fly and Dan. Further he claimed for them near human intelligence and understanding. These two became "his team" more than any other horses.

On at least one occasion, Per felt he owed his life to Fly and Dan. He had taken a load of grain to LaMoure in the morning, but by the time he was back on the trail for home it was afternoon. He was still some miles from home near dusk, and the wind suddenly shifted its direction. Snow began to fall. In a matter of minutes, a blinding blizzard had developed. Per had diffuculty keeping his directions straight, but he was dead sure the team was wrong.

"No, that's the wrong way!" he exclaimed in exasperation. "You're not going to get home that way. Get back on the trail now."

At the same time, he pulled hard to the right on the reins. Both Fly and Dan fought hard against their bits and continued on their way. Per became angry and treated them much more harshly than usual, but again they fought back and literally refused to go in his direction.

Suddenly, Per changed his mind and decided to give them their heads. He did so with some apprehension, knowing getting lost on such a night would be very dangerous.

"You're smart horses. . .must know something I don't. . .," he mumbled. "I've never seen you act so strangely before."

Fly and Dan paced themselves to a fast trot, as Per turned his back to the howling wind. He wasn't so sure anymore what direction the wind was from, but he had thought it to be the northwest. That would be normal and usual. Per was nervous and fretful.

Ten minutes later, he nearly lost his balance as the horses came to an abrupt stop. Per looked up in the semi-darkness to see the outline of his barn just ahead of the team. They were home!

"Thank God! We'd be far from home, if you had gone where I wanted to go," admitted Per.

That night he watered, fed, curried, and rubbed down Fly and Dan with special care. After their sweaty bodies began to cool, the horses were covered with blankets. As he worked, Per spoke to them.

"It's a good thing you're both smarter than me," he declared, "or we would still be lost out in that snowstorm."

Fly and Dan nickered as if to answer Per. He believed they understood every word he said.

As the months passed, Per found he greatly missed Anne. She had been good company and a great worker. He did not relish being a bachelor again. This was especially irksome when he was busy in the fields. Anne's occasional letters and her short annual visits were small consolation.

His relationship with Amund had also changed. They were still brothers, but the kinship of two bachelor brothers was different. Amund and Josephine already had one child named Emma, and Per was certain that Josephine was pregnant again with a second child.

One day while Per was busy in the field, he noticed that the same neighbor who had stolen wood from the riverbank had stopped in his yard. When Per unhitched and came home a few minutes later, he found his fancy buggy harness missing from the peg. Without hesitation, he quickly hitched Fly to the buggy and followed the culprit.

"Why that damn hypocrit!" exploded Per. "He hasn't changed a bit."

Seeing no one around the place, Per went directly to the barn. There, sure enough, hanging on a wooden rack was his prized buggy harness. Without a word, he pulled it down and carried it to his buggy. As he drove off, Per was sure that he saw someone peering from a window of the house.

In the spring of 1896, Fly gave birth to her first colt. The foal was pure black when it was born, and for a time this puzzled Per. He knew a black horse is not that color at birth. Soon he discovered the colt was to turn gray as it grew older. He named the little foal, "Jim."

Sometimes Jim was a terrible nuisance when Per was doing field work. He was tempted to leave him home in the barn, but decided that would be too long a time without nursing at his mother's nipples. The colt had a habit of getting directly in front of the horses such that he stopped all forward motion. This he did with a great show of innocence. Per believed the colt knew exactly what an annoyance he was. There were times when Per was aggravated enough to use certain choice words on him.

"You damned little troll, you!" he threatened. "I have a good notion to sell you for the first bid I can get."

Per's threats were not too serious, as he petted and spoiled his new foal just as he had the others. If anything, Jim grew more impudent than ever.

He saw the girl again at church services. Per remembered seeing her several years earlier. She was younger then. Her family had recently immigrated from Norway. Evidently the father was related to some of Per's neighbors. Later on, the oldest sister had married Johan Paulson, and those two came to church quite regularly. Per remembered she and her sister had sung beautifully in two part harmony. The tones were clear and pure.

Now he heard them sing again, and he could distinguish her alto voice. What a sweet and true voice she had! She was older now and more filled out, but she was still slender, and Per thought she looked very nice. He came back to reality with a start.

"You better pay more attention," he admonished himself. "The pastor is preaching a sermon."

Suddenly Per was angry with himself a second time, as he realized he had nearly spoken out loud. What was the matter with him anyway? He didn't seem to be able to concentrate on the sermon.

During the rest of the service, Per looked over at the young woman several times. He tried to convince himself it was just simple curiosity.

As the people were leaving the schoolyard, most of them stopped to chat a few minutes with friends or relatives. Per spent a few minutes talking to both Bent and Christ as they left the church service. When he turned back to his horse and buggy, he saw the young woman with her sister, who had two young children with her. Near by Johan was unhitching his high spirited mare from a hitching post.

As Per came closer, he turned discreetly to look once more at the girl. For a brief moment her eyes turned to meet his, and she gave him a quick shy smile. He noticed that her light brown hair had a tendency to curl. She seemed more refined than most of the girls around, he thought. That idea appealed to Per.

Just as he was about to drive off, he heard her sister call to her. She used the name, "Serianna."

CHAPTER TWELVE

Serianna

Serianna turned again to look in the direction of the young man. As she did so, he turned also and their eyes met again briefly. She smiled shyly. Serianna had heard his name called "Per." She could see he was very well dressed and she thought he was attractive. Yes, he really was an appealing young man.

She had not been to the schoolhouse for worship services for nearly three years. She had been to visit her sister but not on a Sunday morning. Her own family attended the Standing Rock Church at Fort Ransom. During her visit with them, both Johan and Bergit had spoken of plans for building a new church.

"Oh, that would be nice for the people of North LaMoure," said Serianna. "Everyone needs a real church to worship in on Sunday morning."

Her thoughts went back to the young man. She had seen him when her family first came from Norway. He was dressed in a black suit and a white shirt. A little unusual for the frontier. She could remember being curious about who he was, but she dared not ask anyone.

What was there about this man, that she should feel so attracted to him? At the moment, Serianna could not understand her own emotions, but she realized that they had something to do with Per.

"Come, Serianna!" exclaimed her sister, in Norwegian. "What are you dreaming about?"

"Why, nothing. I'm right here," declared Serianna with a start. But a tinge of rose was creeping into her cheeks.

"Well, you looked like you were a thousand miles away. Here is Johan with the buggy. We mustn't keep him waiting."

"I'm sorry if I kept you," murmured Serianna meekly. She gathered up Clara, the older child, and crawled up into the buggy next to her sister.

Bergit was holding the baby, Anna, in her lap.

Serianna's self consciousness was relieved as everyone's attention turned to the spirited young mare. Gypsy was impatiently fighting the reins, since she especially liked to run toward home. Suddenly the buggy lurched forward as she started off at a jumping gallop, and everyone hung on until Johan settled her down into a trot.

Little Clara, who was nearly two years old, seemed to find the fast ride lots of fun. After a bit, she snuggled back against her aunt contentedly, as they covered ground rapidly.

In a matter of minutes, Serianna could see they were nearing Johan's homestead. They had traveled at a brisk trot from the school.

"Well, that certainly didn't take very long," complimented Serianna; "you surely do have a fast horse."

"Yes, that he does," agreed Bergit. "Johan races with her every chance he gets, and sometimes he isn't above putting a bet on the race either."

"Well that's true," admitted Johan, "but we have to have some fun. Besides, Gypsy almost always wins."

Johan thought horse racing to be a good form of recreation. Most other homesteaders lucky enough to have a fast horse did too. Sometimes Bergit scolded him for betting, but that did very little good.

The first year in Dakota, Serianna had worked for her uncles, Nicolai and Ole, to pay for her passage. After that she worked for wages to help her parents get a new start. During the depression year of 1893, she had given them money to buy a cow and calf. Her brother Nils, had helped them buy a yoke of oxen, Tom and Jerry. In the spring her parents purchased the rights to a homestead from a Yankee in the Bear Creek area. Because times were so hard the price was low. From that time on, this quarter section became their new home in America.

At first Serianna found the new country strange and different from her old home. Now she was getting used to it. The past winter, she had worked in LaMoure at a hotel, because the settlers were too poor to hire help during the winter months. Now that spring was here, she was back among her own people again.

After the midday meal, as Serianna laid Bergit's baby asleep on the bed, she looked at herself in the mirror on the nearly new dresser. She had always been afraid that she wasn't pretty enough. She knew Bergit was prettier, because she had heard her mother say so. Until now it hadn't mattered so much.

"My hair is nice, and I like my eyes," she said, looking carefully at her image; "but my face is too long, and my mouth is simply too large."

Again her thoughts strayed off to the young man. She couldn't seem to get her mind off him. As she discovered this, her face flamed a guilty red.

"You are just being silly!" she scolded her counterpart in the glass. "More than likely, he wouldn't even look at you."

* * * * * * * * * *

Serianna was born in the Vesteralen Islands 21 years earlier. This was near the world famous Lofoten fishing grounds in Nord-Norway's coastal waters. During late winter and early spring, this was a major spawning area for codfish. The islands had a maritime climate, but at times storms and bitter cold came. During the winter, polar fronts swept down from the artic to meet the warm currents. The result was storms and turbulent waters. Otherwise the climate was mild for a land that lay well above the Arctic Circle. Average January temperatures were near 30 degrees fahrenheit.

Vesteralen was Serianna's homeland. She had never lived anywhere else. This was where she grew into young womanhood, and here she attended school until confirmation.

Serianna lived on a small gaard on Seloter with her parents, Kristopher and Anne, and her brothers and sisters, Bergit, Nils,

Wilhelm, Alice and Anna. For several years, the old couple, who previously owned the gaard, lived with them. One of the provisions of the purchase was that the Harsakers should care for the old couple as long as they should live. Such an agreement was quite common and not considered unusual.

Their farm was very small, but a source of some sustenance. The family owned several cows, a few pigs, and some sheep. They also owned one horse in partnership with a neighbor. He supplied the power to raise potatoes, root crops, and a little barley and rye. The climate was not the best for grain crops, but most years they raised enough for their own needs.

Her father, Kristopher, had been a young fisherman from Trondjhem, who had later moved to Vesteralen to be near the fishing grounds. There he met Serianna's mother, Anne and they were soon united in marriage. About a year later, they purchased their new home on Seloter, where they lived until the family sailed for America in the spring of 1892.

During the summers, Serianna worked on the *seters* in the mountains. The cattle were pastured in the lower mountains. During her younger years, she herded the animals, but later she milked goats and cows and made cheese and butter. The long days on the seter were busy ones. During the midsummer, the nights were lighted by the midnight sun. Serianna grew to love the mellow sounds of the cowbells. On the seter, the sky seemed so blue and the grass so very green. She could remember looking up at the mountains higher up, and down at the farms below in a distance. It had been a good and peaceful life, she thought, close to nature and close to God.

Norway was a poor country. From age 14, or after confirmation, boys and girls were expected to make their own way in life. For an entire summer's work, Serianna received only enough for her own simple clothes and a few necessities.

She could still remember the excitement that spread through the family, when her father began to talk of going to America. "America Fever" many called it. Kristopher's long and rigorous life as a fisherman had left him in poor health. He had already written to his brothers in America to ask for help. Ten years earlier, they had emigrated to a place called Dakota.

In time, word came back from the brothers that they would

send money for three tickets. The older children could work for the price of their passage after they came to America. This was commonly done.

"Norway is a poor country. I have worked hard for 30 years, but we are still poor. The life of a fisherman is getting too hard for an old man," explained Kristopher. "America is said to be a good land. Our children will have a better chance. Even if it takes all we own, it is better that we all go there."

The older children were ready for adventure, and readily agreed to work for their passage. The parents found it harder to leave their home of twenty years. They knew they were no longer young; new ways would be difficult.

Since Serianna was able to go to the New World with her family, she did not suffer the same pangs of leavetaking that others did. Still it was not easy to leave the place that had been home for 17 years. Some of her mother's relatives would be left behind, and she didn't think it likely they would see them again. The tears flowed again, when she took leave of her best friend, Beret. The two girls had been classmates in school, and they were confirmed in the church together. Before parting, they clung to each other.

"Dearest Beret," Serianna said through eyes dimmed with tears, "I hope its God's will that you and I shall see each other again one day."

She turned and walked rapidly away without looking back.

Serianna did not find it arduous to get her possessions together. She didn't have many. Other than a scant supply of clothing and other essentials, she owned a Bible and a small wooden chest, with hinges and lock. In it she placed everything she owned, except what she was to wear on the first day.

The spring was warm and sunny, when the family began their long trip. Serianna's father had rented a horse and cart to take them to the boat, from which they would board a steamer bound for Trondhjem. All of their earthly goods were in the cart, except for the tickets that would bring them to the Promised Land.

There was something final about leaving Seloter. Serianna shared with other members of the family, the feeling they would never see the island again.

Hours later, Serianna stood on the deck of the steamer, watching the coastline. The day was clear, and the water calm and blue. There were continuous little islands and skerries along the way. Now and then a steep walled valley opened into a fjord.

"Norway may be a poor country, but it is a beautiful land," she said to her mother, as they both stood together by the rail.

Anne smiled wistfully, as she looked at the coastline. "Yes, Serianna, Norway surely is a most beautiful land."

At Stadsbygd, near Trondhjem, the family visited with Kristopher's half brother, while they waited for the ship that was to take them to England.

A few days later, a second steamship began the journey from Trondhjem to Newcastle, on the east coast of England. There they stayed overnight at a boardinghouse provided by the steamship lines. The following day, a railroad carried them across Britain to the seaport of Liverpool. There they were transferred to an ocean liner from the Cunard line, which was to carry them to New York City. Amid the crowding, noise, and confusion, they soon found their places in the steerage of the ship.

Bergit wrinkled up her nose. "There is a smell in here I can't stand."

"It isn't a very inviting place," agreed Serianna.

The family was not allowed to be quartered together. Bergit and Serianna found themselves in one end compartment, while Nils was placed in the opposite end with the young men. The parents and small children were put into the middle compartment with all the other couples.

While they were up on the deck designated for immigrants, the two girls became aware of the cabin passengers. They were amazed at how elegantly the women were dressed. Surely they were creatures from a different world from the one they had known, the girls thought. Bergit and Serianna agreed that cabin passengers must all be very rich!

After a few days, the time began to pass more slowly for the family. One day Kristopher began to tell of some of his early experiences as a fisherman. All the children gathered around him on the deck.

"When I was a young man, we all gathered near Trondhjem

just after New Years to prepare for the yearly trip to Lofoton fishing grounds," he said. "We brought along *flatebröd*, butter, cheese, pork, and coffee to last us for three months, since we would be very tired of eating only fish."

"During the late winter and early spring, hundreds of fishermen came to Lofoten. We all stayed at camps called *rorbus*, where we could cook and sleep. Most of us worked in boats about 30 feet long. When the fish were running, we set out our strong homemade nets at twilight. We used glass balls for floaters and lead ballasts to keep the nets in place overnight."

"In late winter, when fishing was the best, the days were still short so far north. At the crack of dawn, we were out to haul in our nets. Since darkness was soon upon us, we worked very hard to haul in the fish and get the nets reset so that we could get back and anchor safely in the inlet. After that we had to clean all the cod we had caught. Some we hung on *hjelles* to dry. The best cod was saved for *lutefisk*. If the weather was good, the fish cured well, but if rains came, the fish might spoil."

The children leaned forward, anxious to hear more of his story.

"During late winter and early spring, big ships came from Bergen to take the fish back to the city. From there it was shipped all over the world. Once when I was twenty one, they let me go along to sell the fish. I had never seen a city before."

Serianna shuddered. She was thinking of the many times they had prayed anxiously for her fathers safety, when sudden storms came up while he was fishing. She knew only too well that the lives of the fishemen often hung in the balance until the *hovedsman* could bring the vessel into an inlet.

"When I was a young man, we often went north around the Cape, after the fishing season ended at Lofoten," Kristopher went on. "We went as far as the Barents Sea, near the Russian border. That was the home of the cod. From May until August, the sun never set there."

"I'll never forget the first time I saw a great cliff at the North Cape. It stood out against the Arctic Sea, nearly a thousand feet high. We stood stunned and silent. There aren't any words to tell you how great it was!"

* * * * * * * * *

The crossing itself passed relatively uneventfully. Since the family was used to boats and rough seas, none of them became seasick.

Serianna's little sister, Anna, caught a very bad cold. They all worried that she might have pneumonia. The mother thought it fortunate that the baby was still nursing. Because of this, she felt Anna would recover.

Thinking back, Serianna thought the first day they sighted America had been the most remarkable one in her life. Word that land was near had spread like wildfire among the immigrants in the steerage. A commotion followed as everyone packed up their belongings to carry up on the deck. Wooden chests, bags and bundles were everywhere. Some were tied with a rope.

Since the younger children were not well, Anne stayed below with them. Serianna felt guilty about not staying to help, but she couldn't resist the excitement of going up on the deck to get the first glimpse of land.

They found the immigrants already crowding up on the deck. A fine early morning mist prevented them from seeing clearly in the distance. They knew only that a pilot had come aboard and the ship had entered the harbor. The passengers were straining their eyes to see.

Suddenly a great shout went up, joined in by many other tongues. Several pointed up and to the left of the ship. Serianna turned to see an awesome hundred and fifty two foot statue, holding the torch of freedom in upstretched hand. She stood stock-still staring. Serianna could not describe how she felt, but somehow the view promised hope in the new country. The immigrants were very quiet, as they looked in awe.

"It's the Statue of Liberty," she heard someone say in her own tongue.

Serianna turned around to see a distinguished man standing on the upper level just above. He began to recite in book Norwegian. The words sounded so strange and beautiful. She strained her ears, yet amid the noise could hear only parts of it.

"Give me your tired, your poor. . . Your huddled masses. . . Yearning to breathe free. . . Send, these, the homeless. . . I lift my lamp besides the golden door. . ."

Serianna tried to remember some of the words. They had such a poetic sound. The man must be a cabin passenger; he didn't look like an immigrant.

"Where is Wilhelm?" asked Bergit, with sudden anxiety in her voice. He was nowhere to be seen.

"We must be careful not to get separated. Bergit, you stand here with this red scarf. Now don't go too far," said Kristopher, sounding anxious.

Serianna tried to push her way through the crowd. First she went one way and then the other, but she did not see anything of her little brother.

"Dear God," she prayed silently. "Please help us find him."

Shortly after that, she found the lost boy standing by the rail. In a few minutes the little group was back together again. Serianna doubted not that her prayer had been answered.

As they moved up the channel, she glimpsed ships of all sizes and descriptions. The dull sounds of foghorns mixed with the bright sound of bells.

A few minutes later, they had their second awesome sight of the morning. Forming like a ghost out of the morning fog, was the skyline of New York City! Never had Serianna ever seen anything to compare!

"In school we learned that New York is one of the biggest cities in the world," said Nils, with wonderment in his voice.

"I've heard that almost all immigrants land here," added Kristopher.

A new disturbance began on board ship, as officers came to separate the immigrants into lines. Serianna heard loud shouting. One official tried to force Kristopher and his family into line to disembark. When he resisted and tried to explain, the officer cursed at him and gave him a hard shove.

Because of the sick children, the Harsakers were among the last to leave the ship. Alice was found to have measles, and so she had to be taken to quarantine. The family decided Bergit should stay with her, while the rest of the family should push on to Dakota.

Serianna could still remember the four towers of the immigrant station on Ellis Island. The slate roof was blue and the walls painted in buff. Inside, the immigrants were herded around like cattle from one pen to another. Finally they were pushed into the great registry hall. Here the inspections and the processing began in earnest.

Because of delays, the family had to stay overnight at Ellis Island. The men slept in one great room, and the women in another. Eight bunks were set up in each group, four on the floor level and four directly above. Hundreds of immigrants slept in the same room.

For the evening meal, they were served stale rye bread and stewed prunes, ladled out of pails with small dippers. The men who served, walked on top of the tables from one end to the other. The immigrants were fed by private persons who contracted (for certain sums of money) with the United States government.

The next day, Serianna and the others waited again in long and wearisome lines. She was becoming more conscious of being a foreigner, unable to understand the language. The doctors and inspectors didn't mean to be cruel, she decided, but perhaps there were just too many immigrants. In their impatience, some of the officials equated her inability to understand with lack of intelligence. So much was new and strange. Even with an interpreter it was easy to have a misunderstanding. Before the ordeal was completed, her ego had been bruised, and she found the experience exhausting.

Finally she was allowed to go on through, only to wait for the other family members. Before long they were huddled together again. Serianna could see her father was nervous as he cautioned the family.

"We've been warned to trust no one," he cautioned. "Sharks lie in wait for us, if we should be careless. Some speak Norwegian. We could be robbed, beaten, or even carried away if we are separated."

As they waited, Kristopher told a story that he had heard while on the ship.

This story was about an immigrant, who had been swindled out of his money. Because they were out of money and unable to continue their journey, the man had to leave his wife to go out and look for work. After failing to find any work for several days, he signed up with a work crew bound for Chicago. Suddenly he found himself on a train headed out, without a chance to tell his wife what had happened. She knew nothing but later did discover he had left for Chicago. That was all she could find out about her husband.

For a year she worked very hard in a garment factory, scrimping to save enough money for train fare to Chicago. When she reached the city, she was unable to locate her husband. Two years later, she had nearly given up hope, when a man walked by her basement window. Something about the lower part of his body reminded her of her lost husband. She ran out to see and found that it was indeed her husband at last.

The children were mightily impressed with the urgency of Kristopher's warnings and the story of the immigrants. Perhaps that is the reason why they were able to make the journey in safety.

After a few more hours of waiting, they were loaded into an immigrant car, headed for Chicago. After a long and tiresome trip, they finally reached Minneapolis and then Fargo. Yet another train would bring them to LaMoure.

At the depot in Fargo, the women slept on the benches. The men slept on the floor. In the morning, the men were surprised to find they were literally crawling with body lice!

The last day of the journey, they took the Fargo-Southwestern through Leonard, Lisbon, and on to LaMoure. When they arrived at the depot, Kristopher's nephew, Johan was there to meet them. He brought them the last eighteen miles with his team and spring wagon.

After a long and arduous journey, Serianna was glad to be back into the farm country. She found North Dakota's weather beautiful in June, even through it was very different from Vesteralen.

At first Serianna worried that Bergit and Alice might have trouble, but at last they came too. Serianna held her young sister on her lap. Little Alice began to tell about her stay in the hospital at Ellis Island. She also told of her Swedish playmate, whose family could speak no English. Both their boy and girl were in the hospital with a serious case of measles. Later when the parents came to get their children out of quarantine, they could find the boy but did not find the girl. In complete bewilderment, they finally came to ask little Alice if she knew anything about Hilma. "Well, could you understand them? asked Serianna. "What did you say?"

"Oh, yes, I understood them," answered Alice. "I told them I didn't know much about it, but I did see two men put a white sheet over Hilma and carry her out."

Serianna soon had a job working for Kristopher's brothers. The first summer she was paid $10 a month for the busy season, until threshing was done. She thought that very good. It was about five times as much as she had made on the *seter*.

There was a good deal of monotony in her work. Meals were made from scratch. This meant baking bread, churning butter, tending garden, caring for chickens, and preserving foods. She carried water from the pump, and wood from the woodpile. Clothes were scrubbed on a board and ironed with a sad iron heated on the cookstove. During the busy season, she helped with the milking. Serianna felt lucky not to have to help with the work in the fields.

Often, she wondered if she might meet a man in America that she could marry. Most of the men she had met seemed so rough and ill mannered. Serianna was a gentle person, who tried her best to live her life as a Christian. Perhaps God might help her find a husband too, she thought.

Serianna's parents were deeply religious. Her father believed that God had spared him from a cold and watery grave many times, while he worked as a fisherman. Early in 1893, word had come from Lofoten, that the boat on which Nils and Christopher had worked, was lost with all the men on board. Late in January a terrible storm had hit suddenly, while all the fishing boats were out at sea. Other friends and neighbors were lost as well. Serianna felt certain that God had sent them to America in time, so her father and brother could be spared from death.

* * * * * * * * *

While she was visiting with Bergit and Johan this last time, Serianna was offered a job by Anders Rorvig. His wife, Karen, was her aunt. The Rorvig's farm was only one mile from Per's place. When Serianna accepted their offer of work, it did seem that she might be trying to make it a little easier for the Lord to help her find a husband.

Serianna saw Per often that summer, although he didn't actually court her. They both attended the same church on Sundays, but not in each other's company. Sometimes Per found an errand at his neighbors and ended up talking with Serianna. In the fall, when Per needed someone to milk his cows during threshing, she agreed to do it without counting the cost.

Serianna's Aunt Karen, perhaps guessing the reason, agreed. Four hours a day she would work for Per, and the rest of the time for them. Her aunt also subtracted a proportionate part of her wages each week.

The two mile walk twice a day wasn't so bad. She found that she could walk the necessary distance and do the work morning and evening in the four hours of time. Besides milking the cows and caring for the stock, she sometimes pumped water when the small water tank was low. Best of all, she liked to go into Per's house for a few minutes and tidy up a bit. For a bachelor, she thought that he kept things up well.

There were times when Serianna daydreamed a little on these trips. She felt close to him here. What he really needed, she decided, was a wife to help him.

CHAPTER THIRTEEN

Wolves on the Prairie

Per was a little surprised when Serianna agreed to milk his cows while he was away threshing. He was pleased also. There was something about this girl that was most difficult to forget. Her kind and gentle ways reminded him of his mother. He had to admit, though, that his feelings for her were quite unlike those he had for Petronilla.

During the past summer, he had seen Serianna and talked to her often. She seemed like such a sensible woman, who never prattled on about nothing, as so many did. She had curly brown hair, becoming blue eyes, and a good figure, he noticed. Her shyness reminded him of a doe. Per realized he was strongly attracted to her.

"It's really too bad she isn't from Hadeland," he remarked to himself, with a note of real regret.

Near the end of September, Per paid her for the work. During the past five weeks, she had worked twenty eight days. He figured 25^c a day. Per felt quite generous, since top pay for a hired girl in the neighborhood was only $3.50 a week for a seven day week and a twelve hour day.

When Serianna was about to leave, he was anxious to say something to keep her a little longer. He just couldn't think of anything clever to say, and so what he did say was not what he intended.

"Would you be willing to work for me next summer?" he asked.

"No, I don't think that would be such a good idea," she said carefully, as she turned to walk away.

Per stood watching her as she went, but she did not turn to look back. Had he seen a disappointed look in her eyes? Had it been his imagination? He could not be sure. Already, he was getting angry with himself for not being able to think of something better to say as she was leaving.

For the next several days, Per was busy with his plowing. His four horses were hitched to a two bottom walking plow. Because the gang had wheels and levers, Per didn't have to steer or hold it in position with the plow handles. He did walk behind the plow, but this rig could plow four acres a day.

Per couldn't get his mind off Serianna. On the following Sunday afternoon, he hitched Fly to the buggy. He wanted to talk to her again. Perhaps he might go as far as to ask her to go with him for a buggy ride. She was no longer at Rorvigs. Serianna had gone home to her parents three days ago.

Per set out again. At the end of the six mile drive, he climbed out of the buggy again. Kristopher came to the door. His answer proved disappointing to Per.

"No, Serianna isn't here. She was home but she went to Enderlin. Dr. Olaf Sherping has hired her for the winter."

Per was crestfallen as he turned homeward. Momentarily, he toyed with the idea of setting out for Enderlin to find Serianna, but it was sixty miles round trip. That wouldn't be fair to his horse; she had worked in the field all week without a day of rest.

Luckily Per was soon involved in the presidential election of 1896. He read everything about the two candidates he could find in the newspapers and magazines. Making up his mind was difficult. This election became an interesting, and yet troubled one for Per.

William Jennings Bryan caught his imagination. In him, Per found a kind of hero. Bryan's pictures showed an attractive young man. Undoubtedly he was a gifted orator and often quoted from the scriptures. Per had read some accounts of the "Cross of Gold" speech, made by the 36 year-old Nebraskan at the nominating convention. The delegates had gone wild! Per came to accept his words that this was a contest between the eastern bond holder and the western plow holder. Bryan seemed to be for the common people and the farmer. Per wanted to cast his vote for him.

Yet there were other considerations. Per had never voted for a Democrat in his life. He associated the party with the cities and the South, and perhaps with the Irish Catholics. He didn't know any Norwegians who were Democrats. Besides even the "Normanden" had spoken against the idea of free silver.

"How can a poor immigrant know what is right?" agonized Per, to himself. "One editor even called Bryan a madman!"

At the polls, Per voted Republican, but he had many doubts and misgivings. He felt no enthusiasm for McKinley whatsoever.

After the returns were in, Bryan was easily defeated in North Dakota. In a way this eased Per's mind and conscience, since he felt his vote made no difference anyway. Reform would have to come from within the Republican Party he decided.

The first snowfall of the winter came on election day that fall. This proved to be only a harbinger of what was to come. Much more snow and several storms came to Dakota in November of 1896. By the time winter was official, snowdrifts were piled as high as some buildings.

Shoveling out after each storm and hauling dabs of hay on his sleigh kept Per busy much of the time. Having a well in his new hay shed proved to be a blessing all the rest of the winter.

The unusual winter gave him plenty of time to think about Serianna. The heavy snow made a trip to Enderlin out of the question. Before long, he realized that he missed her greatly.

Per saw few people except his nearest neighbors that winter. It was an effort to get to Griswold for supplies or to the post office for the mail. Again, the newspapers were his main link with the outside world. On occasions when he saw Amund or some of his neighbors, he exchanged news and borrowed as many papers and magazines as he could.

Luckily Per had laid in some coal earlier in the fall, when he sold a load of wheat. Since he had the house banked high with snow, it did not take much fuel to keep it warm. However, he did worry about the fact that he had no cash remaining, since he had been unable to get to LaMoure for some time.

"I simply have to get in with a jag of flax the first chance I get," he thought. He would have to watch the weather closely.

Later in the winter, the weather moderated for a time and settled the snow. Anders passed the word that some neighbors to the south had gone through to LaMoure by working in a group. Knowing there would be a trail to the south until the next snow or storm, Per determined to get to town.

The next morning, long before the first glimmer of dawn, Per had finished his chores. With the first gray streaks in the east, he was on his way.

By the time he got into town, it was nearly noon. He did little loitering although the temptation was great after so confining a winter. On the way home he carried the usual supplies and a small amount of coal. His load was not heavy.

Since the days were still short, dusk was falling when Per was still several miles from home. Suddenly, as he passed the Sjulli pioneer graveyard on the open prairie, several wolves came out in a fast run of pursuit. The horses, who had already been acting very nervous, broke into a flat gallop. Per looked back to see the thin gray forms gaining.

In a few more seconds, the action began. Two of the larger animals neared Fly on the left side. The next instant one of the wolves had hurtled himself at her head, while the female tried to move in for a hamstring at her heels. Per let out a bloodcurdling yell, and caught the female beast across the neck with the ends of the leather lines. She swerved to the side. The other wolf at Fly's head hung on for an instant, and then dropped to the ground. For a bit, the wild animals were distracted by the yelling human in the sled, who was trying to protect his horses by whirling the long ends of the leather lines toward them. Then once more, they closed in for the kill. Per screamed and caught one with the lines again, distracting her. Fly and Dan were now fairly flying down the snowpacked trail. The wolves followed the sleigh closely for another quarter of a mile. Gradually they were losing ground, and suddenly they fell back and gave up the chase.

Now that the danger was past, Per began to react. He could feel the cold sweat over his body. His stomach turned over and over, and his hands trembled. Such an attack was unbelievable!

This was not a real life experience!

"Why they must be starving!" he exclaimed aloud.

Per soon pulled his team down to a fast trot. Darkness was beginning, but he was sure the wolves were far behind. In the last stages of twilight, he recognized his neighbor's buildings. Soon they would be home.

In the safety of the barn, Per looked carefully at Fly, holding the lantern close. He was shocked to find the bridle torn nearly in two, with less than a quarter inch of leather holding it together. The mare had scratches on her neck, but there were no signs of injury to her leg.

Per stood lost in thought. The happening seemed more like a nightmare than a reality.

After that, Per carried a gun with him during the winter. The rest of the year, he was careful to carry a good whip. He also traded in his old muzzle loader for a single shot, 12 gauge, breech loading shotgun and a supply of new shells. He felt it would be very effective at close range.

"I'd sure like to blast them with this," he told Fly and Dan, as they passed the graveyard. However, he saw nothing more of the prairie wolves.

Late in March, the last of the winter storms quieted, and the warming sun melted the great mounds of snow. The creeks and sloughs were filled and then overflowed with icy water. Newspapers told of great flooding in the Red River Valley, along the Sheyenne, and the other rivers.

On a Sunday in April, Per saw Serianna again. After a long and lonesome winter, he had a more realistic idea of his feelings for her. Besides he had come to the realization that she would make a much better wife for him than Sigrid. Now Per was worried about her response. Somehow Per found the courage to step right up to her at the schoolhouse, in front of several people. It was not easy. His Norwegian conservatism warned him to hang back and wait until a safer and better time.

"It surely is nice to see you again, Serianna," he said. "I've missed you all through this long winter."

Serianna turned to him with a smile. "I have missed you too, Per," she said quietly.

Per fumbled with the hat in his hand. "Would you go with me

for a ride in the buggy, if I should come this afternoon?'' he queried.

Once more Serianna smiled shyly. ''Why yes, of course I would.''

He was in jubilant spirits! Fly was allowed to run all the way home. Per could not get there fast enough.

It was still early afternoon when Per began his ride to Johan's farm. When he stopped at the house, it was Johan rather than Serianna who came out to meet him. Per knew that, after all, it wouldn't be proper for Serianna to appear too eager by rushing out. The two men went through the formalities of small talk about the weather, the prospects for crops, and politics. Both of them knew the purpose of Per's visit, but neither was willing to speak openly about it. Finally, Per could wait no longer.

''Do you suppose I could speak to Serianna?'' he asked a little nervously.

''Serianna?'' Johan asked, as if in surprise, ''Yes, I think so.''

Only a minute later, Serianna stepped out from the house. Already there was a kind of radiance about her. As Per looked at her, he thought she was the prettiest woman he had ever seen. However, his Norwegian background kept him from sharing this thought with Serianna. Instead, he smiled politely as he helped her into the buggy.

This was the beginning of a short courtship. On that very first Sunday afternoon, Per ended up by asking Serianna to be his wife. She accepted. It was as simple as that. When Per first kissed her, he thought perhaps he heard violins; but when he kissed her the second time, he was quite sure of it.

Per wanted to get married right away, but Serianna preferred to wait until June. He had to be content with that.

Later he was to see the wisdom of that decision. As he went to see her each Sunday, they grew to understand each other. He found her to be an intelligent as well as a religious woman. From the beginning, she tended to have a soothing effect on Per.

Sometimes when they were together, Per's young blood was aroused for her. Those times were not entirely unappreciated by Serianna, as her own passions awoke in response to his. Per found, however, that she could be decisive and firm. Some things would simply have to wait until after the marriage vows had been said.

Little was said about love, but both appreciated the deep affection of the other. Between them was a certain security, unnecessary to speak about. Per wanted to know all about Serianna's life, and she had a similar interest in his.

Late in June of 1897, they were quietly married. The ceremony was simple, as was the custom with common folks. They agreed that only the wealthy made a big thing of a wedding. Bergit and Johan went with them to Fort Ranson, where Rev. Anderson read the ceremony. Afterwards, they stopped at the home of Serianna's parents, which was on the way home. Rather than a wedding feast, they shared a simple meal much as usual, and yet there was a certain reverent festivity among them.

Per and Serianna, now husband and wife, were home from their wedding in time to do the evening milking and other chores. They simply spent their honeymoon on the homestead. Neither considered this strange, as it was usual in their neighborhood during the 1890's. Both of them were satisfied and happy just to live together.

Serianna was pleased when she looked at her husband. She saw a man, fully six feet tall, who weighed near 170 pounds. He was wide across the shoulders but fairly slender otherwise. At the time she married him, Per was a 34 year old ambitious and hard working man. At times he tended to be nervous and high strung. She could tell it was important to him to be well thought of by others, especially his neighbors. She was glad he was a Christian man, although he did not make a big display of it. Besides all this, he was good and gentle with her.

After so many years of bachelorhood, Per was delighted with his new wife. She was tall and slender and Per though her good to look at. She was only 22. He saw in her a truly practicing Christian. Not only was she a good companion and helpmate, but he found her warm and delightful as a woman. She was not to be hurried, but there was a natural earthiness about her. Again, she reminded him of a doe. The fact that she was not so industrious about the place as Anne had been seemed an unimportant detail.

"Serianna, you are so dear to me," said Per, with appreciation in his eyes.

"And I am content with you as my husband," answered Serianna, smiling.

After his experience as a bachelor and her years as a hired girl, both seemed quite satisfied to settle down together on the homestead. They took pride in planting more trees and making improvements on the place.

During 1896, Per had taken part in several meetings to discuss the possibility of building a new Norwegian Lutheran Church at North LaMoure. From a small suggestion by Rev. O. K. Anderson, the seeds of inspiration began to germinate. The meetings grew in size and enthusiasm.

The cost in money was estimated at $3600, in addition to necessary volunteer work. Lumber and materials would have to be hauled from the distant railroad. All recognized there would have to be sacrificial giving, if the money were to be raised.

At first the cost seemed out of reach for many. Building a church would be a major effort for the settlers, who still had only the bare necessities of life. Most of them still lived in one room homes.

"What do you think of this new church? $3600 surely is a lot of money. Do you think we could build a smaller church for less? Well, we do need a place to worship God out here on the prairie. We haven't had more than two good crops in the last ten years. If only times were better." These were all questions and comments heard when the pioneers met and spoke to each other.

The women were especially interested in a new church. The nine year old Ladies Aid voted to give all the money in their treasury to the new church. They also voted to pledge their annual sale to its support.

At the final meeting, Per thrilled to the words of men such as Johan Oien and Anders Kjelby, as each stood up to speak in favor of the new church. He too, added his own voice to the others and voted with the rest of the pioneers to go ahead with the building.

During the fall, Per and his neighbors hauled a great pile of rocks for the foundation. In the late fall and early winter, many worked to crack the stones with great two handed sledgehammers made for that purpose.

In the spring of 1897, the actual building began. Per and the other men made many trips to town with teams and wagons to haul materials and lumber. Other times, they helped with the actual building.

Serianna was most supportive of everything Per did toward the building of the new church. She was gladly willing to go without, so that they could give extra to the building. Like most of the women, she was overjoyed at the prospect of having a real church in the neighborhood.

Since the site was only two miles away, Per and Serianna could see the new building grow. Often they and others went to see the progress made. The emerging church continued to be a topic of conversation with the settlers.

As Per watched the crops that summer, he was filled with optimism. A good crop with good prices would be a Godsend to North LaMoure and to all of Dakota. Per thought the Lord must be approving of what they were doing.

"Just think, Serianna!" he exclaimed. "If the crop is good, we can give generously to the church and still build our house. We need more room before the children began to come."

Better times came slowly. Yields improved and prices increased in Dakota. Although many of the old problems remained, some changes benefited the farmer. The cost of machinery moderated, and freight rates began to reduce.

Per became interested in the attempts of the new railroad commissioners to gain some control over the railroads. With the help of superb lawyers, the railroads won most of the court cases, but the publicity of the trials turned up much evidence of questionable practices on their part. It became known to Per and his friends, for example, that the stock of the Northern Pacific was watered so much that rates had to support values five times the actual value or cost. Dakotans also learned that not one high official or director of the line was from North Dakota. Newspapers printed these and other damaging bits of information, often with commentaries. As the people came to realize how accurate the charges of the reform group against the railroads were, they turned against the lines.

To regain support, the railroads reduced rates, sometimes as much as 20%. The service in North Dakota was improved as well. Most surprising, customers came to be treated with common curtesy. Per was among those who benefited, as he received a few cents more a bushel for his grain.

After threshing, Per and many others hauled grain to market and lumber to the church barn on the return trip. The new low, long barn was intended to hold forty teams. Horses and oxen needed shelter during the winter months.

By late fall, the church was completed. Per and Serianna could now see it plainly from their home. The high steeple pointed toward heaven, and the white paint gleamed in the sunlight.

As they started for the church for the first service, the clear and mellow tones of the church bell pealed out across the prairie. In just one-half hour the service would begin. As they came closer, Per could see teams and people gathering. Spring wagons and buggies were parked in small clusters. At the church, Serianna went inside with the other women, while Per stayed outside to talk with the men. After he tied his horse, he joined Amund, Bent, and Christ in talking about the new church.

Soon the bell called them again; it was time to worship. Per saw that the church would be filled. Inside, the women and children sat on one side and the men and older boys on the other. All was quiet except for a few coughs and a child that wimpered. Per bowed his head with the other pioneers.

The first service became an emotional experience for most. There was no formal dedication, but O. K. Anderson preached a sermon based on the Norwegian translation of "Built on a Rock the Church Doth Stand". By the time he had finished, there was scarcely a dry eye in the congregation.

Another important event in 1897 was the coming of Rural Free Delivery in that part of the state. In order to get the mail route, each family had to take a daily paper. Per and Serianna still had a mile and a half to the mailbox, but that was much less than the distance to Hans Jacob Hanson's old inland post office.

A daily paper brought Per even closer awareness of state, national, and even world events. He became aware of the second "Dakota Boom" that brought thousands of immigrants and other settlers to western North Dakota. Early range country was now homesteaded by newcomers, and many became permanent citizens of the state.

Per was concerned that there might be trouble with Spain over Cuba. Eastern newspapers, fighting for circulation, spread rumors to excite the American people. Then came the bombshell!

"The battleship "Maine" has been sunk in Havana Harbor!" he exclaimed, looking up from his newspaper. "Many blame the Spaniards. I'm afraid we might have a war."

"From what I've read, the Spanish don't want war," Serianna replied, thoughtfully. "If that's true, why should they want to sink the 'Maine'?"

Dakota newspapers cautioned moderation and spoke of peaceful solutions. Not so with the yellow press of the east. They printed sensational horror stories-some of which had already proven to be false. Now they continued to stir up the people and demanded war. On April 19, 1898, Congress and the President gave way to popular demand with what amounted to a declaration of war. President McKinley had already received a most conciliatory message from the Queen of Spain, but he knew that the mood of the country was not for peace.

Once the war started, Per felt he should support it. He even became enthusiastic about Roosevelt and his rough-riders. Since Roosevelt had spent several years in North Dakota, he knew that many westerners joined the group in admiration of the leader. Per thought the charge up San Juan Hill almost as important as Dewey's victory at sea.

Serianna did not share Per's enthusiasm for the war. "I wonder what God thinks when he looks down at us," she said quietly.

Before harvest, the fighting ended with a victory for the United States. Later, Per was puzzled when he heard of the territory the United States was to take from Spain. There seemed to be a sharp disagreement in the Senate. Some called it imperialism and claimed it contrary to the spirit of democracy, but their warnings were drowned out by those who favored annexation. The new territory was added.

The new home Per and Serianna built was quite modest. The building was a story and a half and 14 feet by 28 feet in size, with two rooms downstairs and two unfinished rooms upstairs.

The former one room house was attached as a kitchen. The new construction was finished with lath and plaster, and with wainscoating added to the lower walls and ceiling.

On a chilly and windy April day in 1899, Per and Serianna attended the funeral of Kari Smedshammer. Bent had told Per earlier that she never fully recovered from her last childbirth. The pioneers understood that she had fallen victim to the rigorous life of the frontier and lack of medical care. However, few if any, would have been able to put those thoughts into words.

Per thought her death a tragedy. Bent and Kari had been his special friends. Their bond of friendship went back to Hadeland. He looked at the family with sympathy and sadness. Jacob, the baby, was only a year old; and Anna, aged fourteen, had to assume the mother's duties. Per was especially worried because Serianna was soon to have her first child. It grieved him to think something similar could happen to her.

A month later, Serianna said quietly to Per, "I think you better go and get Oline now. It seems that my time has come."

Childbirth was hardly a stranger in most Dakota homes, but now that it was Serianna's turn, Per was nearly unnerved. Dan acted surprised when Per used the whip on him, but his trot seemed like a snails pace to the impatient driver. After the whipping, the horse did not need further urging to cover ground.

When he returned with the midwife, Per discovered that Serianna's pains were coming with more regularity. Oline spent several minutes seeing to her comfort and then bustled around getting everything in readiness. She ordered Per to heat a large pot of boiling water. In the meantine, she laid out some clothes and a towel.

For a while, Per tried to comfort Serianna. He held her hand firmly. Every so often, she bit her lip to hold back the sounds and grasped his hand hard in return. As her pains became gradually heightened, he became more concerned and nervous. The midwife looked at him in distain, as she ordered him from the room.

"This is a matter for women," she said tersely. "Husbands don't belong in here. They are worse than no help at all."

This was the first child for Serianna. The chances were good that it would not be an easy birth.

Per awaited anxiously in the next room. Sometimes he sat and then again he stood. Other times he paced back and forth. The palms of his hands were clammy.

After what seemed to him an eternity, Per heard his new baby cry. Serianna's groans and screams had stopped. Was she all right? His relief was enough to hide his momentary disappointment that the baby was not a boy. Sons were important on the frontier farm.

Some minutes later, Serianna was asleep. The ordeal had ended and everything seemed to be all right, Per thought. Suddenly, he felt tired.

"Don't you want to hold your new baby?" asked Oline, with the first trace of a smile since she came.

Carefully, although rather clumsily, Per took the precious little bundle from the hands of the midwife. Then he looked down into the tiny face of his firstborn.

CHAPTER FOURTEEN

Beginning the 20th Century

The coming of the baby, "Christine" brought changes to Per and Serianna's lives. The new life, which was part of them both, drew them closer together. Yet in another sense, she became an intruder, making her own demands. She asked them to be responsible and to make a new commitment to the future.

The new child thrived. Serianna was a natural mother. The infant was not wanting for attention, love, or breast fed milk. Per for his part soon learned to hold the little one with tenderness and ease. The baby was a fine blend of both parents, but relatives disagreed as to whom she resembled.

Anne came from Mayville to care for Serianna and the new baby, as well as to visit her brothers. Her opinion was definite.

"She looks exactly like Per," she declared, after taking one good look.

The first year of the new century was one of severe drought in southeastern Dakota. The crop was a complete failure. Because Per had harvested three good crops in the past five years, with reasonable prices, he had some money in the bank and wheat in the grain bins. This was a help, and yet a crop loss was a serious setback for any settler.

The dry year brought one unexpected result. Ray Bomberg, a neighbor, came to see Serianna and Per. He soon got down to business.

"I'm considering selling my tree claim, if I can get my price," he said. "As you know, it's the quarter just south of yours."

Although Per was fully aware of the desirability of the land, he cautiously responded with a question.

"How much are you asking for it?"

"The land is worth at least $10 an acre, since more than half of it is broken for cropland. but to a neighbor like you, I would consider selling it for only $1500."

Per pondered a moment before answering. One cannot be too careful, he thought.

"That's still a great deal of money in such a bad year. Could you give us three days to think it over?"

The first day, Serianna and Per struggled without coming up with a decision. The land would be ideal, right next to their own. Besides Per believed the soil to be excellent. Yet both agreed it was too great an outlay in a year of crop failure. They would have to mortgage, not only the new land, but their own homestead also. Per knew the bank would lend only up to half the value of the land, besides he needed money to operate through the following year.

"Ten years ago, when I proved up my homestead, I vowed that I would never mortgage it," declared Per, looking down at his calloused hands.

"Should we have more poor crops, we could lose all our land," agreed Serianna. "It's hard to pass up the land, but the risk is too great."

On the following day, Per had an idea. "Let's find out if Bomberg will sell us 80 acres. Maybe we can buy the rest later."

At first the seller was hesitant. Later he agreed to sell the north half at a price of $775. He was unmoved at Per's attempts to further dickering. Per was able to borrow $400 on the new land, and the bank agreed not to forclose so long as he paid the interest. This greatly lowered the risk, he thought.

Another event of considerable importance took place that year. A branch line of the Northern Pacific was built some seven or eight miles north of Per's homestead. A new townsite was surveyed a few miles further west and a town began to form. Hans Jacob Hanson moved his rural post office and general store from section ten in Litchville Township to the new town on the railroad. Since his post office had the name from the township, Hanson now gave the name of "Litchville" to the new town.

Per was pleased to have a town within ten miles. Getting his grain to market would be much less arduous, and it would cut other trips to town by half. What a stroke of luck, he thought.

There was considerable merriment among the old time natives, when they first discovered the exact location of the townsite. Because 1900 was such an extreme drought year, much of the surveyed acres was bottom land and an old slough.

"Those city slickers have done it again!" chuckled one old timer. "The land is of no earthly use for anything else!"

"The land speculators know how to turn a fast dollar," agreed another.

"Just wait 'til we get a wet year with heavy rains. The ducks will be swimming right here in main street," promised a third.

By the end of the year, many businesses had started or were getting ready to open. There was a post office, two general stores, a hotel, the beginnings of a lumberyard, a new bank, two blacksmith shops, and several other businesses. Many of the buildings were moved into town. Others hauled in the lumber and built at the site.

Just after the new year, Amund came to see Per. He had just been to the new town of Litchville.

"Did you hear that the first train came to Litchville yesterday?" he asked. "They had a big celebration. You would never believe there is a law against drinking alcohol."

Per felt a little left out. Since Serianna was big with child again, he had been staying close to home. Her time would come any day now, he thought, and he didn't want to worry her by being away. Serianna, however, seemed to have a serenity that both pleased and surprised Per.

It was Per who showed the worry and anxiety. Serianna's young cousin, Ida, was staying with her, but there was always a chance that a blizzard might prevent him from getting the midwife, when the time came. In that case, the childbirth might prove most difficult for them to handle.

Early in January, the second child was born. The weather was cold but not stormy. With two women in the house to help Serianna, Per found himself in the way. For a second time, his silent prayer for a boy was not answered.

After he had held the infant in his arms Per soon relented, and all of his disappointments were forgotten. She was a healthy baby. Before many weeks passed, they christened her "Pauline". Per did hope the next one would grow up into a strapping young man, who might help him with the farm work.

In the spring of 1901, Per had a chance to buy a small gray mare. The owner needed cash, and besides the young mare was too high spirited for him. Per was surprised to judge her part mustang and part Arabian. He had developed a good eye for a horse, and this one looked as if it might be a dandy at $75. With the added acres, he needed another young horse, and another mare to raise foals. Since this mare was also named Fly, Per renamed her "Gray Fly", to distinguish her from his other mare.

As the year progressed, he was pleased to find the new horse everything he had hoped for. Her spirit more than made up for her small size. Together with Fly, Dan, and Jim, she made up a mighty lively four horse rig.

During the summer, Per came home from his brother's place with a serious look on his face. He shared his concern with Serianna.

"Amund was hurt. A mad bull came after him and got him down on the ground. If Josephine hadn't come running, he might have been killed."

"Josephine? How did she save him?" questioned Serianna.

"Well you know she grew up in the mountain *seters* back in Norway, and so she handled cattle from girlhood. She got the bull away from Amund and after herself. Then she ran him through the gate before the bull knew what had happend."

"Is Amund hurt bad?"

"Yes, he is. He went to the doctor and some ribs were broken. They were afraid it might be worse, but the doctor could not find anything else."

The settlers lived close to nature. During the summer of 1901, the weather seemed perfect. Per watched the crops closely, as he did every year. As the time came close to the harvest, his grain stood tall and heavy in the summer breeze. The kernels were filling plump and full. Almost too good to be true, Per thought, as he began to hope for another bumper crop.

During threshing, Per heard news that startled him. His friend Anders was the first to tell him.

"Have you heard that the president's been killed?" he asked. "They think a crazy man shot McKinley!"

"My God!" exclaimed Per. What is going to happen next? What is the country coming to?"

At first he was stunned by the news. That the president could be killed in a civilized country seemed impossible! In Africa or Central America perhaps, but surely not in the United States! McKinley had taken office for the second term only five months earlier. Now he lay dead!

Quite suddenly Per had a different thought that brought excitement to his voice.

"Theodore Roosevelt will be president! I think he'll make a dandy president."

Since Roosevelt became his hero, Per had read a lot about him. Party bosses were not excited about Roosevelt. In fact one editorial had suggested that Per's hero was made vice president in order to bury his political career. No so. Now he was president of the United States, and the best part was that he already had a strong reputation as a reformer. He would not do as he was told, since his political career strongly suggested otherwise.

"Yes, I think he will make a dandy president," repeated Per with conviction. "He will have a feeling for the common people of North Dakota."

Almost all of Per's friends and neighbors felt as he did about the new president. Many Dakotans were highly pleased to have "Teddy" as president.

The years that followed were the best ones that Per had experienced in Dakota. One good crop followed another, and prices remained comparatively high. He and Serianna easily paid off the mortgage.

In 1903, when Per went to see Bomberg about buying the other 80 acres, the price had increased. After three good crops, the owner wanted $1200. Per offered him $1000. After some haggling, they agreed on $1100. This time Per could pay cash. In order to farm the additional land, Per also bought another team of horses. One was a gangly roan gelding named Jerry, and the other a clumpy brown mare called Dolly. He knew they were not the best, but he figured they would make good field horses. Besides they were reasonably young and the mare was with foal.

In February of 1903, Per and Serianna's first son was born. Per was jubilant, as was Serianna. She had sensed her husband's disappointments, and she knew well how important sons were to pioneer fathers. Now she smiled as she watched Per holding his new son. The boy was named Leonard.

As a president, Roosevelt did not disappoint Per. He managed to be in the news one way or another. As the youngest president ever to take office, he was a good deal more energetic than any other. In fact it seemed as if he were bubbling over with energy. Per felt he was winning the trust of the common people without being a radical populist. Roosevelt often said he was for big business. He only wanted corporations to be accountable before the law of the land, like anyone else. Per wondered if this were possible. He was afraid big business would find a way around the law.

The great majority of Dakotans cheered the president on. They like his decisive action, and applauded his efforts to control trusts and railroads. People in the state swelled with pride at his public statement that he never would have been president except for his experience in North Dakota. The citizens claimed him as their native son.

"Roosevelt is the best president since Abraham Lincoln," bragged Per.

"Yes," agreed Anders, "and it sure doesn't look like the party bosses can control him at all."

In 1896, Per had misgivings, but now he was happy to be a Republican. The reformers had long needed such a powerful leader, he thought.

Dakota was in a wet cycle and good times continued. However, even during the good years, Per and Serianna con-

-188-

tinued to live frugally and simply. They produced their own food as always, with the exception of such staples as salt, sugar, oat meal, rice, corn meal, coffee, and dried fruits. During the late fall, Per purchased a barrel of apples and its contents were doled out carefully so as to last until spring.

The children all ran barefoot during the summer, partly to save on shoes. Clothing and shoes were purchased sparingly from Sears Roebuck and the general store for winter. Serianna knit mittens and socks from woolen yarn, first carded and then spun on the spinning wheel. Work clothing usually had patches. The small amount of store bought finery served strictly for Sunday best.

One Sunday, while returning home from a picnic, Per discovered a discarded sandwich on the road. He pulled Fly to a stop, gave the reins to Serianna, and climbed down from the buggy. Yes, there in plain sight lay the dastardly evidence for all the world to see.

"The bastard, who threw the bread on the road, has never really been hungry," grated Per through his teeth. "With all the starving people in the world, it's a damn dirty shame to waste food."

"Per, you mustn't swear like that," admonished Serianna, quietly.

Her husband was such a good man, she thought, and yet he swore when he became angry. Sometimes she cringed, when he took the name of the Lord in vain. So far her efforts to get him to stop had been fruitless.

Many improvements did go into making a better farm. One windmill was erected in the pasture to pump water for the cattle, and another placed on the feed shed to grind oats and barley for the stock. High grade red poll cattle gradually took the place of low grade cows. Imported brown leghorn hens laid eggs by the score and were the envy of the neighbors. Some begged to exchange eggs so as to hatch out their own chicks. A new riding gang plow and other machinery saved on hired men and helped work the bigger farm.

One of Per's larger projects was a large hip-roofed barn. The number of horses and cattle had long since outgrown the old stable, and hay supplies had become a problem during blizzards or unfavorable weather. Per had plans to build a 30' x 64' building with fifteen double stalls, plus a good sized feed bin and stairway to the loft. The upper portion was to hold a full thirty tons of hay. The new barn was to be double walled and have a heavy plank floor. A small window would light every stall.

The building went well until the skeletal structure was complete. About that time, a severe windstorm came up unexpectedly. As Per watched from the window of the house, his stomach turned over faster with each passing moment.

"Looks like the whole thing is going to go down!" he cried.

"It seems to be twisting from the wind," agreed Serianna.

"Everything is all twisted out of shape already!"

Since builder's risk was an insurance totally unknown to Per, he would have to sustain his own loss. He simply had to wait out the storm to see how badly damaged the unfinished structure was.

At the end of the storm, the building was still standing, but it was leaning badly to the lee of the wind. The skeleton barn would have to be straightened. The carpenters did their best to undo the damage and to restore the building. Turnscrews and long steel cables were brought in, together with large wooden beams, to bring the framework back into position. To hold the lumber skeleton in place, four stout iron rods, equipped with turnscrews, were set in concrete and attached to the upper part of the barn. Two of these were set on each side, about sixteen feet from each corner. The turnscrews could be tightened or loosened as was necessary. After that the building was double braced with lumber and spikes, and completed with roof and siding.

Per was never entirely happy with the end result. When he looked closely, he saw the new barn leaned slightly to the southeast. The windstorm had struck from the northwest.

During January of 1905, a third daughter was born. This was the fourth child for Serianna and Per in their eight years of marriage. They named the infant girl "Carla".

The pastor was invited for Sunday dinner after church and the baptism. Per handed him a dollar in a white envelope. This was customary for a wedding or a confirmation, but not so usual for a mere baptism. Since the salary of the pastor was only $300 a year, these extras from the parishioners who required such services were necessary. In the congregation, Per knew there were those who thought the pastor ought to prove his sincerity by a lack of interest in a salary. He noticed that they were invariably the same ones who showed a healthy interest in worldly possessions themselves. Just for a little moral support, he often slipped a sack of oats into the back of the pastor's sleigh or his buggy.

The new North LaMoure Church thrived as a religious meeting place and as a social center. Even though services were held in Norwegian, other Scandinavians came to join the congregation. In time even the yankees took part in the social events held there. Per and Serianna were active in the church. When the first Sunday School began, Serianna was the superintendent. Per was a trustie.

Each year Per's sister Anne came to visit her brothers during her vacation. The rest of the year, she worked for an Elkin family at Mayville. During the times she visited Per and Serianna, she assumed complete control over the entire household. Anne was still a terrific worker, and had no thought of resting during her vacations. Serianna did not seem to mind her sister-in-laws intrusions. She thought Anne must enjoy being the boss and organizer for a few days each year, since she had the role of a hired girl the rest of the time.

One year, Anne did not seem the same. She seemed unhappy and spoke in critical tones of her boss's new wife. It was evident that she was considering changing jobs. By the time she left, Per guessed the truth.

"Poor sister. I think she's been sweet on her boss," confided Per to Serianna. "She seems terribly disappointed that she isn't his new wife."

"Oh, that's too bad," said Serianna. "I could tell she was not herself."

"He married a younger woman."

One serious drawback of the frontier was a lack of good doctors and hospital care. In the earlier years, the nearest qualified doctors, in Per's opinion, were at Lisbon, Enderlin, or Valley City. Each of these towns were about 30 miles away. Usually the settlers did not think in terms of a doctor unless they were afraid a family member might die. Normal functions of life, such as childbirth, were attended by a midwife, and usual illnesses sometimes rated a neighborhood practical nurse. The result of this brinkmanship was frequently early death. Per and Serianna were no different from their neighbors in this respect.

During the early spring a near tragedy came to them. Their young son, Leonard, came down with a hard case of pneumonia. They were afraid they might lose him, since he was very sick during the night.

"I am going to Valley City for a doctor," Per said in the morning. "We must do everything we can to save him."

"Yes, I think you should go," agreed Serianna, "but you better hurry or it may be too late."

Per chose his super-mare, Fly, for the trip. She was no longer young, but so far had shown no signs of aging. Sensing the anxiety and urgency in her master's voice, the mare set a record for a farm horse that was to stand a long time. They traveled the thirty miles in just over two hours.

Once there, Per quickly stabled the tired horse and went to find the doctor. At first the man was reluctant to go so far out, but as he listened to the urgency in Per's voice, he consented. "As soon as my driver gets here with the team, I'll come with you."

In a short time they were on the road. Once again Fly showed her remarkable qualities by setting a fast pace for the tall and rangy team driven by the doctor's hired driver.

After the physician had examined the boy, he spoke in low and grave tones. He stayed for several hours, doing everything he could, but nothing he did seemed to make any difference. In the later afternoon he picked up his coat and hat.

"I'm afraid there is nothing more that I can do," he said gravely. "I'm sorry but I seem unable to save your son."

Before dark, Per decided he would have to do his chores. For some time he worked to feed and water the stock, milk the cows, and finish the many farm chores. As he started for the house, the message that he was dead tired from the day penetrated his senses.

Serianna met him at the door. In the dim light of the kerosine lamp, he saw the dark circles around her eyes. She sensed the unspoken question.

"No, he is still alive," she said quietly, "but he may not last until morning."

As Per clasped her hand, they both kneeled together at the side of the little boy's bed. The child seemed to be breathing with difficulty. Only a miracle could save him now, Per thought.

Some time near midnight, Per lay down to rest for a few minutes, fully clothed. Almost instantly, he was sound asleep. Looking at him with soft eyes, Serianna returned to her son's bedside. She could not accept the doctor's word, and was determined to keep vigil through the night. Earnestly and persistently she sought Divine intervention.

Awakened by the first light of dawn, Per looked up to see Serianna standing by the side of his bed.

"Leonard will live," she said quietly.

The tears rolled town Per's face. He believed a miracle had occurred.

Not long after that, Serianna's sister, Bergit, was found to have tuberculosis. Every indication was that this was an advanced condition, as she seemed unable to combat the ravages of the disease. Tuberculosis was considered a very serious illness, and no remedy could be found for her. Serianna found her prayers were of no avail.

During the late summer, Bergit grew thin and wan. She, who had been so vibrant with life and so good to look at, now wasted away. In September, she had a serious hemorrhage that resulted in her death.

Both Serianna and Per found this a most sorrowful event. Bergit was only thirty two years of age, and she left behind a husband and seven children. Clara, the oldest, was only eleven, and Willie, the youngest, was six months old. Like so many others on the frontier, the funeral was a grief filled day.

For others in the neighborhood, typhoid fever, diphtheria, blood poisoning, appendicitis, and other illnesses became deadly. In some families, only half of the children reached adulthood. Yet for those pioneers who remained, life went on. Premature deaths and disasterous events often brought them a little closer to God. There was nowhere else to turn. The births and deaths went on- both common occurences at North LaMoure.

Both 1905 and 1906 were great crop years. In the fall there was not enough room for the grain. Box cars were short, and the three elevators at Litchville were filled to overflowing. For the time being, prosperity for the settlers, including Per and Serianna, continued.

Some predictions for the town of Litchville came true. During the spring, the main street became a quagmire. Ropes had to be stretched across the ends of the street to keep the teams and wagons out. The high board sidewalks were caked with layers of black mud. Yet the same black soil gave the town rapid growth. Its three elevators shipped record breaking amounts of wheat to eastern markets, and a great many other business flourished as a result. The most optimistic prophecied that the town would soon grow into a city of several thousand people.

In the fall of 1906, the only remaining French-Canadian settler in the neighborhood confided to Per that he planned to sell out and move. His quarter section lay directly across the road to the west of Per's homestead. As a result of good times and crops, land values had risen again. Per's neighbor was asking $2400 for his 160 acres and he would not accept less.

"It has 80 acres of good cropland, and we can use the hayland too," reasoned Per. "Whatever hayland we don't need, we can break up. I think we should buy it."

"We still live in Dakota; hard times may come again," cautioned Serianna.

"That may be true, but if we sell some wheat, we can pay cash," countered Per. "We won't need to borrow."

"Have you thought of buying half of it?" queried his wife. "Surely 400 acres of land is enough, even for a *stor bonde* like you."

Per came to agree with Serianna. Even with 400 acres, he was likely to need two hired men during harvest and threshing. His son would not be of any help for some time, and the other children were girls.

The Frenchman agreed to sell half the land to Per, as soon as he found a buyer for the other half. The deal was closed and the deed transferred. Per knew his relatives back in Norway would never understand the meaning of that much land. It was far beyond the largest land holdings in Hadeland.

Per had often thought of a visit to his family and homeland, but each time good and valid reasons seemed to present themselves against the idea. Serianna had little desire to go back, since her family was in America. It wasn't fair to go without her, yet the children were too young to be left without parents. Even for him alone, the cost would probably be at least $300, and that money could better be used for the family, he thought. He did not propose to go by steerage (or third class) this time. To make it worth while, the trip would perhaps take two months, and that was a long time to be gone from one's family.

In the fall, Per found a letter in his mailbox. It was from Norway. Such a letter was still very special, and so Per broke the red wax seal and opened the envelope there on the road. For a long time, he stood reading, and then he began to walk slowly towards home. Per was lost in his thoughts. His mind was going back to the day, now more than twenty five years ago, when he had last seen his family in Norway. Their images were still quite clear.

Per stopped again. He pulled the letter from his pocket and re-read it. As he did so, a sad and far-away look crossed his face. Yes there it was. No doubt about it. His father, Erik, was dead.

CHAPTER FIFTEEN

Age of Reform in Dakota

Immediately after returning home, Per went to see Amund. As usual the two brothers spoke to each other in their native tongue.

"Have you had a letter from Norway?" asked Amund. "Have you heard?"

"A letter came today," replied Per, and now I'm thinking of *Mor.*"

"It is a hard thing to say, but her life may be easier now. Erik's drinking was worse lately, than when we were home."

"Mother told me once that when she and Erik were young, drinking was a terrible problem in Norway. The law allowed alcohol to be made on every *gaard.* The government thought this would help the poor, but instead it was too much of a temptation for many who were struggling with the hard times."

During the latter part of December, there were heavy snows and blizzards. 1906-07 turned out to be another year of deep snow and storms. Per experienced difficulties getting his grain to market. In January, all train service to Litchville stopped, and soon the elevators were too full to accept any additional grain.

Other hardships were experienced because of the blocked rail lines. The supply of coal and wood and other supplies began to run out. However, it was not until stocks of tobacco and snuff

ran out, the the situation was considered to be critical. Per joined with a group of about a dozen neighbors, who set out with
several teams and sleighs toward LaMoure. They carried scoop
shovels and broke new trails through the snowdrifts. Word
came later that a similar group from near Litchville had made
their way north to Sanborn on the main Northern Pacific line.
From then on some supplies were brought through on a fairly
regular basis by convoys of men, sleighs, and teams.

Over a period of several years, Per had raised four fine foals.
Dolly's Morg was now a sturdy full grown gelding. Gray Fly's
three foals were all a beautiful dark dappled gray, with light
manes and tails. They were sired by the same exceptional
stallion that produced Fly and Dan. Polly was a beauty that gave
promise of unusual quality, and Nellie showed definite qualities
of another super-mare. Both of the mares had somehow managed to combine the stamina of the mustang with the beauty of the
Arabian ancestry and the super genes of the stud. Only the
gelding, Ned, was disappointing by comparison with the others.

The entire family was proud of the dappled gray mares, and
Per often drove them to church or to town. Whenever he did,
they were quickly noticed for their show horse appearance.
Among others, several of the neighbors were envious and most
anxious to buy them.

About the same time, Per made a horse trade with his friend,
Anders, in which he traded Morg for a sorrel mare named
Queen. The gelding was younger and larger, but the mare was
more lively and nimble. Per liked that in a horse. Besides he
wanted another mare, since she might produce several fine
foals. He was convinced the best horses by far were those he
raised from his own mares.

One day during the plowing, little Leonard followed the men
and horses out to the west 80. He was not yet four years old.
When the men began to plow, he intended to return home.
However, instead of turning towards home, he set out in the opposite direction. Before very long, he was hopelessly lost and
wandering about the prairie.

In the evening, when the men came in from the field, Christine
came running to see about the boy.

"Where's Leonard?" she asked. "Isn't he with you?"

"No," answered Per, surprised, "we thought he went home!"

"I'd better unharness Fly and go out to look for him before it gets too dark," volunteered Thorstein Stenbraaten, the hired man.

"Run inside and tell them! See if Alice can come and help us look."

Per and Serianna's sister, who was the hired girl, set out on foot to see if they could find Leonard. The young sisters looked worried. They were afraid maybe a wolf might get their little brother. Serianna worried too, as she knew it would soon be dark.

The sounds carried clearly in the quiet of the evening, as each of the searchers called out as he went. Per found he could easily hear the others in the distance. Before too long, he caught up with Alice. All at once, they both heard Leonard cry further to the west. The louder voice of Stenbraaten, on horseback, carried clearly.

"Giddapp, Fly!" . . . "Leonard?" . . . "Is that you, Leonard?" . . . "Whoa, Fly." . . . The crying stopped. The lost boy had been found.

In the fall of 1907, Christine was seven years old. Being good Norwegians, both Per and Serianna knew it was time to send her to school. Some time earlier three schools had been built in Litchville Township, and so now there were very few children with more than a mile and a half to go to school. Cross country, as the crow flies, Christine was within one mile.

During the fall and early winter, she walked back and forth to the school. After that, when the weather was unusually cold or stormy, Per took her in the bobsled. Sometimes even on very cold days, she walked home, with the wind.

Roosevelt was everything Per had hoped for in a president. He tried to bring the trusts under the law of the land. Per was pleased when the Pure Food and Drug Act was passed. He had read about meat from cows with tuberculosis or equally infectious diseases, being sold to unsuspecting customers. Also of butter being reprocessed from the storekeepers old tubs in the back room. First the butter was strained to take out the filth, bugs, and mice, and then was treated with chemicals to take away the smell. Last of all, it was mixed and churned in sweet milk to be sold again with the label "Sweet Milk Butter." This law required truthful labeling, and sought to prevent spoiled food or diseased meat from being sold.

When Roosevelt began a national forest conservation program, Per cheered again. He had read of lumber barons taking great stands of virgin timber on government lands for a pittance in payment, with the help of dishonest public officals.

He laid down his newpaper with a smile. "The food companies and the lumber interests are crying, "Socialism," but it sure looks fair to me."

"It seems like they should be stopped by someone," agreed Serianna.

When Roosevelt chose Taft as his successor for president in 1908, Per voted for him without the slightest hesitation. The best years Per ever experienced in Dakota were those of the Roosevelt Administration.

During the same years, the age of reform was taking shape in North Dakota also. The author, Rex Beech, had exposed Alexander McKensie in magazine articles, which were widely read. The wiley politician had been saved from prison only by President McKinley's pardon, which had been arranged by powerful political cronies. As a result, "Honest John" Burke was elected governor of the state, despite frantic opposition by McKensie and his followers. The reform Republicans united with Democrats to vote for Burke. He vote was especially strong among the Scandinavian and native American voters in the eastern third of the state, while McKensie's main support came from party stalwarts and newer immigrant groups further west.

Per's only regret was that the reform candidate was not a Republican. At first he was reluctant to accept "Honest John" because he was a Democrat, but as time went on, his respect for the new governor increased.

"John Burke is being called the Abraham Lincoln of North Dakota, without any regard to party politics," he grudgingly admitted.

Per and his friends were highly pleased with the report of the Banker's Association and other investigations of the grain trade.

"When we complained, the bankers called us "hayseed

socialists," but when our senator said the state was losing millions because of dishonest grain trade, they got busy, declared Per.

"Yes, and they found out that what we said was right," added Christ.

"They found out some of the big elevators sold twice as much No. 1 hard wheat as they bought," explained Amund.

"Some elevators sold thousands of bushels for use in flour, that was bought as 'reject' from us farmers in Dakota," added Bent.

"An elevator in Duluth sold nearly three million bushels of wheat in one year that it never paid for," asserted Per. "Do you wonder that we often thought our weight was a little short?"

"Do you really think these reports will change anything?" asked Amund.

"No. Nobody believes in reform for the farmer. Often in the past, the bankers have been hand and glove with the millers and the elevators," answered Christ. "They won't change now."

"Even when we know what's going on, we can't get it changed," grumbled Bent, looking disgruntled, "but it helps to have them admit it's true."

Several times, Per and Serianna had talked of building a better home. Another daughter, Marie, was born in 1907, and the pattern was another child every two years. Their own family, together with a hired man and sometimes a hired girl, were too many for their modest home. Besides Per was becoming quite conscious of the fact that many of his friends and neighbors were building sizeable homes.

That same summer, they had an important decision to make. Amund had offered them his old home for $300. He was going ahead with his building plans, and they would have to make up their minds right away.

"The main parts of both houses are sound," reasoned Per. "For another $300 we can put the two together and add on a kitchen."

"So we could have a ten room house for $600," answered Serianna. "How much would a new one cost?"

"It depends on how big and fancy it is, but one big enough for us might cost between $2000 and $3000."

Before long, they agreed to buy Amund's house and add it to their own. The habit of frugality was too strong, and they found the price difference simply too great to ignore. To do the work Per hired a carpenter, whose main qualification was that he came from Hadeland. Per had this weakness. There was never anyone quite like someone from his own part of Norway.

Syvert moved the other house three miles without difficulty, but he had insurmountable problems putting the two houses together. Somehow, he managed to talk Per into setting them four feet apart, and building the two together by means of a hallway and an attic. The two parts were thus separated forever. A kitchen addition was built 32 feet long, including an entry and pantry.

Serianna was seldom, if ever, critical of Per or anything that he did. This was one exception. She was totally unimpressed and let it be known.

"Syvert may be from Hadeland, all right," she remarked acidly, "but he has a lot to learn about being a carpenter."

Still Serianna found the larger home nice in many ways. It was ideal for large gatherings at Christmas, or for having the threshers. For most of the year there were six bedrooms. However, during midwinter, the family found using only one part of the house the most practical.

Per thought his luck changed with the new president. He felt a marked change in the country, as grain prices fell despite lower yields. In 1909, a part of the crop was lost due to hail; some feed crops came back by harvest. 1910 was a drought year and the harvest was a poor one. In 1911, rust hurt the hard wheat and oats. Wheat, the main money crop, was hurt the most.

"Farming costs almost as much in a poor year as in a good one," Per explained to Serianna. "The difference is mostly in harvest and threshing."

"You need hired help every year," nodded Serianna.

The first of the three years went on much as before, since there was some crop, and other grain still in the bins. Per had money in the bank. Besides, they were milking eight cows, and there were steers to sell. Per mowed some of the poorest grain fields to make hay for winter use. A poor year was something a man had to learn to live with, every now and then.

The second bad year, life could not go on as usual. Expenses, hired help, and taxes had to be paid first. The bins were empty now, except for next year's seed, and no improvements could be expected that year. Savings had to be used for living expenses, coal, and operating expenses in the spring.

During the third year, the total crop amounted to only a few hundred dollars. Even with cattle, there were shortages to get everything paid. It took an effort to get the land taxes paid. The family faced an austere winter.

Per continued to get offers for his team of dappled grays. One of his neighbors was especially persistent. Paul was an ambitious young bachelor, who had done well and saved his money. Not only was he envious of the mares as a show team, but he also knew something of their super qualities. In spite of the hard times, his offers increased. Per did not want to sell the mares but the offers grew more tempting.

A kind of ritual developed between the two. Each time they met, a discussion of the possible terms of sale followed. Finally in exasperation, the younger man turned to Per demanding the obvious answer.

"All right then, make up your mind! What will you take for the mares?"

Per was caught off guard. It was up to him to give an answer.

"Five hundred dollars!" he exclaimed. "Five hundred spot cash!"

He was positive he had set the price so high, it could not possibly be accepted. With times so hard, that was simply too much for any team of mares.

"I'll take you up on your offer," said Paul quietly. "I'll buy them."

Per had ambivalent emotions. How could he part with his beautiful and wonderful horses? Still $500 was a lot of money, and there was the family to think about. He had set his own price. Could he back out now?

When Paul came to claim the horses, Per stood looking at them as they went down the road. Suddenly he turned vigorously back to his work.

Shortly after that, Per received a letter from his former hired man, Thorstein Stenbraaten. The letter was short and very clear. So far his homesteading venture in Manatoba had not turned out so well; but if he could hang on for another year, the land would be his. In the meantime he was near starvation. Could Per possibly lend him $100 until he could prove up his land?

Not only was Thorstein from Hadeland, but Per considered him a good friend and the best hired man he ever had. Besides remembering his own painful experience so long ago, he wanted to help the man hang on to his land.

"At least now I do have the money to help him," he said to himself.

During the lean years, two more sons were born to Serianna. The first was born in March of 1909. He was called "Edgar." The second was born in July of 1911, and he was christened "Joseph." They were both so lively and healthy from the beginning, that Serianna found them difficult to control.

Per and Serianna did not use Norwegian names for their children. Both agreed to use American versions or names that would sound more native than their own. Because their names could always be identified as foreign born, they had often wished for American names. This was especially true of the earlier years in the new country.

"You will have two workers here," said Serianna marveling at the ceaseless energy of the two younger boys.

"We will have plenty of help now, when all the children grow up," Per assured Serianna, as he looked at his seven children.

As the youngsters grew they came to believe that Per was an ideal father. Other fathers drank and failed to provide for their families, but certainly this was not true of their "Papa." They learned that he was kind, although he could be stern at times. In fact, if there was ever anything wrong with Per, the children never found it out from Serianna.

By 1911, three children were in school, Per was elected director of the school nearest him. Carrie Smedshammer was the new teacher. Most of the year she walked the nearly three miles from home, But during midwinter she boarded with Serianna and Per. The children grew most excited to think that the teacher was to stay in their home!

The school itself was a white frame building about 16' x 32' in size. In the entry was space for coats and overshoes, with shelves to hold caps and dinner pails. Two neat outhouses in the back took the brunt of the midwinter cold and northwest wind. None of the children made unecessasry trips there. A slope roofed horse barn with three double stalls also stood to one side in the back. It served a dual purpose, doubling as a backstop for ballgames and other exciting games such as anti-i-over.

Inside were two rows of well carved double desks, ranging in size from small to adult. The smaller ones were near the pot bellied stove that stood to one side in the front. The teacher's desk and captain's chair were on the other side. Hanging from the ceiling was a round twelve inch globe of the world, and centered on the front wall was a rectangular blackboard. The only light in the room came from four windows on either side. For an evening meeting, a lantern was hung high up, near the center of the ceiling.

The children wrote on slates. Each one had a reading book, and the older ones also had an arithmetic book. For other classes, only the teacher had a book. Writing lessons and spelling lists were written on the blackboard.

At noon Christine went with the other children to the cloakhall to get the gallon sized syrup pail containing the children's lunches. One person might use a half gallon pail, but there were three to eat from this one. On cold winter days, the sandwiches or the apple might be partly frozen from the morning walk or the cold entry.

The children enjoyed a recess for fifteen minutes both in the forenoon and afternoon. Everyone hurried to bundle up and run outside. During the cold weather, they played running games such as Fox and Geese. Sometimes they went sliding on the big hill near the school. Often in the spring or fall, the boys tried to play baseball, but they lacked most of the equipment.

"The best time at school is the last hour on Friday," said Pauline.

"Why do you say that?" asked Carla.

"Then we can draw or sing, or the teacher might read a story or have a spelldown."

"I think school programs are the best times, when we can speak our pieces," chimed in Leonard. "Afterwards we can sit and eat our lunch with the grownups."

"Basket socials are the best," declared Christine. "It gets exciting when someone bids on your basket."

"Oh, you're just hoping some nice boy will buy your basket, so you can sit and eat with him," teased little Carla, skipping past.

"Don't be so smart. We'll see what happens when it's your turn."

The basket social was popular with grownups as well as the young. The baskets brought in by the single girls were often elaborately decorated with colored paper. Usually, they contained a delicious lunch, carefully planned and prepared. The auctioneer made a great show of spurring on competion between the young men, who bid on the baskets. The younger children were interested in how couples paired off after the auction. Sometime a basket social led to a new romance between two young people.

One day Per was visited by an encyclopedia salesman. In order to sell his merchandise to the schools he first had to persuade the several school board members. Per listened attentively to his enthusiastic pitch, at the end of which the man moved in for the clincher.

"Here, I have a note for you from the chairman of the board, Nils Linn," he said, fully expecting to get a sale.

Per opened the note to read it. "HAVE NOTHING TO DO WITH THIS MAN" was written in Norwegian.

One morning Per came rushing in from the barn, ashen-faced and excited.

"Gray Fly was kicked by Queen!" he exclaimed. "She is hurt so bad that I don't think I can save her."

Both mares had been bred the year before, and each gave birth to an early spring foal. Queen's colt was a jet black and later called King, while Gray Fly's filly was to be a dappled gray named Florie. Queen was an excellent mare in many ways, but Per didn't realize that she could also be a most vicious kicker. Unknowingly, he placed the two in the same pen at night, and on this morning he found Gray Fly badly injured. Later on, her wounds became infected and the poor mare had to be killed. From that time on, the little gray filly was fed cow's milk from a bottle.

Per was able to find some consolation in the new foals, and in the fact he still had Fly and Dan. The two horses were now at or past twenty, but still in excellent condition. The new foals showed great promise.

"Most horses grow old, but Fly and Dan will live forever," declared Per to Serianna one day.

"It almost seems so," agreed Serianna.

One summer day, Pauline watched the horses bunched together from the upstairs window, as they stamped and swished to fight the flies. Then she saw one of her younger brothers, who for some reason or another wandered into the horse herd. She held her breath for fear the young boy might get hurt, but seemed rooted to the spot and unable to move. Suddenly, he received a buffet from Dolly that sent him reeling into loud wails and tears. It was then that she saw old Fly came to the rescue, as she nudged him out of danger with her nose. As she finally flew into action, the young girl came running out of the house in time to see Fly walking behind the boy, escorting him safely through the gate.

"You are the best and smartest horse in the world," she declared, patting Fly on the neck.

The mare nickered softly. Pauline was certain she understood every word.

Over the years, Per had grown in interest and understanding of political matters. From the time he studied for citizenship, he had read political articles and editorials. Unlike many others, his interest did not wax and wane with the fickle fortunes of Dakota depression or prosperity. Every winter, he exchanged and borrowed books and magazines with friends of similar interests.

He found a practical education in reading. Together with friends he had read a series of articles in McClure's magazine, dealing with dishonesty in business and politics. He also read *The Octopus* by Frank Norris, describing the struggle between the farmers and the railroad. *The Pit*, by the same author, exposed the bad effects of speculators in the grain trade on the price farmers received. *Wealth against Commonwealth* by Henry D. Lloyd, gave many facts about how big businesses bribed public officials to destroy competition.

"Teddy Roosevelt should still be the president," grumbled Per. "Big business is ruining the free enterprise in our country."

"I can't understand why people are so dishonest," added Serianna. "Most of them have so much more than they need."

All that Per had read and experienced confirmed his suspicion that men in politics were usually not to be trusted. The main reason for this was that most voters didn't care that much. So long as they were doing all right, most people were too busy with their own affairs to be bothered with political matters, Per felt. Since they were not informed, most voters could easily be fooled by a self serving politician or his clever follower.

Per believed people were being fooled in another way too. They were being prompted to feel patriotic by simple and naive acts, such as standing up at attention before the flag. At the same time they were encouraged to ignore their real responsibility as citizens in a democracy.

Taft was not a president to catch Per's loyalty. After the young and energetic Roosevelt, he seemed much too tame and stolid. Per understood that Taft had supported some reform, but he just didn't think it was nearly enough. He felt that reform was slipping back, rather than forging ahead.

Per was better satisfied with state politics. The Norwegians in eastern Dakota had become a strong force in the reform movement. Not only were the voters better informed, but their leaders were more able and better educated. Now there were editors, lawyers, and professors among them. These men were not always outwitted by the political bosses as earlier leaders had been.

During this strong reform mood, "Honest John" Burke was elected governor three times. He served from 1907 through 1912.

"It's getting so that even the McKensie Gang pretends to be progressive," scoffed Per, as he laid down his paper.

"They can't be against reform and get into office," answered his wife.

In the summer of 1912, Per was glad to read that Roosevelt was back from Africa. When he announced his hat was in the ring, Per was elated. Once again he gave Teddy his loyalty and support. After the Republican convention, he was indignant when his hero declared the nomination had been stolen away from him by the party bosses.

"We can clean up politics in North Dakota," groused Per, "but I don't think it can ever be done nationally."

However, when Roosevelt was nominated at the "Bull Moose" convention, Per felt he was as good as elected. After he read in the newspapers that the delegates marched around the convention hall singing "Onward Christian Soldiers", he felt quite sure of it.

Mother Nature smiled on Dakota again in 1912. The rains came and the weather was near perfect for growing crops. Per's best wheat went 30 bushels to the acre, and he threshed 300 bushels of oats from a three acre field. In the fall and winter hauling grain to market became a major task.

Per was not so pleased with the presidential election. Because the Republicans were divided, the Democrats won and Woodrow Wilson was elected. That his candidate came in a strong second was only a small consolation to Per. He did find a little comfort in the fact that three-fourths of the votes had been cast for reform candidates. Taft received only one-fourth of the total votes.

During these years, Per's health began to bother him. He was having stomach discomfort, indigestion, and heartburn. His habit of chewing one pound of J. T. tobacco each week did not seem to be helping matters. Per thought a lot about quitting, but an old habit like that was hard to break.

He suspected that he might have an ulcer. Because he was concerned that the doctor might want to operate, he did not go to one about his stomach. He had such a young family; Per felt he had to keep going. It would not do for him to get laid up in a hospital, or to have something happen to him.

Per began to take patent medicine. It made his stomach feel better after he took it, at least for a time, so he thought that it was helping him.

CHAPTER SIXTEEN

The Northern Lights Grow Dim

As the first pale rays of the morning sun shone through the window, Per arose quickly from the breakfast table. If he were to reach the elevator before long lines began to form, now was the time to get on the road.

"Serianna, will you get my heavy clothes ready, while I hitch up? When I come back send Leonard out to hold the team, while I come in."

Serianna carried in the huge dogskin coat and the muskrat fur cap. She went back a second trip to pick up the four buckle overshoes, the laprobe, and the long woolen scarf, and added them to the stack next to the stove. Last, she brought the foot-warmer. To fire it, she selected a good sized piece of charcoal from the box, lit it from the coals of the fire, and placed it into the drawer at the bottom of the footwarmer.

"I surely hope this lasts until he gets to town," she mused; "it must be below zero outside this morning."

In a matter of minutes, she saw Per coming with the team. He hitched them to the bobsled that stood before the two open doors of the granary.

"Hurry up now, Leonard, and get your coat on," she prompted. "Go and hold the horses for your Papa, while he gets into his warm clothes. You can finish your breakfast when you come in."

Leonard hurried out just in time to see the sorrel and the gray pull the sleigh away from the granary. First he ran to close the two big doors and then he came around to the front of the bobsled.

"You had better hold Queen by the bit," cautioned his father. "Jim will stand fast, but Queen can't wait to get on the road."

As Per started toward the house, Leonard watched the white breath steaming from the nostrils of the horses. The cold stung his bare face. He shivered and looked impatiently in the direction of the house.

Inside the house, Per pulled on his warm traveling clothes, and stooped to pick up the footwarmer and the laprobe. As he did so, he spoke to Serianna.

"Do you have the list ready? I must get going. There's much to do in town, besides I have to haul home a load of coal."

"Don't forget the kerosine can. We're out. Can you bring home a lamp chimney without breaking it?"

As Per drove away, Serianna's brow creased into a frown. She was worried. Obviously, her husband was having problems with his health. Because he was suffering from rheumatism, he was wearing woolen underwear both summer and winter. So many of the early settlers had rheumatism. She thought it must have been caused by long exposure to extreme weather. In the early days, a trip to LaMoure with a load of grain had taken a very long day, and most of the time had been spent traveling back and forth. Per had not had the warm clothes either then, she thought.

Something else worried her even more, since he was trying to keep it from her. She knew him well enough to understand his stomach was bothering him, and she was well aware of the patent medicine he was taking. When she asked about this, Per only smiled and said he had been a bachelor too long. It was really nothing much at all, only a little gas on the stomach.

"Well, Per usually knows what he is doing," she reflected out loud. "I hope that's true in the matter of his health too."

The sharp northwest wind stung the upper part of Per's face, as he turned the horses to the north. Well, it was cold all right, but he simply could not sit by the fire, waiting for the weather to warm up. There was too much grain to be hauled. The heavy load pulled quite easily by sled and the horses trotted often, and yet it took some time to go the ten miles to town.

"When I was young, I ran alongside the sled to get warm," reminisced Per to himself. "Now I'm fifty. Too old to run in the snow."

Two hours later, they approached the elevator. The frozen snow crunched under the iron shod hoofs of the horses, and the runners squealed as the bobsled hit a few bare spots on the plank ramp. Per brought his team to a stop and jumped off the sleigh. He was chilled to the bone.

"Hello Pete!" called the manager. "Damn cold this morning isn't it? Watcha got on the sled?"

"Morning! Ya, it sure is cold," agreed Per, his teeth still chattering. "That's durum wheat in the sacks."

Before Per had finished his business and loaded coal, it was two thirty. He double checked his list again, and cradled the new lamp chimney in a nest of empty sacks. The weather had warmed some since morning, and the trip home would be a half hour shorter.

These were busy years for Per. Managing a 400 acre farm was a big job. Even with a hired man, and sometimes two, the work kept him going constantly.

In two months springs work would start again. Wheat and oats had to be sown just as soon as the ground warmed up and mellowed enough to be worked. Per felt wheat had to be planted by the first of May, if it were to make a crop. After that, he seeded oats on double disked corn ground and the barley on spring plowing. If there was new ground, the flax was planted last.

During the first years, weeds had not been a problem, but later they had become a nuisance. Per summer fallowed ground each year. This he disked or cultivated to kill weeds and conserve moisture. He also checked in his corn rows, so the field could be cultivated both ways to kill weeds.

June was no letup. That was the month for summer fallowing and for cultivating corn. Usually some grain was hauled out and the coal bin filled directly from the railroad car. Coal was cheaper that way. June was also the month during which he fixed fences and buildings and did necessary painting.

Better equipment took some of the hardest labor out of haying, but the weather was usually hot at haying time. Stacking hay in the haymow was always a sweaty job, even with a hay carrier and slings.

One day just before harvest, Carla came running out to the grain binder that Per was repairing for the harvest.

"Papa! Papa!" she exclaimed. "Come quick! They're here with a piano."

"A piano?" queried Per, rising from his knees. "What are you saying?"

"The Rud Company from Valley City! They have a piano and want to show it to you."

"A piano from Valley City? What in the world can a man expect next?"

Per hurried off to the house and there, ready for inspection and demonstration, stood a shiny new piano. The salesman was an excellent musician, who made playing the piano seem easy. The music sounded marvelous!

"No, of course I didn't buy the piano just because Rud is from Hadeland," Per explained afterwards. "Our girls should be taking piano lessons. Just think—if one of them could learn to play in the church, Serianna!"

The girls were besides themselves with glee! What a good Papa they had! Now they could learn to play the piano.

The boys were not neglected either. The same summer, Per brought home a beautiful, near orange colored, pony with a light mane and tail. "Birdie" soon became a favorite with the entire family. She was used for riding and to pull the cart and buggy.

The summer passed, and another crop was harvested. Dakota was in a wet cycle, and rust was more of a problem than drought. Industrious farmers who practiced frugality prospered.

"The threshers are here! The threshers have come!" called out Marie, running into the house. She pointed her pudgy finger toward the field, where men with teams and hayracks were loading bundles from the shocks.

"I just can't wait to see the big steam engine!" chimed in little Edgar, plainly showing his excitement.

When the threshing rig came across the field, the children found the new little red house on the tender a fascination. Down below, a wooden tank carried water for the steam engine, and up above sat the little red painted house partly filled with straw. The fireman fed the straw, a small forkful at the time, into the burner. On a move from one farm to another, the tender followed directly behind the steam engine. So as to be on hand at the crack of dawn, the fireman and sometimes the engineer slept in the red house at night.

The children loved threshing. Men and teams were everywhere, and the boys could ride on wagons or hayracks. Best of all, the young ones liked to sit on the back of the steam engine to watch the threshing. Burning straw and hot steam had its own peculiar smell. Added to this was the fresh smell of new straw, and the more pungent odor of fresh horse manure, sweat, and urine. So once experienced by several of his senses, threshing was forever etched in a child's memories.

After threshing that fall, Per brought home a good used sulky plow. This riding plow had one 16'' plowshare and was designed for three horses. With it, a boy of 10 or 12 could plow three acres a day.

'''Leonard, come and see the plow I brought for you,'' called Per.

By this time, Leonard had learned to expect quite a lot. After all, he had been the only boy in the family for some years.

''Shucks, I thought it was going to be a brand new plow,'' he replied with a marked lack of enthusiasm.

Yet in a sense, Leonard became a man that fall. From that time on, he sat on the sulky plow and drove three horses, while his father drove five on the gangplow up ahead. For the first time, Per did not have to hire a man.

Per's love of horses lasted his lifetime. King and Florie had both grown into exceptional mature animals. They were the last of what could be called the super-horses sired by the same male as Fly and Dan. However, more foals were born almost every year. Some grew up to replace older horses, but Fly and Dan remained strong. There was an ageless quality about them, as they approached their middle twenties.

During the summer of 1914, the family was the object of a prolonged sales campaign by Embertson and Olson of Litchville. One Sunday, the entire group was loaded into a 1913 Model-T Ford, and taken to Fort Ransom for an outing. The children were so excited! How new the leather cushions smelled. How fast the automobile sped across the countryside at speeds of 25 to 30 miles an hour! Why, they could travel from one place to another in almost no time at all.

Afterwards, Per and Serianna seriously discussed the purchase of an automobile. Soon they discovered that both were interested in the same idea for different reasons.

"Just think, we could get to town in twenty minutes!" exclaimed Per. "In the busy season, when we need repairs for machinery, time is important."

"A car would be nice for Sunday too, both for church and visiting," added Serianna.

That they could pay cash for the auto was an important consideration. Neither one would have been willing to borrow any of the necessary money. They seldom borrowed, even for the best of reasons, and certainly they would not have borrowed for such a luxury. Besides at $600, they thought it a good buy. The automobile was only one year old and used as a demonstrator.

This was a Touring Car with a buggy style top and open sides. It was ideal for good weather. True, there were side curtains provided for rain and cold, but they flapped in the wind and often came loose. Per did not consider this a hardship, since he was used to an open buggy and twice the traveling time.

The new car was a four cylinder, with an engine cranked by hand. Since it operated on a magneto, the automobile was hard to start in cold weather. Jacking up a back wheel, made starting easier. Since the lights also worked by means of the magneto, they were bright when the engine ran fast and ridiculously dim when it slowed down. Should the motor run too fast in low gear, the bulbs might burn out, plunging the driver into total darkness.

Per had some rudimentary instructions, but he needed practical experience. He had heard of strange happenings to a first time driver. Getting the vehicle into motion wasn't so difficult, but stopping was quite another matter. Per practiced diligently in the cow pasture, until he began to get the hang of driving the car.

"What are the three pedals on the floorboard?" asked Leonard.

"One is the low pedal, the middle one is for reverse, and the third one is the brake," explained Per.

"Do they call this the gas lever?"

"Yes, that has to be set or moved for high or low speed. The big hand lever on the left side floor here, is to put the machine into high gear."

"A driver can't forget that."

At first Per found it difficult to remember everything at once. Since the automobile traveled so fast, there was little time to think while driving. A person had to be alert and keep a sharp lookout so that he did not run into anything.

Most of the roads Per drove on were simply two well worn wagon tracks in the sod. Some of these were original buffalo and Indian trails. Most of the roads followed section lines, but avoided sloughs and steep hills, simply by going around them. Usually prairie roads were passable even in wet weather, unless small potholes formed from water standing. The few main roads that were graded had no surface except the dirt and clay from which they were made. Those were faster during dry weather, but muddy and sometimes impassable when wet.

Within a few weeks after they had bought their new auto, Per and Serianna experienced something new. As they were driving along, a loud report much like a gunshot occurred. Per pulled the car to a stop, and Leonard was first to jump out to see.

"It's a flat tire!" he yelled. "We just had a blowout."

Sure enough, Per found the tire flat. The 3" x 30" front tire carried 60 pounds of pressure, and all the air was lost through a hole blown in the inner tube. Since no spare came with the automobile, the blown out tire had to be removed from the rim for repairs. A patch was discovered in a repair can in the tool box. This was placed over the hole in the tube according to the directions on the can. Well over half an hour had passed before the tire was pumped up with the hand pump and ready to be driven again.

Every day, the newspapers told of international tensions in Europe. Per had read enough to understand that there were two armed camps, both armed to the teeth and ready for war. Instead of gaining the security they sought by the arms race, many European nations were virtually sitting on a powder keg. One false move on anyone's part could spark an explosion, and each country lived in fear of a strong neighbor.

Near the end of June, Per looked up from the newspaper just brought home from the mailbox.

"It says here that the arch duke of Austria has been killed in Serbia!" he exclaimed.

"Do you think there will be war in the Old Country?" asked Serianna.

"It sure looks like it. We are lucky the Atlantic is between us."

Within weeks, he read that war was declared by the Dual Monarchy. A tense time followed in Europe. With so many military alliances for protection, it looked as if many countries would be drawn into the war.

Per was pleased with the stand of the North Dakota newspapers. With few exceptions, they called for a policy of peace and neutrality.

Because Norway was not in the war, Per found it easy to stay neutral. He realized that it was not so easy for the German immigrants, whose mother country was in the struggle. He knew many west of Griswold, who were newcomers like himself.

Late in the fall, Per jacked up the wheels of the new Ford, and put it up on blocks for the winter. Snow had fallen, and snow plows were not yet in use. Neither Per nor his neighbors considered trying to operate an automobile during the winter months.

Midwinter came and the shadows lengthened. Christmas came and went. North Dakota slumbered under a thick blanket of snow.

With the following spring came more news of the war, and in May the Lusitania was torpedoed by a German submarine. American citizens were on board. While many began to clamor for war, most Dakotans felt it best to stay out. Per shared with many of his friends the fear that if war came, the reform movement would be forgotten. Now that the people were finally in control of the state, Per thought it unthinkable for them to lose that advantage.

"Shady politicians stand ready to move in and take over the minute that the people lose interest in government," Per cautioned the others.

"Yes, that's right, Per," the others agreed.

As a neutral, the United States shipped grain and other food supplies to both the Allies and the Central Powers early in the war. This increased the exports of grain and kept the price up for farm products, even considering the excellent crops.

Per often hired newcomers for farm help. He was especially concerned for those who came from his own district, but he also gained a name for being sympathetic and helpful toward others. Since many came directly to Dakota from their homeland, he often helped them with their struggle to become Americans.

During the summer of 1915, Per hired two brothers. Anders and Gulbrand could scarcely believe the scale on which Per and Amund operated their farms. Anders looked first at the hay-loader and then at the hayslings which he was expected to use for hauling hay into the barn.

"This will never work," he declared in pure Hadeland dialect.

The self tying grain binder was another wonder to them. Both were amazed that one 8-foot binder could cut, tie, and lay in neat rows enough bundles to keep them both busy shocking in the very heavy grain. The brothers were equally surprised at the large size of the fields and the great expanse of the farms.

At first the threshing too, became near impossible to comprehend, as they saw a quarter section of heavy grain threshed in one day. The machine also weighed the grain and stacked the straw, without the help of men.

"This isn't the Old Country. You are in America now," laughed Per.

Another interest caught up the newcomers. Tales of the Old American West greatly intrigued them. At first, both valued the wild west magazines for their pictures alone. Eventually, they not only looked at the sensational pictures but learned to read the stories in English as well.

"Aren't Anders and Gulbrand spending a lot of money for

guns and bullets?" asked Serianna. "They seem always to be out there shooting."

"Yes, they have bought frontier model Colts and repeating Winchesters," agreed Per.

"They're shooting all day Sunday it seems."

"It must take many boxes of bullets every week."

The two immigrants practiced marksmanship diligently at every spare moment. As a result of this untiring practice, they soon developed amazing skill. Before long they were ready to put on an exhibition.

"Have you seen Anders and Gulbrand shoot?" asked Carla.

"One holds up a matchbox, and the other shoots a hole through it," said Leonard, very impressed.

"Gulbrand can set up a knife with the blade towards him. Then he steps back ten paces and splits the bullet by shooting at the sharp edge," added Pauline.

About this time, Per and the Smedshammers decided to attend a "Hadlenings Laget held at Fargo. This was one of the many groups formed by Norwegians who came from the same district in Norway. For Per, traveling by Northern Pacific, this was a major event that took three days. In addition to the time he spent at the meetings, Per also learned a great deal about the city of Fargo.

"Our girls are going to go to school at Oak Grove," declared Per, after he returned home from the trip.

"Oak Grove? What are you talking about?" queried Serianna.

"It's a Lutheran school I saw when I was in Fargo," he explained.

Per's boast was not an idle one. The following fall, the two older girls did in fact, attend school at Oak Grove. There the girls found life different from anything they had known on the open prairie of North LaMoure. Serianna and Per were only able to guess at the wonders of the open window, through which their daughters were privileged to look. For the sisters, it was an adventure into another world, limited only by their own lack of curiosity and experience. Besides the regular studies, Christine came to excel in the art of sewing and dressmaking, while Pauline practiced untiringly to learn piano from a gifted instructor.

Each time the girls came home for a holiday, the event was a learning experience for the entire family. The younger ones listened with open mouths to hear and share the wonders. The changes in their daughters that Per and Serianna perceived, seemed to make the sacrifices worth while.

During April of 1916, the last child was born. The others had come with marked regularity every two years, but this one was almost five years behind the next one. Per was called in from the field. For this childbirth, he was able to call Dr. Stixrud at Litchville by means of the telephone on the wall. Serianna's sister was there to help, and Christine was allowed in the room.

The younger children huddled together in the parlor at the other end of the house. They sat in a cluster, pretending they didn't know what was happening. The tension and worry mounted until, at long last, they clearly heard the lusty cry of an infant.

In a few minutes, Christine opened the door and said, It's a boy!'' with a grand flourish of her hand.

The parents were pleased with the youngest child. They hoped that he might take care of them in their old age.

That fall, Thorstein Stenbraaten came to see Per. He was still most grateful of the loan of $100 several years earlier. Due to Per's help, he had survived the hard times. Now when better times had come, he had done well.

"I'm making a trip back to Norway," he said. "Why don't you come too?"

The idea was a tempting one for Per. The plowing was nearly finished, and they could be back in time for Christmas. Mor was now in her eighties, and Per had not seen Engebret or Kari since he had left Norway in 1881.

After a struggle, Per decided to stay home. The money could better be used for the family, he thought. This matter of education, for example, was important for the children. Also there was the war. His boat could be sunk by a German submarine, and the family could not get along without him. Most of all, he did not want to leave Serianna for such a long time. He really didn't want to go without her.

Politics in North Dakota was taking a new turn. Under the leadership of Arthur Townley, the farmers of the state were being quickly organized into a new political organization. The objective of the group was to take over the Republican party. Most of the leaders were former Socialists.

The new Nonpartisan League became a paradox for Per. The speeches stirred the same flames inside him as the Farmer's Alliance had done earlier, but he could not make up his mind about the leaders of the organization. Townley spoke most eloquently for the farmers, but Per could not feel the same degree of trust toward him he had in some leaders. He was not confident that Townley was another Lincoln, Roosevelt, or John Burke. The man seemed too radical. Per paid his $6.00 membership, but with reservations.

That winter, Per's health continued to deteriorate. He worried about it, but did not see a doctor. More than likely the doctor would want to operate if he did go to one, he was quite certain about that. Surgery might be too risky. Several of the people he had known had died on the operating table. However, early in January Per had serious bleeding from his stomach. Dr. Stixrud had to be called out from Litchville.

The doctor informed Per that he had a very serious ulcer, and ordered him to stay in bed. Dr. Stixrud looked at the patent medicine with disgust and at the J. T. tobacco with even greater distain.

"Quit taking this confounded patent medicine. The high alcohol content irritates your ulcer," he asserted. "While you're at it, throw away this chewing tobacco too. It's just as bad for your ulcer as the alcohol."

The doctor was not satisfied to let Serianna be the nurse, and recommended that a nurse be brought in to care for Per instead. He would arrange for one and bring her along when he came the next day.

Olga, as she was called, turned out to be a domineering woman. Her experience was somewhat limited, but she was strictly a no-nonsense person. She took immediate charge of the sickroom, demanding that Per's heavy woolen underwear be stripped off at once.

"First we have to get those dirty underwear off," she h
"and then we'll change these blankets for some n
sheets."

Having accomplished this, she opened the bedroom
Since it was January, the weather was very cold outside.
not had his woolen underwear off, except to bathe and
for years; the only difference was that he wore heavy on
ing the winter and lighter ones in summer. Soon Per be
have chills, and his voice grew hoarse. Serianna was the f
realize he had come down with pneumonia. In his weak
condition, she knew this could be very serious. She called
doctor again.

In spite of everything they tried to do, Per did not seem to
prove. He developed a dry hacking cough. Finally, it was
himself who understood that he was not going to get well.
the realization dawned on him, he became greatly agitated. Th
would never do! He must get well again!

Olga tried her best to quiet him, but the effort proved futile
As she stood helplessly by, Serianna came to talk to him, bu
she also was unable to calm or soothe him. She hurried to bring
the family Bible and took Per's hand in hers. With tears rolling
down her cheeks, she began to read in a quiet, firm voice.

"Fear thou not; for I am with thee. . . I am they God; I will
strengthen thee. . .

"I am the resurrection and the life. . . he that believeth in me,
though he were dead yet shall he live. . ."

"Serianna, is it getting dark in here? Please get the lamp. The
darkness seems so forboding. . ." His voice was hoarse but
more calm.

Serianna laid down the bible and went to get the kerosine
lamp.

As Per lay desperately ill upon his bed, he thought for a moment that he saw a small farmyard. He squinted and tried to
focus. Could it be Elvestuen? Yes, that must be the *elv* and the
old blacksmith shop. It was all so dim and so far away.

Serianna set the lighted lamp on the chiffonier. Again she took
Per's hand in hers and began to read quietly from the Bible.

"For God so loved the world, that He gave his only begotten
Son, that whosoever believeth in Him should not perish but

ve everlasting life. . ."

"Serianna," said Per in a raspy voice, "call the children. I must speak to them"

With a hushed voice, she went to gather the children. They could easily tell that something was wrong.

"Your Papa is very sick. He wants to talk to you. You have to be quiet when you go into the bedroom."

Solemn faced and wide eyed, the children filed into the sickroom. How pale and weak their Papa looked. He must be very sick.

"Soon I will be gone from this earth and with our heavenly Father," he began in a hoarse voice. "You must all help your Mamma. Christine and Pauline, you must carry part of the load, and Leonard, you will have to be the man of the family now."

Per paused for a dry hard cough. His face looked flushed.

"I hope it will not be too hard for you without a father. . .in years to come. . .May the Lord bless each one of you."

As the children left the room, Serianna kneeled beside the bed. She took his hand in hers again. He looked so weak.

"Soon I will come too; then we'll be together again," she promised.

Per tried to signal that he had heard. His eyes turned with a wan smile, as he tried to squeeze her hand.

"Our Father, who art in heaven. . ." she prayed.

Not long after she had finished, Per died. A few days later, Fly and Dan drew the bobsled that carried his coffin to the church-yard. There his body was laid in the bosom of the North Dakota prairie, that he had learned to love.